the Adventuress

THE ADVENTURESS
Copyright 2022 © by Lori Bates Wright
www.loribateswright.com

ISBN 978-1-7326738-9-2 Ebook
ISBN 978-1-7326738-8-5 Paperback
Print Edition

Scripture quotations and references are taken from the King James Version of the Bible (The King James Bible), the rights in which are vested in the Crown, reproduced with permission of the Crown's Patentee, Cambridge University Press.

All Rights reserved. No part of this publication may be reproduced in any form, stored in any retrieval system, posted on any website, or transmitted in any form or by any means without written permission from the author, except for brief quotations in printed reviews and articles.

This is a work of fiction. Names, characters, incidents, circumstances, and dialogues are products of the author's imagination and are not to be construed as real. Any resemblance to actual events or persons, living or dead, is entirely coincidental.

Library of Congress Cataloging-in-Publication Data

Cover design by Roseanna White Designs

SierraVista Books
113 Traveller Street
Waxahachie, TX 75165

To my sister, Sheri,
who borrowed my clothes,
raided my candy stash,
let me put my Donny Osmond poster
on her side of the closet door,
and who always loves
with a heart as big
as the New Mexico sky.

Do nothing out of selfish ambition or vain conceit.
Rather, in humility value others above yourselves.

~ Philippians 2:3

"Blessed are the curious for they shall have adventures!"

~ Lovelle Drachman

Books by Lori Bates Wright

THE SABERTON LEGACY
True Nobility
Field of Redemption
Sacred Honor

A MATTER of INTRIGUE
The Songstress
The Adventuress

A MATTER OF INTRIGUE

the ADVENTURESS

LORI BATES WRIGHT

SierraVista
BOOKS

Prologue

Mission San Gabriel
New Mexico Territory
January 1842

STORM CLOUDS WITH downy-white centers burst over the Sangre de Cristo Mountains resembling a fine, fur-trimmed cloak. A howling wind surged through Cimarron Canyon flinging shards of sleet and snow against the old adobe mission.

Father Miguel De La Torre struggled to pull in the wooden shutters, then blew a visible breath into his cold-stiffened hands. Despite the storm's shrewish tantrum, he had faith that the morn would find them safe. *La Tormenta* would rage, but he knew from experience the thick walls of the mission would hold them in an ever-protective embrace.

With a nudge, the hood covering his head pooled in woolen folds around his neck. His hand stilled as something prickled his senses. Something beyond the winter's blast. Tilting his head, he listened again. There, barely perceptible above the constant roar of the north wind, a weak thud and an odd scratching sound.

Most likely another displaced branch, yet, instinctively he knew it was more. A visual check of the windows revealed each was completely secure.

The noise came again along with a pitiful whine.

Perhaps a kitten had lost its way. Following the cry to large pine doors at the arched portal, he drew a heavy bar from its hasp. Instantly, he was forced to shield his face with an arm as the door blew in on an icy gust.

A caped bundle toppled inside, crumpling in a heap at his feet.

Father Miguel threw his meager weight against the heavy doors to bring them back together, heaving the bolt into place. He dropped to a knee and carefully examined the unexpected visitor, searching for a face.

"Who have we here?" Father Miguel brushed aside damp hair, fair as winter wheat, to reveal the ashen features of a young woman twisted in pain.

She clasped a handful of cloth covering her middle, writhing closer to the warmth he provided with an agonized moan.

"You're half frozen. Come warm by the fire." He laid a bronzed hand over hers, noticing how very small and milky white it was against his own. "A warm meal is what you—"

The words froze in his throat when her cape fell open to reveal a distended belly, heavy with child. A dark spot stained the material beneath her, confirming her time had come.

Despite his shock, Father Miguel gathered a steadying breath. He must remain calm. The young woman was panic-stricken. It was imperative he keep his wits.

"You are safe here." He lifted the gold crucifix from around his neck and placed a kiss on it before laying it upon her breast. "Hold tight to this and do not fight the pain. God is with you. Let Him bring comfort."

"P-please." She looked up at him with luminous gray eyes, obviously terrified of what was happening to her. "Save the baby."

A LUSTY WAIL echoed through the choir loft as Father Miguel dipped his finger into a bowl of holy water to trace a sign of the cross over the babe's brow. "What name shall we call this babe with such the ferocious cry?"

Chuckling, he looked across the tall stone altar at the somber face of the child's mother. Her eyes fixed unseeingly at a statue of Our Lady of Sorrows.

Gently, he patted her hand to gain her attention. "*Mija?* Have you considered a name?"

Silently, she shook her head. The girl had divulged nothing these past five days since her arrival. The nuns tried tirelessly to coax a name from her, and still they did not know it.

"Very well, then. Shall we name him for his father?" He kept his voice gentle.

With this, her eyes met his, and he watched them cloud over. His heart ached for her, however, he could not help if she would not speak.

Disclosing this name in particular seemed especially painful.

"You are safe, but you must trust me. I must know what to call the child for his christening into the Holy Faith." Father Miguel hoped his voice conveyed the compassion he felt toward her. He gave her a moment to contemplate the question and did not continue until she released a quivering breath. "Only the father's familial name if you wish."

"Wolf." She whispered with shimmering eyes and a quivering chin. Clearing the thickness in her throat, she tried again. "His father is Gray Wolf, son of Chacon, the Apache chief."

Aye que mi.

The priest whispered a silent prayer, looking down at the squirming infant with new understanding. "This demanding *niño* that has captured our hearts has blood of a true warrior. Is that it?"

A couple of the mission's orphans stood from the front bench, hoping to catch a closer peek at the baby, who chewed hungrily on his fist.

"Wolf." Father Miguel repeated the name. Hearing it spoken aloud obviously disturbed her. With good cause. It would not be easy for a young woman such as herself to raise a child named after Gray Wolf. He must guide her carefully.

An idea suddenly formed. "I was acquainted with a fur trader with this name, Wolfe. He added an *e* on the end, as with the old language. This is an honorable name, *si*?"

Clearly struggling to avoid a surge of tears, she finally consented with barely a shrug.

Father Miguel waved for the children to be seated. "*Bien, bien.*" He must press forward while she was agreeable. "What then of a Christian name? Perhaps that of your father's?"

"No!"

The priest exchanged worried glances with a nun standing beside him. This was the loudest she had ever spoken. Even in the throes of childbirth she'd shown remarkable restraint.

The girl reddened at her outburst. "What I mean is, I-I want him to have my brother's name. He passed on when he was little, but I loved him dearly."

Father Miguel noticed that she avoided looking down at the babe, as if it somehow pained her. Perhaps it merely pained her to see someone else in his small face. "What was your brother's name, *mija*?"

"Nathan." The baby grabbed a fistful of her hair, and with this she did glance down at him. She smiled weakly. "Nathaniel Lee."

"*Muy bien!* I baptize thee Nathaniel Lee Wolfe in the name of the Father, the Son, and the Holy Ghost, amen." He quickly crossed himself while tiny voices along the front bench echoed his "amen."

Father Miguel watched a tear make its way down her pale cheek as she tugged her hair from little fingers. When she turned from the altar, he motioned for Sister Consuelo to take the babe, who had again taken up his deafening appeal for nourishment.

A wet nurse had been found from the village when the *señorita* refused her motherly duty. It had not taken the genius of Fray Lamier to discern the girl's intentions. She planned to leave the child in the care of his mission.

"Please, *hita*, ... must it be this way?" He caught up with her halfway up the aisle as she headed for the vestibule. "Surely there is room in your home for one more. He is not very big." He held his hands inches apart to prove his point.

The young woman stopped and faced the priest with shimmering eyes. "Papa said if I dared bring the brat home—he'd kill it."

"*Que lastima!*" Father Miguel was appalled. "What manner of man would speak such a thing? Surely you are mistaken."

"No mistake about it, Father. Papa despises Gray Wolf. He doesn't know him like I do." On a ragged breath, she hurried on. "I haven't yet turned eighteen. I have no way of providing for a baby. I won't let him suffer because of my mistakes." Her gaze briefly lifted to the tall cedar cross at the head of the sanctuary in search for understanding. "God knows I have live with what I've done. But you can take care of the baby. Papa will never have cause to do him harm. Please, Father, say you will help me!"

"Yes, of course. Of course." He slipped a comforting arm about her. "I will see that the *niño* is cared for. But I am concerned for you. Is it safe to return to the home of such a man?"

"Papa's good-hearted enough. He just has no use for the Apache." She responded to his frown, managing a faint smile. "He will make sure I regret this for a long, long time. You can count on that. But he won't hurt me."

Sincerity shone brightly in her pewter-colored eyes and the priest had no choice but to trust that she knew what she was doing. "Then what can I do to help?"

"I wrote the baby a letter. Will you see that he gets it? I'd like him to have it when he gets bigger." She nervously swiped at her hair falling across her brow. "It tells about the way things are. I think he should know about his papa and mine, too. Gray Wolf doesn't know anything about this baby, or he'd come and take what's his. He's proud like that."

The priest nodded. "Perhaps it would be best for the *niño* if he were to go to his father."

"Oh, no. Please. That baby doesn't need to grow up confined to Indian land. Things are bad for Gray Wolf's people and will only get worse. I want little Nathan to go wherever he wants, be whatever he wants to be." Turning, she grasped Father Miguel's arm. "He needs schooling, Father. So he can learn to make it in this world. I want him to have fine manners, too. And a proper upbringing so he's accepted wherever the Lord sees fit to take him. You'll see to it, won't you?"

"*Si*, of course." He led her to sit beside him on a back pew. "It's in your mother's heart that he be the best God has for him."

"But I can't be a mother to him. Don't you see? I can't have Gray Wolf, or his child anywhere near me." She shook her head and shuddered a sigh.

"Yes, but surely—"

"It's no use, Father. I've had plenty of time to think this over. The church can find him a good, respectable home. Even if he stays here with you at the mission, you see that the children get a decent education. They are always clean, never hungry …" Her breath caught in her throat, and she turned aside.

He witnessed her valiant effort to be brave and gentled his voice to a near whisper. "From time-to-time young people need a chance to determine for themselves what's most important. One day soon, you will come to see that you are much stronger than you realize."

Sniffing, she took a Sunday handkerchief from her pocket.

Upon closer inspection, he saw it was carefully hand stitched with pink rosettes and the initials A.R. embroidered in one corner. "Will you see that he gets this, too? It's the only thing I have that's mine to give him."

"Certainly, and I will give him your letter, as well." He used her handkerchief to dry her cheek. "He will grow into a fine man—a hearty man, your Nathaniel Wolfe. Inside and out. He will know of his mother's courage, and someday when things change for you, *mija*, he will be right here waiting for you."

Chapter One

Hays City, Kansas
21 April 1870

"NATHANIEL WOLFE, YOU'RE under arrest."

The brim of his black Stetson slowly inched upward as Nathan squinted at the lawman standing across from him.

"What's your gripe, Ranger?" Marshal James Hickok shifted a cigar to the other side of his mouth and slapped down his cards. "Give me two."

Captain Cade Matlock stepped forward. A little beauty in a fancy hat stood close beside him. "Lobo has a warrant on his head down in New Mexico Territory. I've come to bring him in." Cade tossed a parchment to the table. The print stood out in bold black ink.

Wanted: Dead or Alive
Nathan Wolfe
Known as the fast draw, *El Lobo*

"Perhaps it's best if we discuss this elsewhere." The lady watched Nathan's hands, making sure both were visible above the table. "I suggest you come along peaceably, Mr. Wolfe."

Nathan had no intentions of going back to New Mexico, peaceable or otherwise. He drained the contents of his mug, watching her over the rim of his glass. Whoever she was, she wasn't a local. Only saloon girls wore silk and lace around here. Just a whole lot less of it. If guessing, he'd say she was a Pinkerton working alongside Cade Matlock.

Tense anticipation rippled through the elaborate gaming room as Nathan rose to his feet. A crowd began to gather, all eyes trained expectantly on the controlled movements of his hands.

"Suits me, Matlock." A hush fell when Nathan spoke.

Even the piano man ended his jaunty tune, swiveling on his stool for a better look.

Lightning fast, he flipped a short blade from his sleeve and stuck it in the middle of the handbill with a thud.

Those close by scattered.

With the parchment dangling from the tip of his knife, he offered it back to the lady. "After you, ma'am." Nathan's voice was smooth and composed.

A chorus of guffaws drowned out Hickok's curse as he slapped his cards face up onto the table and leaned back in his chair. "Four of the prettiest little queens you ever did see, Matlock. Gone to the dogs. You two better have something better'n this to show for it." He yanked the poster from Nathan's knifepoint and ripped it in two.

"There ain't four queens here, Marshal. Only two." A trail-dusted old codger shuffled through Hickok's discards, lifting a pair of red queens.

"Yeah, well, them other two were up next, Pate. I got a hunch about these things." Hickok winked at a couple of girls lounging at the bar. "McCoy, mind if we use your stockroom? This oughtn't take long."

At the saloon proprietor's nod, Hickok led them into a room under the polished banister.

Once inside, Nathan's mood immediately turned serious. "What's this about, Matlock? I haven't been down to New Mexico since I left the Rangers."

"You know good and well he's been right here in Hays. Been my deputy for as long as they pinned this badge to my chest." Hickok smoothed his blond, long-handle-bar-mustache, admiring his image in a tarnished mirror on the wall. "That'd be what? Nearly a year now, Lobo?" Turning from the mirror, he frowned at the lead captain of the Texas Rangers. "We all went huntin' elk two years back in Colorado. You know he ain't been out murdering no one. I never seen a man try so hard to keep from shootin' these young fools around here."

As far as Nathan could see, there was no credibility to this warrant, so what was this really about?

Waving off their questions, Cade pulled a chair over from the corner. "Relax, Lobo. We know it's not you DeLaney's after."

"However, someone is murdering innocent landowners at an alarming rate." The lady next to Cade spoke up. "And whomever they are, they've taken great pains to make it look like it is you."

"No offense, ma'am, but I don't believe we've met." Nathan's brows drew together. It was high time she stated what business this was of hers.

"Meet my wife, Mrs. Juliana Matlock." Cade swept a hand out toward Nathan. "Jules, you're looking at the famous gunslinger, *El Lobo*."

"Howdy do. Pleasure to make your acquaintance, Mrs. Matlock." Hickok was quick to take her hand, but clearly thought better of placing a kiss on her cheek. "A real pleasure indeed."

So his ex-commander had gone and gotten himself married. That would explain why they hadn't heard from him in a while. Still, it did not explain why the two of them were here trying to serve a fake warrant for his arrest.

As always, Cade Matlock picked up on Nathan's hesitation. "Juliana's a Pinkerton. Washington called in Federal detectives to make sure you accompany us back to Cimarron."

"As your prisoner?"

"If need be." Cade matched his tone.

Nathan pulled a timepiece from the top pocket of his leather vest. "You're wasting your time. The stage south leaves in half an hour. If you two hurry you can just about make it."

"Mr. Wolfe, someone held up a federally insured payroll stage outside of Cimarron. The driver was gunned down in cold blood." Juliana Matlock took a step toward him. "The killer was dressed in solid black, tall, with raven black hair, and a surly scowl. Much like the man I'm looking at right now. He never spoke, but every passenger on that stage swore he was *El Lobo*."

"Yet you both know it wasn't and apparently the Federal government does, too. So, what was the point of that show out there?"

"We need your help in solving this case, Mr. Wolfe." Juliana's gaze never wavered when Lobo's attention swung back to her.

Matlock leaned forward in his chair, resting a forearm over his knee. "Smoking out this killer is only a drop in the bucket compared to the illegal dealings going on down in the Territory. Now that Pinkerton has gotten involved with the lawmakers concerning that million-acre land grab, seems their hands are tied to do anything about it. Jeb Hollinger put together a gang of gunmen, and they're forcing innocent families off their land as fast as they can get settled. The territorial government's choosing to look the other way. Appears like every corrupt politician and businessman from Santa Fe to Washington has their hand in it. No one's raising a finger to stop him."

"Make no mistake." Juliana crossed her arms. "This warrant is real. You are formally accused of master-minding the Wells Fargo stage robbery and murder. A half dozen landowners have been shot down, and as many as fourteen others have gone missing. For whatever reason, someone in New Mexico sees you as a threat and they've gone to great lengths to frame you for these murders. Allan Pinkerton is well aware of it. He simply chose to use this to our advantage."

Nathan's short laugh was anything but amused. "How would my hanging be to his advantage?"

"Relax, Lobo. We won't let it get that far." Matlock sat back in his chair. "But since they've singled you out, you'll make for mighty good bait."

Nathan frowned. Nothing he'd heard so far compelled him to want to put his neck in a noose to humor any of them.

"Don't you see?" Juliana placed a gloved hand on her husband's shoulder. "By publicizing your arrest, the imposter is forced to give up his crime spree. He can't go on with it, or everyone will know he's an imposter."

Hickok smirked at the lady's gullible suggestion. "So you figure this two-bit bandit's just gonna give it all up? Go back to where he came from with his tail between his legs, and that'll be the last you hear of him, is that it?" Placing a well-worn boot on a whiskey crate, he leaned an arm across his knee. "Just maybe, he'll get to feeling so bad for sullyin' up your good name, Lobo, that he'll come beggin' to turn himself in."

Nathan grinned at Cade's look of exasperation. Hickok was just getting started.

"'Course, by that time, they'll likely have you danglin' from the nearest cottonwood." No one found James Butler Hickok more amusing than Hickok himself. "Yes, sir, sounds like you've got yourself a real good plan there, Mrs. Matlock."

Nathan almost felt sorry for her. By the time she realized she was being strung along, Hickok was past return.

"Yessir, with Lobo out of the way, that good-for-nothing is sure to see the error of his ways. Most likely give back every penny he ever took."

"All right, all right, Hickok. You've made your point." Cade stood with a lifted hand. Hickok could be at this all day if they'd let him. "Like we said, it wasn't just the express driver. Good men are being picked off—some disappearing into thin air. The authorities down there are knee-deep in corruption. It will take a whole lot of government intervention to get this straightened out. That's why we need your help, Lobo. We need you to come to New Mexico Territory and join the case."

"Who was killed?" Nathan caught a cockroach under the tip of his boot. Being accused of killing was nothing new to him, but in every instance he'd been in the clear. There had never been any question about it. "Anyone I know?"

To her credit, Juliana never lost her composure as she closed the gap between Nathan and herself. "A very good friend of yours, as a matter of fact."

Cade presented his back to Hickok. "They got Augus Jamison out near Cimarron."

Now they had Nathan's attention.

Augus Jamison wasn't just a seasoned Texas Ranger, he was a close personal friend. A highly skilled lawman in his day. This imposter had to be mighty practiced to have taken him down. "And no one saw who did it?"

"Sadly, no." Juliana spoke when Cade simply shook his head.

Straightening, Hickok was sobered by the news as well. "Livin' with the reputation of a dead shot is hard enough, Matlock, without your wife here addin' coal to the fire. Puttin' a price on Lobo's head makes him a target of every bounty hunter worth his spit."

Nathan pushed off from the barrel he was leaning against to stand at full height. "Every young gun out there is looking to put a hole through me for free. If you offer to pay them for the pleasure, I won't last a day in the Territory."

Turning a hard glare on the lady, Nathan was done listening. "Seems to me you two ought to head back to New Mexico and look to catching an outlaw."

"That's exactly what we intend to do." Cade took the heat off of his wife. "But you're coming with us."

Nathan rested a hand on the hilt of his gun. "I seem to be the only one here with high stakes in this game. If someone down there is parading himself as me, getting away with murder, there's no need to fake an arrest. I'll ride into town on my own and dare the coward to show himself."

"Very gallant of you." Juliana patted his back like he was a good dog. The gesture put him to mind of Lily Valentine. Lily obviously trained her well. "But that's exactly what they're hoping you'll do. Mr. Hollinger pushed hard for this warrant. He obviously has an interest in luring you back to New Mexico to defend yourself. We want to know why."

Hickok shook his head. "That wanted poster says dead or alive. Lobo can't just go waltzing into town. That coward'll shoot him dead in the street. Collect a nice big reward for it, too."

"Please understand, Mr. Wolfe. We will make certain nothing—and I mean nothing—happens to you. Right, Cade?" Juliana peered over at her husband, and he gave a nod. "We'll make your arrest public. The killer will have no choice but to refrain even if only for a little while. In the meantime, you will be free to scout around. Hopefully you can find us some connection to the murders and this new corporate investment group the Hollinger man is a part of. Commander Pinkerton assures us that no one knows the area down there like you do."

"I'll attest to that," Cade agreed. "Plus, you have favor with the Apache and Ute. They have great respect for you. Anyone else nosing around on their lands would likely come back without a scalp."

"Hollinger was here about six months back." Nathan ran a hand over his dark hair. "Tried to recruit me to head up some band of 'enforcers' he was putting together. He's paying a tidy sum for their services. I turned him down flat."

No amount of money was worth what Hollinger was looking for. He made it clear Nathan would have full discretion as to whether to shoot first or run them off.

Nathan wanted no part of it, and told him so in no uncertain terms.

"Bet that made him furious." Matlock smirked. "Hollinger doesn't take well to being turned down."

"Sure did," Hickok piped in. "Stormed outta here like his tail was afire. All his little yahoos following right behind."

"So he does have a score to settle." Juliana raised a trim brow. "That would explain why this bandit calling himself *El Lobo* is suddenly terrorizing stage routes. Revenge must be his motive. Plus the money that was stolen must fund his band of enforcers quite nicely, wouldn't you say?"

"Surely you have enough lawmen down there to do the job." Hickok frowned. "Call in the cavalry from Fort Union. They're always looking to get in on a good squabble."

"Won't do any good. The army has their hands full keeping peace in those rowdy mining towns along the trail. There's a steady stream of pan-handlers around Cimarron looking for gold, and plenty more looking to take it away from them." Cade paused before going on. "And, truth be told, no one's sure who can be trusted in the Territory anymore."

Hickok released a low whistle.

"As I said, you won't actually have to sit in jail." Juliana renewed her appeal. "Think of it as a visit back to your childhood home. Cade and Lily said you're legend in those parts. You do want to defend your reputation, don't you?"

"You can stay out at your mission near Elizabethtown." Cade's tone was mindful. He knew how much the place meant to Nathan.

"I won't put the Padre's place in danger."

"No one will know you're there. As far as anyone is concerned, Lobo will have been arrested and held up in

Cimarron until Cade brings you to Texas for trial. Sheriff DeLaney will see to it that your empty cell is well-guarded." The lady was persistent.

"Before it's all over with, Pinkerton will make sure your reputation is fully restored." Matlock's voice took on a softer edge. He was one of a very few who knew how much an honorable name meant to Nathan. As a kid with no past, he had no family to lean on. No legacy to leave, except the name given to him by a woman he never met. "Matter of fact, the newspapers will likely write glowing reports all about it. Those El Lobo dime novels will look like alphabet primers in comparison."

Nathan spent most of his life taking the long way around trouble, but it always found him anyway. He never went looking for it, but stayed ready at all times. Along the way, his only loyalty had been to the memory of a lonely kid and the wise priest who raised him.

Surely Father Miguel didn't believe he had anything to do with those murders. Or did he?

Nathan rubbed a hand over the scruff along his jaw.

"With DeLaney tied up in Cimarron, Juliana and I will be back in Texas gathering support from the Rangers. We'll be waiting for the go-ahead from Pinkerton to return to make the arrests."

Once again, Nathan's hand instinctively rested on the hilt of his gun. "That's tough territory down there."

"That's why Commander Pinkerton has asked for your help." Juliana seemed encouraged and was quick to press on. "After your arrest is made public, you'll have a couple of weeks to scout around for clues and come up with a connection we can make stick."

"With a price on my head? That will make for some

pretty fancy detective work."

"Not if no one knows who you are." Juliana looked confused.

"How do you plan on making that happen? They know me pretty well down that way."

Clearing her throat, she went on. "Mr. Wolfe, Lily has this whole thing worked out."

"Lily Valentine." Hickok slapped a knee and gave another whistle of a different kind, adding a waggle of his brow. "I just may ride down with you, Lobo. I wouldn't mind having another gander at that little gal, myself."

Cade continued, "Lily's already in Cimarron waiting for you. Staying at the big hotel and stage depot Augus owned. She's intent on figuring out who's done this. We all are. Augus deserves nothing less."

"Cade and I are only there for a couple of weeks to help get things rolling after your arrest. Lily will stay in Cimarron with you until the killer is caught." Juliana stepped forward. "Keep in mind, it was her idea to put you out at your mission in disguise."

"What kind of disguise?" The question rumbled from Nathan's chest, controlled but direct.

She eyed his jaw. "You'll need to shave a bit closer. Clerics usually don't go for facial hair."

Nathan's gaze shot toward his longtime friend. "Father Miguel will never go for it."

"Lily tells me he wasn't fond of the idea, to be sure." Juliana smiled. "But he's not completely opposed to it either. He isn't at all happy that innocent men are being killed. Especially given that someone has gone to great lengths to pin all of this on you."

So much had happened since he'd left New Mexico. If

truth be told, he was tired of Kansas. Keeping one eye over his shoulder just to stay alive. A good talk with the Padre right about now would do wonders for his soul. Father Miguel spent years trying to convince him all he needed in this life was to keep his faith and keep his word. Make a decent effort to treat every man equally. He promised that if he did, Nathaniel Wolfe would be welcomed—and accepted—wherever the Good Lord led him.

Nathan stifled a laugh.

He'd done a fine job of messing up that crazy notion. He was accepted all right. Accepted as a quick ticket to fame for anyone daring enough to catch him off guard. Somehow, somewhere he and the Good Lord seemed to have parted ways.

This Lobo imposter went after the very thing Nathan was most protective of. His name. Such as it was, it was still his and his alone. The prospect of personally nailing the man who was making a mockery of it was tempting.

Obviously, Allan Pinkerton had not given up on him. Maybe the Padre hadn't either.

Nathan looked up from where he'd been studying the shine on his boots into the expectant faces of his most loyal friends.

"When do we leave?"

Chapter Two

"SHE GOT 'EM! Antelope stew for supper!" A couple of boys popped up from behind a clump of mesquite.

"I told ya Jessa could do it. She once lassoed the wings off a hummingbird." Bucky Jamison vaulted over a dry pebble creek with Wheezer Phillips fast on his heels.

"Steady, boy." From atop her paint pony, Jessa Jamison ran leather-gloved fingers along her horse's long neck while the end of her rope wriggled frantically against the pommel of her saddle. "Careful, this one's feisty. Use your knife. Be quick and be done with it."

The boys disappeared into a scrub of piñon bushes to claim their prize.

Jessa backed her mount to tighten the slack. She hadn't gotten a good look at the antlers, but if the skirmish he was kicking up was any indication, this was surely a pronghorn.

"Jee hoshaphat!" Wheezer Phillips sprang backward from the brush, landing with a thud on his backside.

"Gosh Amighty, Jessa!" Bucky shot out behind his friend, stumbling over to his sister's horse. "Let him loose! Quick!" Frantically grabbing at her rope, Bucky caused her pony to sidestep.

"What on earth's gotten into you?" Jessa swatted his grimy fingers with her reins. She hadn't been keen on helping these two catch themselves an antelope in the first place. But now that she'd agreed, she wanted to get it over with. "Don't tell me you're scared of finishing the job."

"T-That ain't no antelope," Wheezer stuttered, pushing at his wire-rimmed spectacles with one hand and yanking at his oversized britches with the other.

A rise of alarm prickled the hair at the back of her neck. Her gaze shot to the rustling brush. Sliding from her saddle, she steadied her horse, continuing to peer at the source of the racket.

True, she hadn't actually set eyes on it, but she'd seen a herd of antelope heading this way. As soon as his brown head appeared just over the top of a small piñon tree, she'd roped him. It hadn't been big enough—or furry enough—to be a bear. So, what had the boys so spooked? Both were talking so loudly and so fast she couldn't make out a word either of them were saying.

Nearing the fracas, the strange sounds coming from the thicket took on an almost human quality. Her heartbeat kept pace with her hurried steps as she followed the lead of her rope.

Parting the bushes, Jessa gasped.

The small priest from the mission down the way was trussed up like a Christmas goose.

"Father Miguel!" She rushed to his side, removing the dark hood that had fallen across his face, muffling his protests. "Oh, my heavens! Are you hurt?"

"You'll go to the devil over this, sure as shootin'." Bucky stood back with eyes wide.

Wheezer nodded in solemn agreement.

Jessa ignored their prediction, working the rope free from Father Miguel's chest where his arms were pinned snugly to his side.

His usually gentle eyes snapped with indignation.

"Honest to goodness, Father, I didn't see you there. We thought you were a ..."

"Wasn't me. Jessa did it. Papa always told her she'd never catch a man unless she lassoed him on the run." Bucky was as worked up as a politician on Election Day. "Well, she caught one alright. A holy one, to boot!"

With a stiff arm, Wheezer stood at attention, offering an awkward salute. It was painfully obvious the boy was unfamiliar about how to greet a man of the cloth.

"Put your hand down, Wheez. He ain't the president." Bucky threw an elbow at the thin boy's side, causing him to crumple over.

With an exasperated shrug, Father Miguel rid himself of the thick twine.

Jessa recovered the priest's Indian blanket from the ground and handed it back with a sheepish grin. The nuts sprinkled inside were evidence that he'd been shaking down the piñon trees before his feet were yanked out from under him.

"I am truly sorry, Father." Sincere regret warmed her cheeks. "I hope you know I wouldn't set out to hurt you for the world."

His look of irritation softened as he accepted the woven spread. "Come, walk with me." He held out an arm to allow her to precede him from the brush. "You two *vaqueritos*, as well. Come along."

The boys took up the procession, balancing themselves on a wheel rut as they walked along.

"Let me make this up to you, Father." Jessa rolled her lasso and retied it to her saddle. "I'll have Miss Ramsey whip up one of her apple cakes. I'll even bring it out to the mission myself."

"No, no." He patted her arm and kept moving. "No need for a peace offering."

"I promise to borrow Wheezer's glasses next time I go trapping an animal in the brush." Father Miguel responded to her embarrassment with a short chuckle. "And I will keep my head up to make certain I am seen."

"Hey," Bucky called out over his shoulder. "You ain't Meth'dist, are ya?" He played hop along in the rut. "That's what we are is Meth'dist."

"Pa says we're German." Wheezer trotted along behind him, trying to sound impressive.

"I trust you boys attend church regularly?" Father Miguel smiled as they exchanged puzzled looks.

"I made sure they went whenever the circuit preacher was in town." Jessa grew quiet as she walked alongside her pony. "But ever since Reverend Emerson was gunned down, I do the best I can teaching them from Mama's old Bible."

"Reverend Emerson was a cherished friend. His death was a considerable loss. As I recall, he was going to meet with your father in Taos. Neither of them made it home." Compassion in his brown eyes tempered the sting of his words. "I was greatly saddened by *Señor* Jamison's passing. You are left with great responsibility raising young Bucky. This will not be an easy task."

Jessa slipped a golden wisp of hair behind her ear. In all the ruckus, the neat ribbon tied at the nape of her neck now hung low and slightly off to one side.

She wasn't ready to consider that her father might be gone for good. His body was never found. He could just as easily be out there on a new adventure. Still, folks meant well with their sad wishes and promises to pray, so she learned to redirect their attention. "Bucky is mischievous as the day is long. But he's a good boy. Papa would have it no other way."

"Augus Jamison was a fine man. He and your mother stayed a short time with us at the mission upon their arrival from Texas." He smiled kindly. "And you. You were an infant, but beautiful even then."

"Well, I suppose if chubby and toothless is beautiful, then I was a beauty." She smiled thinking of the baby painting her father hung over the mantle. She was never certain whether the artist merely lacked talent or if she really did have a big ol' Benjamin Franklin head on a tiny little body.

Hearing Father Miguel laugh somehow eased the guilt she felt at her horrific blunder. "Papa always speaks well of you and the mission."

They moved to the side of the dirt road to allow a couple of riders past, waving off the dust kicked up in the wake while the boys galloped after the horses on pretend ponies.

"Your father was a good friend to our mission. Always generous with his time and contributions." Father Miguel spoke louder to be heard over the boys' excitement. "He often sent food and clothing for our children."

Jessa calmed her pony. "How many children do you have now, Father? I'd like to ride out and visit them sometime."

He stopped at the fork splitting the roads between Cimarron and Elizabethtown. This is where they would part company. Jessa spotted the mission's adobe walls in the distance.

"We have five *niños* living with us at the moment, aged two to eight." He used his weathered hand to show the differences in height. "They get lonesome for new faces.

They would enjoy your visit very much."

"I'm thinking of becoming a missionary." Jessa smiled at his obvious surprise. "I've submitted an application to the Women's Missionary Council in New York. I hope I get to go to Persia, or India, or somewhere far across the ocean."

Her heart was to help people, or as Papa would say, "a natural care-taker." She would see Bucky through his formative years, then she'd set off on her own.

Papa told story after story of the places he'd been and people he'd met. He made it a point to leave folks feeling a little better about themselves everywhere he went. She believed with all her heart that's why God had so richly blessed him all these years. He was like a beacon of hope. That's what she wanted to be, too.

Suddenly an idea sent a wave of excitement through her, and Jessa stopped abruptly. "I've got it!"

The Father shielded his eyes to better see her face.

An incredible thought surfaced at the mention of the mixed bag of children staying at the mission. "I'll bring some books and read to them. And if the hot weather holds off, we can bring a picnic lunch down by the riverbank. I'll have Miss Ramsey pack us a basket full of treats. Do you think they'd enjoy that?"

"*Maravilla!*" Father Miguel seemed genuinely pleased. "They would be delighted to have a lovely *señorita* take such interest in them. Is reading something you enjoy?"

"I love it. I have a few children's books with pretty pictures. I will definitely bring those. And I have the latest copy of Harper's New Monthly, too. There's a story about life out here in the West."

The priest raised his bushy eyebrows in amazement.

Jessa nodded. "We're considered outrageously wild, according to folks back East. They can't get enough stories about us." She grinned at the misconception most had about the land they called home. "It's an interesting article. I particularly like the political series that comes out every month." The admission spilled out before she could stop herself. Women weren't supposed to be interested in such things. Thankfully, the Father didn't appear inclined to berate her for it. "How about I come out next Monday?"

"*Muy bien.* It's settled then. I will tell the children this evening. Your brother and his young friend there are welcome to come along." Father Miguel stood with his hands folded as if he was about to pray.

He'd need to pray if she agreed to bring Bucky with her. Those poor kids had enough troubles without adding her brother. "Thank you for the offer, Father. But he will be tending to his school lessons ... and then there's chores ... and he promised to help Miss Ramsey plant some blackberries. Maybe next time."

Father Miguel gave her a knowing smile and she felt heat rise in her cheeks. They both knew she'd just danced a circle around his invitation.

"Very well, then. We shall expect you next Monday." With that he put a hand to her face and smiled before turning to make his way down the narrow road.

Jessa watched him for a moment before swinging up into her saddle. How could she have mistaken that gentle man for an antelope of all things? Well, she was determined to make it up to him one way or another.

Wheeling her pony around to head toward home, she glanced back twice.

For some reason, she couldn't shake the feeling that something significant awaited her out at the old pueblo mission.

Chapter Three

THE COOL APRIL breeze fluttered in from an open window, quickly cooling her bath.

Shrugging into a gloriously thick robe, Jessa sank to her knees in front of the hearth to place another log onto the hungry flames. Holding her hands out to the heat, she gazed into the flickering glow.

Ever since she'd gotten a brochure from the Women's Missionary Council, she'd been convinced she wanted to go to Calcutta. India was half a world away and involved a whole new culture to explore. To think of all the good she could do.

Unlike here where nothing exciting ever happened. Or if it did, it usually involved meanness and debauchery. Since the war, Cimarron had seen a steady stream of drifters, most of them bitter or flat-out looney. Every one of them were armed and looking for a quick way to make a buck.

Honest farmers and sheepherders had been thinned out by the bank foreclosing and taking over their land. Seemed like there weren't a whole lot of honest folk left.

Jessa took up a boar bristle brush to begin the painstaking task of removing tangles from her wet curls. She used to love it as a little girl when her mother would brush her hair before the fire. So much was different after Mama was killed.

She'd been working the registration desk of the hotel when an unhappy land owner followed the surveyor inside and shot at him as he signed for a room. The bullet missed its intended target, but with that one shot, Jessa was left without her beloved mother.

"Careful, love. You hack at your lovely tresses as if they were weeds in a garden." In her incomparable way, Lily Valentine glided in from the hallway. Her elegant skirts swirled noiselessly around her as she pulled a padded bench over from the foot of the bed and took over the tedious task herself. "Now, what's this Bucky tells me about you bushwhacking a preacher?" One perfectly shaped brow rose a tad higher than the other.

"The Father wasn't, I mean, I didn't exactly—" Jessa pulled the belt of her robe tighter around her waist. "Not on purpose anyway. Thank heavens he wasn't hurt, just good and shaken up."

"Best you start from the beginning. Who was not hurt?"

"Father Miguel, the priest from the mission."

"I remember him. What on earth did you do to the poor man?"

"It's a funny story, really." With a forced laugh, she reminded herself to tread lightly. "What time did you say your friends are arriving?"

Having brushed Jessa's hair to a silky shine, Lily moved to shut the window. The north wind had picked up and her room held a chill despite the roaring fire. "Four ten. Now, continue your funny story."

With an exaggerated sigh, she began to finger comb her hair to help it dry. "Father Miguel was out picking piñons. I thought he was an antelope. I may have been a bit hasty in throwing my rope. I took him down before he ever saw it coming."

Jessa knew how much Lily disliked careless mistakes, especially when they put others in danger. Everything she did was calculated and measured. She never let impatience get the best of her. This was probably why she was the best female detective alive.

And most probably why Jessa was not.

Lily's stoic expression held, giving nothing away until her lip finally curled in amusement. "He wasn't hurt then?"

"I made sure of it before I left him. He wasn't too happy, I will say that. But he's a gracious man. He invited me to come read to the children out at the mission on Monday."

"I expect he will have a new novice staying there by then. I shall send an invitation for them both to join us for dinner next week. I'm anxious to meet the man."

How Lily knew these things was as big a mystery as Lily herself. Papa said she was the best private investigator Pinkerton had. Tough, yet unquestionably elegant. Brilliant and shrewd. Easily the most beautiful woman in the room on any given day. She never spoke of her past but her speech held a hint of her English roots. Papa said she was a lady of the realm or something that had to do with royalty. She was called Lady Lily Valentine there, just about the most regal-sounding name Jessa had ever heard.

She and Augus Jamison had been working together on a case when Jessa's mother was killed. He'd taken the news especially hard and Lily had been a true friend to them all during that time.

Papa somehow convinced Lily that Jessa was at a tender age—barely twelve—and needed a female influence in her life. He'd convinced her to take her under her wing. Like a godmother, or a favorite aunt, although nothing official or on paper. Just a commitment of the heart.

Lily wrote letters regularly and sent frilly gifts for every birthday. They developed a special bond over the years, and Jessa aspired to be just as daring as she was someday.

"Juliana will be delighted to meet you. You can wear one of the new ensembles I brought you from Chicago." Lily opened the heavy oak wardrobe and took down a stiff lace blouse with a flowery satin skirt and matching short jacket. "No need to make that face, love. As far as I am aware, Honiton lace has never been a viable cause of death."

The woman had eyes in the back of her head.

Here in New Mexico Territory, fancy lace and satin was as out of place as her buckskin britches would be in a palace. Most women in town made their own clothes from calico bought from Phillips General Store, unlike Lily, who special ordered her dresses from Paris and London and New York. She had the figure to pull it off, too.

Jessa was built like a boy.

Lily's every action commanded admiration and respect. She traveled the world over and never let anything hold her back.

With her head cocked to one side, Jessa watched Lily lay out a bunch of lacy underthings. Maybe she should follow in Lily's footsteps and become a Pinkerton detective. She was certainly curious enough, and good at finding answers to things. Signing on with the prestigious agency would surely get her out of Cimarron and away from the mundane life of running a hotel.

Since Lily's arrival, they'd spent every evening discussing her father and the possibilities surrounding his disappearance. Lily was easy to talk to and had an unusual knack for asking all the right questions. Nonetheless, she was an expert at avoiding questions about herself. Jessa sensed she'd experienced great sorrow at some time in her young life.

One day she'd figure out what brought her friend all the way here from the courts of London. And why she was so committed to righting every injustice in the world. And why she seemed to avoid her own happiness. Surely Lily thought about settling down someday. She wasn't old by a longshot, just a bit beyond what most would consider a marriageable age.

Honestly, Lily didn't look a day over twenty-five.

When Jessa was helping her put her trunks away, she had come across the stub of a ticket for a passenger ship from just last year. The listing was for Lady Lily Valentine, female, age: twenty-nine years old.

Folks around here would call that an old maid. But certainly not to her face.

"What has you so far off, love? Surely, the thought of trading your buckskin for the latest fashion doesn't require such deep reflection. What is going on in that mind of yours?"

Jessa's hand stilled. "Lily, how did you meet Papa?"

Lily laid out a soft-sided corset and fresh petticoats on Jessa's flannel quilt. "Though I admire your clever deduction, you are heading down a rabbit hole." Without looking up, she added a pair of stockings. "Augus was a colleague only. One to whom I owe a great deal of appreciation and gratitude. He was unrivaled as a detective. I considered him and your mother dear friends."

"So you're saying—"

"I am saying that after your mother died, there was

nothing romantic between your father and me." She gave a nod to where the latest edition of Harper's Bazaar was laid open on the window seat. "You should stick to your political articles and leave the romantic stories alone."

Jessa frowned. The question had begged to be asked.

"Keep your head and guard your heart well, Jessa. Romance is fickle. Oftentimes, it's nothing more than a figment of one's imagination. That's all I'm saying."

That might be all she was saying for now, but there was plenty more she wasn't saying. Which only fueled Jessa's curiosity. There wasn't time to get to the bottom of this just now, but later on she would find out what dastardly deed had brought this beautiful woman to such a low opinion of love.

For now, she'd keep quiet and endure the useless contraptions she had laid out on the bed.

"How about we agree to a trade off? You wear the corset, and I won't try to convince you to wear your hair up for dinner." Lily watched her in the swiveled mirror over the dressing table as she fluffed the lace on her scooped neckline.

"How about I wear my hair up and leave that thing in the closet?"

Miss Ramsey, the housekeeper, entered with a knock at the open door. "Mr. and Mrs. Matlock have just arrived. I put them in the burgundy room on the first floor. My, but they are a handsome couple. Newly married, and so very in love."

Jessa noticed Lily's reaction in the mirror. With her eyes downcast, she let out an exaggerated sigh before an almost pained expression flitted across her face. If the thought of newlywed bliss caused her that much discomfort, she must carry an awfully heavy burden. Someone needed to help restore her faith in love. Help show her she still had plenty of life left, and whatever had happened to steal her joy could all be put to rights with a little support from people who loved her.

The caregiver inside of Jessa instantly jumped to the occasion. She was just the one to do it. Her missionary dream to India would have to wait. Instead, she'd tag along with Lily as a Pinkerton. All good detectives had a trusty sidekick. She would be that for her dearest friend. Maybe even help her find love somewhere along the way. They would have grand travels together just like the stories her father told.

Solving crimes was a benevolent thing to do. She could still help people in need, they'd just have different sorts of needs.

Mind made up, she decided the best way to convince Lily, and Mister Pinkerton, and Cade Matlock, and his new wife was to go along with her plan.

First of all, she'd wear the dress. Even the petticoats if it meant being taken more seriously as a professional detective. She'd do whatever was needed to show them she was as good as any of their other operatives.

Chapter Four

Lost in quiet reflection, Nathan stood in the cobblestone courtyard of the mission where he'd grown up. Snow-dipped peaks of the Sangre de Cristo Mountains provided a regal backdrop to the old church's bell tower. To the east, miles of rolling plains lay covered in a thick shag of grama grass. Southward, thatches of sagebrush freckled the mesa as far as the eye could see. Along the horizon, a bosque of trees wound vagabond along the Cimarron River.

Nathan took a deep breath from the crisp morning breeze, warming his hands on a steaming cup of coffee. Nothing cleared his head like cool mountain air.

Cedarwood smoke poured from chimneys in the surrounding village. Mingled with the smell of fresh coffee and potatoes frying in bacon grease, this must be what heaven smells like in the morning.

Taking another sip, he reached inside his shirt pocket to remove a tattered handkerchief that he kept with him at all times. Many a man had teased him over the years while most women just assumed it was from an old flame, someone bearing the initials of A.R.

He let them believe whatever they wanted. It made no difference to him. The familiar feel of the well-worn material between his thumb and forefinger never failed to bring a certain calm when his thoughts were unsettled.

Any fanciful notions about the woman who'd embroidered those initials were dismissed a long time ago. The letter she'd left for him had been read, and for the most part, forgotten. But there was something comforting in the feel of the handkerchief.

Nathan propped a shoulder against a giant cottonwood at the center of the courtyard to watch a mountain blue jay searching out a morning meal. The bird had what he could only dream of—freedom. Freedom to move when and where he pleased. Land wherever he wanted to. No thought to danger, merely living day-to-day without a care in the world.

A scrawny yellow dog caught his eye over on the west mesa as it sniffed around a prairie dog mound. With a sudden yelp, the hound leaped backward, and Nathan had to laugh. The pup had a thing or two to learn about sticking his nose where it didn't belong.

Pushing off from the tree, he shook his head. He wasn't usually given to mindless daydreams. No sense fooling himself. There was no rest for men like him. He was destined to keep moving. Had to if he wanted to stay alive. He could dream all day long about settling down, finding a little spread in the valley somewhere. But as long as he was forced to strap on a gun every morning, he knew better than to get too attached to any one place for very long. Inevitably, someone would recognize him, and he'd be forced to move on.

All the wishing and dreaming and scheming in the world wouldn't change that.

The path he'd taken hadn't always been an easy one, but he'd managed to stay alive along the way. More than he could say for most with a quickdraw reputation.

Once again, he studied the clay walls of the mission. Amazing how much he'd missed this place. Solid and secure. For all that felt unstable in his life as a kid, the mission had stood up to it all. His upbringing here had been solitary by most standards, but not unhappy.

As a kid, he'd stood in this very spot watching the local boys play stickball in the road on the other side of the low courtyard wall. They never gave him a second glance until the Padre brought out a plate of sugared biscochitos and suddenly he had a passel of new friends.

Nathan grinned at the memory, taking another sip of his coffee.

Father Miguel had even gone so far as to join the game himself until seven-year-old Nathan felt comfortable enough to hold his own with the older boys. A row of black-and-white robed nuns cheered him on from the side yard. He'd played twice as hard as any of the others to make his audience proud.

Proud they'd been, too. Well, except prune-faced Sister Helena who shook her head and made clicking sounds with her tongue. She was a stern one. But she didn't dare cross the Padre. He'd send her off to make bread or pick apples for supper, so Nathan could play in peace.

Funny the things that come to mind when surrounded by reminders from your past.

"The morning holds a chill, no?"

Nathan tilted his head against the bright sun to see Father Miguel coming toward him. He missed his hat. "Morning, Padre."

"*Buenos dias*, Nathaniel." Father Miguel was the only one who ever called him Nathaniel.

"You caught me daydreaming."

"*Por supuesto.* It is good to visit our memories now and again." The Father's gaze was drawn to the same spot in the road. "The past gives substance to the future."

Typical padre answer. Vague enough to make you have to think, but direct enough to know he was speaking directly to you.

"Or ..." Nathan replaced the treasured handkerchief into his pocket. "... it takes up time better spent earning your keep. What can I do to help out while I'm here? Is that old stovepipe still acting up?"

"She still asks about you, *mijo.*" Father Miguel pointed to the pocket where Nathan had put his mother's handkerchief.

The Padre's words turned his blood cold.

"Why bother?" He held no animosity toward the woman. In fact, he rarely thought about her at all. He'd given up trying to persuade Father Miguel to reveal her identity ages ago. The priest had given his word, and being the man he was, he'd take her secret to his deathbed. Whether or not he agreed or disagreed with her decision to keep it from Nathan, he had always maintained it was her decision to make. "Seriously, I can't figure why she'd care."

It was a fair question.

"You mustn't think badly of her. *Tu madre* has always done the best she could. She cares very much, but she is not able to show it openly."

An ugly laugh was all Nathan could manage. "No, we wouldn't want to disgrace the poor woman, now would we? God forbid someone might guess she'd birthed a kid with savage blood running through his veins."

He ran a hand over his dark hair, instantly irritated at the mere mention of the woman who'd left him here.

Aggravated that she could still stir up that ache deep down in his gut. "But that's about what I've come to expect from the fairer sex, Padre. They love you when it's convenient, get what they can out of the deal, then scramble off before anything more is expected."

"Nathaniel, you are too young to harbor such bitterness." The Father's voice grew quiet. "You have convinced yourself that all women are heartless. This is simply not the case. This hate will destroy you."

"I don't hate women, Padre." It was the truth. He found them highly entertaining at times. "I just don't trust them as far as I can spit upwind."

Father Miguel sighed heavily. "Even as a boy you were cautious. I regret you never had a respectable woman outside of our sisters to draw this trust from. Certainly, the company you keep now is not the proper measure of a lady."

Well, he had him there. The tainted women in Kansas, even the ones he'd encountered on the trail before that, were not the best source of feminine virtue.

"You must realize not all women are the same. *Tu madre* did what she felt was best. She acted with her heart. You have read her letter. Her choice to stay away has always been for your good. She is a fine lady, Nathaniel. Someday, I hope you will see this for yourself."

The Padre's words were a waste of good breath. Nathan had made up his mind on the subject years ago. Dealing with a two-headed rattler was easier by a long shot than putting up with a conniving female.

"I will pray for you. One day you will know the love of a good woman."

Mercifully, the peal of children's laughter saved him

from saying the first thing that sprang to mind. Good women wanted nothing to do with the likes of him.

"I noticed the tower cross could use some tending to." Nathan tossed out the last of his coffee.

Father Miguel nodded. "I am afraid there is much in need of repair. The pump to the water well is loose again. Perhaps you can have a look at it, no?" He patted his former pupil on the back.

"Sure thing. I'll see that things are all squared away around here before I leave." Nathan began rolling up his sleeves when he caught the look of concern marring the priest's brow. "What else is on your mind, Padre?"

"It's nothing, really."

Nathan nodded and turned to begin his work when the Father stopped him.

"Except that it worries me to see you moving about so freely. With no regard to whether you are recognized. Though it is unorthodox, I would prefer that you wear a cassock. There is a large reward for your arrest."

Nathan glanced over at the three girls and two boys playing in the side yard. The smallest of them, wobbling on an older girl's knee, caught his eye and smiled broadly, waving her chubby little hand. "I suppose it wouldn't do for them to see me carted off—or worse."

"Particularly, given that we have recently received threats."

Nathan reached out and caught hold of the Father's arm as he began to walk past. "What threats?"

"There was no need to trouble you, Nathaniel. I have made it a matter of prayer."

"Trouble me anyway." Nathan fought the urge to pack them all up and check them in to the hotel. They'd be a great deal easier to keep an eye on. Out here, they were an open target.

"Twice a rider has come to deliver a message from Mr. Hollinger, the *presidenté* of the bank."

"What does Hollinger have to do with you? The mission is no concern of his. The bank holds no mortgage."

"No, but the man claims to own the land it sits on."

The Padre needn't say more.

The main reason Hollinger decided to take aim at the mission had nothing to do with the church itself. It had everything to do with getting revenge.

This fight was personal. He wasn't about to let the Padre or the kids get dragged into it.

Hollinger would soon find out, Nathan didn't appreciate threats. The Padre might seem like easy prey, but he did not stand alone.

Nathan would defend him to the death.

Chapter Five

B Y TEN O'CLOCK the tower cross once again stood tall, and the handle of the water pump pressed with ease. The sun played hide and seek with a few stray clouds as it climbed higher in the turquoise sky.

Nathan kept himself busy clearing the list of needed repairs. Not an easy task in the priest's robe he wore, which was too tight across the shoulders and at least six inches too short. He refused to give up the shade of his hat, but the absence of his gun belt kept him uneasy.

The children took turns on a play horse he'd rigged up from an old saddle and some rope, unconcerned with the real horse and rider fast approaching from the east.

Nathan, however, had eyed the white and sorrel paint pony since it first came into sight. The rider was too small to be much of a threat, still he wasn't ready to dismiss it altogether.

Chickens scattered noisily in the road as the pony skidded to a halt on the other side of the mission's wall. A red hat atop the mysterious rider's head fell down her back to reveal a cascade of golden curls.

"Hello there, Father." She tilted her head to the side for a moment before sliding effortlessly from her saddle. Buckskin britches hugged her slim hips and long legs. Oddly, it wasn't without a certain appeal.

Nathan straightened. A grip of uneasiness seized him the moment he focused on the lady's bright, amber-colored eyes. Gold as a prize nugget, outlined in a perfect fringe of black lashes. Like the Creator took extra care when putting this one together.

"You are the new priest, aren't you?" Her manner was easy, unaffected, despite his impatient glare. Most men avoided his gaze altogether, but she had yet to look away.

Must not be too bright.

"Father Miguel's inside."

"I'm actually looking for the new priest that's come to train with Father Miguel. That's not you?" She lifted a brow and nodded at his borrowed robe, not bothering one bit to hide her smile. "You dress awfully funny if you're not."

Suddenly remembering his disguise, Nathan silently reprimanded himself for becoming distracted. "Certainly … daughter." He gave her a half-smile, trying to guess at how the Padre would handle this. "What can I do for you?"

On instinct, he watched her closely. No one came right out asking for him unless they were up to no good. She may look all innocent and sweet, but he had a gut feeling she could be a handful of trouble.

"I promised Father Miguel I'd come read to the children this morning. I hope it's still all right." Her vivid gaze was steady and, by all appearances, genuine. "He's expecting me."

"I'll let him know you're here." Nathan led her to the front doors of the mission. He wanted to know why she'd come looking for him in particular, but he preferred to get the details from Father Miguel.

As they turned the corner, she paused beside a bench at the entrance. "If it's all the same, I'd rather read out here in the courtyard, The day is so nice, seems a shame to let all this sunshine go to waste."

Sunshine. That's what she reminded him of.

The golden hue of her skin, honey color of her hair, and gold flecks in her eyes looked like she gained her very life from the sun.

"Are you new to the priesthood?" She untied the chinstrap to remove her hat.

"You could say that." Nathan noticed both boys playing in the side yard circling in for a closer look. He wasn't the only one curious about the new arrival. "Just came down from Kansas a couple of days ago."

"So, you're a novice?"

Nathan laughed out loud. It had been a long while since he'd been called a novice anything. "Well, I'm new to being a priest, that's for sure."

"Then you're the one Lily sent this note for." She removed an envelope from the back pocket of her britches and offered it to him. "She specifically said to give it to the novice priest."

Accepting the note, he saw that it was from Lily Valentine. A quick scan told him she needed to meet and asked that he and Father Miguel come to the Jamison Ranch for dinner the next evening. This bright-eyed beauty was apparently Augus Jamison's daughter. "Jamison, huh? You got another name to go along with that?"

"Jessa." She offered a leather-gloved hand with a smile. "Jessa Jamison. Nice to meet you."

Nathan accepted her hand because it was expected, reminding himself that priests were supposed to be kind and gentle. He didn't need to stir up her suspicions.

The two-year-old toddled up with arms raised to be

held. Without hesitation, she lifted the child onto her lap.

"You smell pretty," the Bradford girl piped up. The smaller girl nodded in agreement.

"It's lilac lotion. Our housekeeper makes it from wild lilac bushes that grow by our house. I'll bring you some next time I come out." Jessa reached over and smoothed a hank of hair out of the little girl's eyes.

Nathan turned away, not entirely comfortable with the tender gesture.

One by one, the other children gathered around her.

"What's your name?" She smiled down at a blushing child of about six or seven.

"Sissy!" the baby on her lap provided, tapping the small girl's shoulder as if it were a game which the others found funny.

"I see." Jessa put an arm around her. "So, you and the baby are sisters?"

"Yes'm. We're Bradfords. That's my baby sister, Nora. I'm Nelly, and over there's our brother, Jacob. He's the oldest 'cause he's already ten." She pointed to a boy with guarded eyes hanging back from the group.

Something akin to pity flooded over Jessa's features as she was met with the reality of the children's predicament. He'd seen it a million times in faces of well-meaning town folk. Pity tempered with a fair amount of curiosity. When he was a kid they used to fawn and coo over him like he was a sideshow at the county fair. "Poor dear. Wonder what happened to his folks?" If he'd heard it once, he'd heard it a hundred times.

Soon enough, the novelty wore off. They'd pat his head and be on their way, returning to their cozy homes without giving the kids at the mission another thought. Thinking about it still made his blood boil.

No one would treat these kids that way. Not while he was around to stop it.

Lifting his gaze, he looked them over one by one. None of these kids appeared the slightest bit offended. In fact, they lapped up her attention like starving pups.

The remaining two stepped forward to provide their names. An Hispanic boy, proudly displaying his missing front teeth, and a little Navajo girl, about the same age. Nelly, the mother hen of the brood, hovered to provide any detail the others might leave out.

Jessa respectfully shook their hands in turn as they came forward to be introduced. "Pleasure to meet you." Her smile brought a warm blush to each of their small faces.

Nathan watched carefully for a condescending frown or a mocking tone in her voice but found nothing. From what he could gather, she genuinely enjoyed their company.

The sound of her laughter brought his attention to an upside-down tree frog hanging by one leg that the youngest boy held out to her. The kid's face beamed with the sincerity of his gift and Jessa Jamison accepted it without qualms. She had an easy confidence, a good-humored way about her. Like friendliness just bubbled up from inside her.

Which made no sense at all. She'd recently lost her father. She should be sad and mourning. So, what made her so quick with a smile?

Even more reason to keep an eye on her. He'd learned to never turn his back on the friendly ones.

"*Señorita* Jamison!" Father Miguel came around from the garden, grinning and dusting off his hands. "I did not hear you arrive."

Jessa stood holding the toddler with one hand and the

tree frog tightly in the other. "Hello, Father. I haven't been here long. We're all getting better acquainted." She looked around at the children before allowing her gaze to settle on Nathan.

"So, I see." The priest also glanced at Nathan before quickly sending the children in for a snack. "I hope you do not mind. They will be much more attentive to your stories if they have something in their bellies."

"I don't mind." Jessa bent to set her present free. "We have friends in town. They'd like for you and your novice to come to supper tomorrow night. They are awfully interested in meeting your new priest."

The Padre would lose his shirt playing poker. The guilt he felt at deceiving her clearly ate at him.

Nathan quickly intervened. "Pad … uh, Father, I need to speak to you. Privately. 'Scuse us, ma'am." Nathan took the small priest by the arm and the two disappeared around the corner.

"It's for her own good. The less people we let in on this, the safer we'll all be."

"But *mijo*, this seems so dishonest." The priest looked up at Nathan, imploring his former student in hushed tones. "She is a fine young woman. I know she will keep your secret."

Nathan shook his head, firm in his resolve. "Can't chance it." Jessa Jamison made him uneasy. He'd been living on instinct too long to ignore the feeling. "Lily chose to leave her out of this, and so did Cade. We'd best do the same."

With a heavy sigh, Father Miguel lifted his hands in surrender. "I will go along for now. But I do not like this. She is far too clever. I see the way she looks at you."

Nathan returned to the courtyard with barely a nod in Jessa's direction. Taking up a hammer, he moved to the other side of the gate to fix a hinge, avoiding her as much as possible.

A useless effort. The memory of her striking gaze was seared in his mind. She was a nuisance is what she was. One he didn't need right now. He'd have a talk with Lily and suggest she keep her home from now on. At least while he was around.

By the time she finished reading to the children, the sun cast long shadows over the mesa. Standing in the side yard, Nathan watched her ride off toward Cimarron with her loose curls flapping in the wind.

"*Muy bonita*, no?" Father Miguel came to stand at his side.

"Nothing special." Nathan wiped his hands on a rag.

Then crossed himself for lying as soon as the Padre turned around.

Chapter Six

JESSA HAD MET Cade Matlock twice before, the last time being five years ago when she was fourteen going on fifteen. For the most part, he still treated her like she was a bothersome kid. So far, he'd been the greatest obstacle in persuading Lily to let her help with the case. Even though Lily had the most sway, Cade still had to sign off on it. Unfortunately, he and Juliana were leaving to go back to Texas on Friday. She only had two days to plead her case.

Suddenly anxious to get on with it, she swept her napkin across her lips then tossed it onto the side table. "Leave the dishes, Miss Ramsey, I'll get to them before I head out to the stables."

The housekeeper handed her a white china cup and saucer with just the right amount of milk and coffee inside. "I won't hear of it. Enjoy your company and don't give the dishes another thought."

The others were already finished with their afternoon pastries and were settled in to enjoy their coffee. Jessa jumped at the perfect opportunity. "You said we could discuss my officially joining your ranks after dessert. So, let's discuss." She smiled brightly to set the mood.

"You can't deny that she has tenacity." Lily was the only one who smiled back.

"Yes, but like Cade said, her unreasonable fear of guns

might put a damper on dealing with bad men." Juliana's glib observation was a tad patronizing for Jessa's taste.

"I don't fear guns. I detest them. But I can outride and out rope any man—bad or good—in this entire Territory. Or in Texas, either, for that matter," Jessa shot back.

"Very true." Lily was perched elegantly on a rolled arm of the sofa. Ice blue silk cascaded from her cinched waist, pooling gracefully around her feet. "I daresay, Jessa could outride most of your own men, Cade."

"Ha! I could outride *him*." Though Jessa mumbled it quietly, the expressions on their faces told her it had not been quiet enough.

"Jessa, I don't see how the ability to ride a horse, or rope a steer could possibly provide the protection you'll need to take on a job like this. This is very dangerous work." Juliana took another dainty bite of Miss Ramsey's blueberry hand pie. "Mmm. This is delicious."

"You forget that as Pinkertons, we are known for our diverse talents." Lily held her teacup and saucer, one in each hand, looking very refined and elegant. "Where one may have a weakness, another has a strength. It's through our combined talents that we are so incomparably effective."

"In other words, until you can ride without sliding sideways in a saddle, Sweetheart, don't dismiss Jessa's distaste for firearms." Cade gave his wife a playful grin. "You two might need each other someday."

Jessa immediately took it as encouragement. "So you'll let me join? Or enlist? Or whatever you do to get an official Pinkerton badge?"

"No badges." Lily frowned as if the suggestion was distasteful. "Just an oath and a listing on the payroll. Followed by an extensive amount of training."

"How old are you, Jessa?" Juliana was determined to be a fly in the ointment.

"About your age," Jessa answered with a quizzical brow. "Why?"

The sound of Cade's deep chuckle filled the parlor.

Juliana set her plate aside, unaffected by her husband's amusement, as she looked to Lily for confirmation. "Really?"

"The two of you are merely months apart."

"I'm so sorry. I just assumed ..." Juliana crossed the room to examine Jessa a bit closer. "Cade always refers to you and your brother as Augus's children ..." She gently lifted the thick rope of hair that Jessa had hastily braided on her way down and pulled it forward over one shoulder. "I wasn't taking your request seriously, but now I can see that you are no child at all. You are actually a very attractive young woman. I would have guessed you to be about sixteen or seventeen years old. Such innocent beauty."

Jessa said nothing, but studied Juliana's face for ill-intent. She found nothing there but a sincere observation.

Juliana spun back around to face Lily and Cade, hooking her arm through Jessa's. "But now that we know, certainly we can use her!"

Lily also stood. "She's clever, Cade, and she knows this town and its people. Plus, she has Augus's inheritance to dangle in front of this den of thieves." Crossing her arms, she turned to Jessa. "She has spunk and determination. We can work around her impetuous nature."

"All right, all right." Cade sat back in his chair. "I can see I'm outnumbered. It's fine by me as long as you take responsibility for her." He pointed at Lily. "And if you're sure Augus would approve." He pointed at Jessa.

"He'd be all for it! Papa encouraged me to help him reason through a case. Taught me to weigh all the clues." Jessa was so excited she could barely contain herself. "He also knew once I set my mind on something, it was only a matter of time." She flashed her brightest smile. "Once we find Papa, I can move on to the next case, and then the next, and the next. Hopefully, to places far away from here. Somewhere exotic or dangerous or mysterious."

"You read too many of these." Cade picked up a stack of *Harper's New Weekly* from the lamp table. "Made-up stories are always more exciting than real life. Sniffing out counterfeiters in Cleveland ain't all that thrilling."

"But, what about Bucky? You can't just leave him here alone." Juliana looked concerned.

"Augus's last will and testament states that Bucky is to go to military school at age thirteen," Lily provided. "Then on to ride with the Texas Rangers by seventeen. At age twenty-one it's for him to decide whether he carries on his career as a lawman. Money is set aside in a special account for him to attend college if not."

"Leave it to Augus to think of everything," Cade said with a shake of his head. "Lord knows the kid could use the discipline."

"But Bucky is only eleven," Juliana persisted. "He still has two years before he is sent off to military school."

A twinge of guilt gripped Jessa's heart. It was a struggle she dealt with daily. Papa was convinced this was the best plan for his headstrong son.

Jessa was not.

"Seventeen months to be exact," Jessa provided. "He turns twelve in November. I intend to spend every minute of that time with him. I figure this case could take a good six months, then I'll just take Bucky with me wherever Lily and I go from here. It would only be for a year."

When she looked around, hoping for understanding, she was met with questions in each of their expressions. For being top-notch detectives, they weren't very good at hiding their thoughts. This was obviously going to need more explanation than they'd been given. On a sigh, Jessa decided to start from the beginning.

"For most of his life, Bucky's been my responsibility. He was two when mama was killed. He's been a handful since the day he was born."

Lily sat on the sofa and motioned for Jessa to have a seat beside her.

"Papa and I had a mutual arrangement. While he was off doing detective work for the Pinkertons or the Rangers, or seeking out land to add to our holdings, or wooing investors for his latest venture, it was up to me to stay home and see that Bucky was taken care of. We were partners. Fifty-fifty."

"Full-fledged partner at twelve or thirteen?" Juliana came to sit on the other side of her, concern shining in her dark eyes. "You were never allowed to simply be a child?"

"There isn't much to keeping things running around here. The hotel and stage depot runs like clockwork, down to the last stage at ten twenty every evening. Papa made sure Miss Ramsey and the managing staff of the hotel have a vested interest in the place by giving them a share of the profits. Because of it, they covet their positions. Everyone takes the success of this hotel personally, including me."

"That's a mighty big burden to put off on a little lady." Cade sat forward, looking intently into his coffee cup as he spoke. It was plain that he didn't think much of his friend's arrangement. "Too big if you ask me."

Juliana quickly continued, "I'm sure he was only doing the best he could given the circumstances. It's commendable that you have taken on such heavy responsibility and have done so well with it. The Jamison Hotel is one of the finest I've seen south of Saint Louis. The stagehouse is opulent compared to the small-town depots we have back home in Texas."

Even though Papa only made it home three or four times a year, Jessa never doubted his love or devotion to them. He was a man driven to carve out a life they could all be proud of.

"He made a promise to my mother. They met in Philadelphia when she was only seventeen. Her father was Franklin O. Murphy. Some big financier up there."

"I've heard of him." Cade spoke as if he was thinking aloud.

"Bucky and I never met any of Mama's family." Jessa would have liked to know them, but she was never given the opportunity. "My mother grew up in high society. She was used to having the best of the best. Papa said he was lovestruck the moment he set eyes on her. The sweetest gal he'd ever seen."

"Sounds like Augus." Cade held out his cup as Miss Ramsey entered the room with a fresh pot of coffee.

"Franklin Murphy disowned his daughter when she ran off with Papa to the dusty wilderness of Texas. Cut off all communication and support. Eventually, my folks came here and settled in after I was born."

"Not surprised he convinced her to run off. Augus could make swampland sound like an oasis once he got to spinning tales." Cade sat back and rested a boot over his knee.

"With wide open spaces comes endless possibilities," Lily quoted one of Papa's favorite sayings.

Jessa appreciated that these friends of her father seemed to understand his many oddities and loved him anyway.

"Mama was heartbroken at having lost the love and support of her family. Papa made a vow that someday he'd become every bit as rich and successful as her father. I'm sure he meant every word of it, too, but fate stepped in before he could provide it for her."

"I'm sorry." The tears in Juliana's eyes caught Jessa by surprise. "I know how hard it is to lose your mother, and now you've lost your father, too. I don't think anyone has stopped to realize how very much you've gone through these past few months."

Jessa didn't want to think about it. There was nothing she could do about Papa being gone. She preferred, instead, to focus on today. And that meant convincing the Pinkertons that she was capable of helping them solve the questions surrounding his disappearance.

Lily, on the other hand, was a picture of composure. "Might someone from Philadelphia have been responsible for Augus's sudden death? Perhaps in retaliation for persuading your mother to leave her family?"

Jessa sprang from her seat. "You all keep talking about him as if it's a foregone conclusion that he's dead. My papa is still alive." She refused to hear differently. "I don't know if he crossed the Indians some way, or if he's been hurt and laid up for the winter, or maybe he is being held by someone. I just don't know. But until they find his lifeless body, I refuse to give up hope."

Not one of the three were inclined to argue the point.

They couldn't. They simply had no proof. Too many questions needed answering before they could put together a solid case that he was truly gone.

"The way I see it, we need to be looking for this Lobo outlaw. I'll just bet he knows what happened to Papa, and to the thirteen other men who've vanished. Find him, then we can look to connecting him to Hollinger's gang."

She had read enough crime stories in her magazines to know they were going about this backward.

"Lobo was brought in a couple of days ago." Cade set his coffee cup aside. "DeLaney's got him locked up until I can arrange to have him transported to Texas for a federal trial."

Jessa hadn't heard anything about it. "The man who may have something to do with Papa's disappearance is sitting in a jail cell across the street? Why aren't we over there questioning him about it?" She dashed for the door hoping at least one of them would follow.

"We've already been there." Juliana hurried to head her off. "He's refusing to talk."

"The man wasn't all that impressive." Cade grinned at Lily. "Just a small fish in a big sea. Hollinger is the one who's giving the orders. He's the one we need to go after."

Lily stood and turned to the window to gaze out into the street. "I'm inclined to agree with Jessa. Until we can prove definitively that murders have indeed taken place, we have no case. Like it or not, Hollinger has been given license by the territorial authorities to enforce his bank regulations. As unthinkable as it is, he cannot be put to trial for the innocent blood he's shed on behalf of his land interests. The Territory chooses to see them as illegal trespassers who were given fair warning. This shareholder corporation he is a part of seems to think they are above the law, and sadly, up until now have been."

"No doubt about it." Cade joined her at the window. "We need bodies to prove murder. We need solid evidence to prove corruption. Right now, we haven't got much of either."

"That's why you need my help." Jessa was more convinced than ever that she'd made the right decision. "We can go through Papa's notes and journals right after supper."

Chapter Seven

AFTER DINNER, THEY convened once again in Augus Jamison's library to pool their information on the case thus far. Jessa didn't wait to be invited, she simply followed them in and held her breath that noone would shoo her back out.

Cade moved to stand in front of the desk, opening a leather folder of Papa's papers. "Augus was set on leaving quite a legacy for his family. Buying up as much land as he could get his hands on. Investing time and money in every outrageous opportunity that came along. Even had dealings with the railroad, trying to get them to build tracks straight through New Mexico then clear on out to California. Always chasing the next big dream."

"Which probably kept him away from home for most of the year." Juliana turned to the housekeeper who was busy stoking the fire. "Was he usually away or home by this time of year?"

"He was home by early spring. He and Jessa would head to the cabin to round up this year's mustangs by now."

Cold dread seeped through Jessa's veins. Papa would never miss their standing date to wrangle in new ponies. This was the highlight of his year. He'd told her so countless times.

"Dear little Bucky always missed them both during that

time." Miss Ramsey offered her two cents worth. "He was never able to understand why he wasn't permitted to go. I believe your father promised next year he would be allowed to go along. Or was it this year? No matter. He misses his papa terribly. Not that Jessa hasn't done a marvelous job considering …"

" … considering Bucky Jamison is the spitting image of his papa—in looks and in temperament." Cade finished the housekeeper's thought, effectively letting her off the hook. "Full of bold ideas. And brazen enough to act on them."

Jessa couldn't argue with that.

"Which is why military school and a stint with the Rangers could be just what he needs to make a man out of him. A good man. One Augus would be proud of." Cade's tone softened to temper his words.

Jessa felt all eyes on her as they waited for her reaction. She didn't like to think about the day when Bucky would leave her. She avoided thinking about it at all, but these three were intent on making her mull everything over. Clearly, they didn't expect her father to come home to make his own decision about these things.

As Bucky got older, he was becoming harder to handle. Growing up here on what felt like the fringes of civilization without a strong male hand to guide him through the rabble was asking for trouble. Staring into the fire for a minute, Jessa hoped for a bit of Divine assistance before giving her approval. If this was her father's wishes, she had no choice but to go along. "I won't contest it."

"Fine. I'll see to the arrangements. We'll get him on the list at the new military institute in Austin. You can come out and see him whenever you'd like."

Lily slipped an arm around Jessa's shoulder and gave it

a squeeze when she saw tears forming in her eyes. "Enough of that. Tell us about your visit to the mission today, love."

So many changes in so short a time. She couldn't let herself dwell on the future or it quickly became overwhelming. What she needed was to keep her mind on the present.

Clearing her throat, she stepped out of Lily's embrace to claim a seat beside the fire. "The mission has six children living there right now. Sweetest little faces you ever want to see." Jessa smiled, remembering her frog. "We read at least ten stories before I had to leave. They seemed to enjoy every one."

"Were you able to deliver my letter?" Lily wanted to know.

"I gave it to Father Miguel's new priest just like you said. He isn't much for talking, but he did say they accepted your invitation and will be here for dinner tomorrow night." Jessa stood to crack a window. The room suddenly felt a little warm. "I liked him. He's very attractive."

"Oh, for Pete's sake."

Jessa instantly regretted having spoken her thoughts aloud. Cade obviously had taken her meaning wrong. "I don't mean to say he's attractive in an 'I-want-to-make-him-mine' sort of way. I just meant he's attractive in an 'oh-look-there's-a-nice-looking-male-person' sort of way."

Lily nor Juliana bothered to hide their amusement.

"You just remember that particular *male* person is off-limits to you," Cade chided.

"Well, of course he's not for me." The irritation in her voice was unavoidable. "He's dedicated to God. I wouldn't even consider him as a real man."

"Oh, he's real all right." Lily tilted her head as if seeing her goddaughter in a new light.

"A real pain in the backside," Cade muttered, though none too quietly.

"Now, Cade, darling, we mustn't speak of the clergy so flippantly," Juliana warned with a twinkle in her eye. "This Father … what was his name again?"

"He never said. But I heard Father Miguel call him Nathaniel."

Lily stood and put herself between Jessa and the other two, who obviously lived in their own newlywed world. "Guard your heart well, love. That's all we're saying." Lily's smile faded. "You know nothing about him."

For the umpteenth time today, Jessa felt chastised by the whole lot of them. For what reason? There was no harm in looking. "Well, priest or not, he struck me as an exceptional man."

Lily's gaze cut over to Cade when he opened his mouth to respond. With a shake of his head, he suddenly kept whatever it was he was going to say to himself.

"You needn't worry about me. Honestly." Jessa stepped around Lily to face them all. "I'm not one to chase after everything that grows whiskers. I have too much of Papa in me for all that. But, I can appreciate a fine piece of art without having to take it home and hang it on my wall, can't I?"

Lily's lips twitched in a half-hearted smile. "Jessa, love, you have no idea how much trouble that kind of innocent thinking might get you into." With a gentle shake of her head she reclaimed her seat. "Be careful. It would kill me to see you hurt."

"Listen to her, Jess." Cade was suddenly serious as well. "Those two priests will be coming over tomorrow night. You'd do well to forget the younger one is a man at all."

That would be next to impossible.

He was definitely a man, and no ordinary man, at that. A highly favored one. Whereas Father Miguel was a dear, saintly little individual, Father Nathaniel ... well, he was an altogether different sort of heavenly.

In the short moment when they'd met, her pulse quickened and her palms grew sweaty beneath her gloves. She was certain that nothing remotely sensible had escaped her lips. Then, when the same thing happened twice again, she knew he was no common mortal. Every time he looked into her eyes, her insides turned to melted butter.

"I won't forget he's a man, I can tell you that. But I promise not to do or say anything to embarrass you, if that's what you're worried about." Jessa took up an armful of her father's journals and papers from the desk to go over in her room. "I'll give you fair warning, though. This Father Nathaniel has been kissed by the heavens. He has an almost angelic presence."

Now, why did that make Cade Matlock laugh like a deranged hyena? Looking to his wife for a clue to his odd behavior, Jessa found her giggling behind her hand as well. Didn't these people believe in such things? "It's in the Bible. It says, 'The Lord bestows great favor and glory and honor to those who walk uprightly.' Kind of like the angels."

Now they were all three laughing.

Exasperated, she was done talking about the new priest. They'd just have to meet him for themselves.

Cade's voice followed her down the hall.

"And she thinks she has what it takes to be a detective?"

Chapter Eight

AUGUS HAD BEEN legend around here. Most of what Nathan had learned about life in the saddle, and especially about being a fast-draw, he'd learned from Augus. The Ranger who'd taken him on as a favor, eventually gave him a chance to scout for his unit. Nathan learned a lot about the nature of people under his watch. He was equally civil to the Apache and Ute as he was to the soldiers at Fort Union. Made far more headway than past government officials who had come in to clear them out like vermin.

As they approached town, Nathan slowed his mount, waiting for Father Miguel to catch up on his grizzled burro.

Cimarron looked about the same as when he'd left.

The Jamison Hotel down at the end of the main road, along with the restaurant and stage station that went with it, was easily the nicest establishment in town. From the looks of the massive poplars lining the drive up to a fancy courtyard, he'd say Jamison had done all right for himself since he'd seen him last.

They'd ridden together for four years clearing the way for the US government to redefine the southwest frontier. Be that as it may, Nathan had never been inside Augus Jamison's home, nor had he ever had the pleasure of meeting his family.

As they approached, he recognized the sprawling Jamison ranch angling off to the side of the hotel. The high white walls and red-tiled roof of the main house were impressive, but the considerable verandah encasing the entire upper level made of ponderosa pine especially drew his attention. Master craftsmanship. Augus never settled for less than the best. A generous split-rail corral circled a red stable where fresh horses for the stage line were kept. Some might say the extravagance of the hotel was a bit much for these parts, but it had an inviting feel.

Today the corral stood empty. Besides a variable breeze blowing through the enormous evergreens flanking every side of the hotel, nothing else stirred. Business must be down this time of year.

Nathan led his horse around to the side yard, stopping in front of the steps below the ranch's porch. He swung from his saddle to help the Padre down from his burro.

Suddenly, he caught movement from out of the corner of his eye. A slight shadow slipped from the porch around the side of the house.

Without warning, a loud noise split the air.

Nathan's hand went for the hilt of his gun, and he was instantly irritated when he didn't find it there. He never went anywhere without his silver-plated Colts and didn't like being defenseless.

"The wind, *mijo*." Father Miguel pointed to a heavy wooden door flapping unsecured against the side of a barn. "No cause for alarm."

"The sooner we get this over with the better." Nathan lowered his voice as they approached the arched doorway. "I shouldn't have let you talk me into wearing this getup. Especially not without my gun belt."

Father Miguel smiled indulgently. "It would cause concern, I'm afraid. A student of the church wielding deadly weapons."

If his instincts were on target, something wasn't right here. But there was no use in worrying the Padre. He'd see him safely inside then come back out to investigate.

Stepping up to the threshold, Nathan lifted a hand to knock when a hard jab stuck him in the back.

"Reach for the sky, Mister," came a muffled voice.

Nathan swallowed a curse.

Only one thing to do—overtake the good-for-nothing coward. Otherwise, the Padre and everyone inside would be easy pickings.

In one swift move, Nathan pushed the Padre aside and knocked away the hand that dared hold a weapon to his back. Yanking the would-be bandit up by the collar of his jacket, he came face-to-face with a squalling brat.

"Jessa!" Kicking his legs, the kid's feet dangled off the ground.

"Ah, young Bucky Jamison. I see that you are up to mischief already this evening." The Padre apparently knew the runt. "You may free the *niño*, Nathaniel. He's not likely to do us much harm with this." Father Miguel patted Nathan's arm to gain the boy's release, holding up a wooden gun coarsely whittled from pine.

Nathan complied and dropped the wailing kid on the part that needed a good paddling.

In the excitement, the front door came open and a lady in a fancy dress glared at him with her arms folded at her midriff.

Lily Valentine. Looking none too happy that he'd just man-handled Jamison's kid. She should thank him for not pinning his rotten little hide to the wall.

"*Señorita*, so good to see you again." The Padre quickly stepped ahead of Nathan to greet her.

As always, Lily was a sight to behold. Fine, store-bought clothes made her look like royalty. Only a few privileged individuals knew she had an equally fancy six-shooter strapped to her calf beneath all those petticoats. That chilling stare of hers was meant to knock the wind out of him, but he deliberately held her gaze as long as she wanted to tangle.

Finally, she stepped aside and invited them in with a wave of her hand. "Welcome, Father." She smiled graciously at the padre and took his hand. "Always a pleasure to see you."

She lifted the fuming boy up by his arm. "Wash up, now, and tell your sister our guests have arrived."

Bucky, obviously empowered by Lily's closeness, marched up to Nathan and reared back with a fist, but froze when he got a solid look at his face, mostly hidden by his Stetson. "You! Y-You're Lo—"

Lily's hand clamped over his mouth before he enlightened the entire county. "I am ever so proud that you're such a bright boy, but let's keep quiet about our guest for now. Our little secret, hmm?"

Defiance shone brightly in Bucky's green eyes until Nathan narrowed his gaze at the kid.

"Bucky, Miss Ramsey's marigolds were trampled last week. If she were to catch whomever is responsible, there would be no dessert for a week. Do you understand?" Her hand nodded with his head. "Good boy. Now do as you're told."

She released the child, and he slowly backed away from

Nathan.

Father Miguel smiled nervously.

"It's those dime novels." Lily smoothed her skirt then moved to close the door behind them, as if dealing with such hijinks was every day's business. "He aspires to become a famous gunslinger someday. I should have realized he would recognize you. Evidently, Lobo is one of his favorites."

The comment was like a stab to the pit of his stomach.

No kid should want to be like him. It was never his goal to make a name for himself—not this way anyhow. When his service as an Indian scout for the Rangers ended, he'd decided to take Hickok up on his offer to help keep peace in Hays City.

Wearing a badge was an easy buck until something else came along. It wasn't hard to outdraw a drunk cowboy, and that's just about all Hays City was known for. Except for the unfortunate few who'd come looking to make a name for themselves at his expense. His reputation had grown with each retelling of the stories, until he couldn't walk across the road without being challenged. He made it a point to be first to draw, but never first to shoot.

No one could say Lobo didn't give every chance to walk away. None ever had.

Regret clung to him like an undertaker's stench.

"You can leave your hat here on the bench." Lily's voice brought his thoughts back to the task at hand as she looked him over from head to foot. "Yes. I see it now. Swooning good looks. But I daresay they will get you nowhere if you always scowl so. Nice of you to join us, by the way."

"I'm here on your invitation, remember?"

"Only because you failed to check in as soon as you

were settled in." She took Father Miguel's arm and led them to the common area at the center of the hacienda-style ranch. "Cade was under the impression you'd decided to do this without us."

Cade came close to the truth. Nathan would much rather run this case alone. "Does this mean you have new information?"

Lily gave him a warning glance over her shoulder. "We have plenty to discuss, but it will wait until after dinner. No one other than Cade and Juliana suspects that you are anything other than Father Miguel's latest novice and I'd like to keep it that way for now."

Lily was used to calling the shots. Thing is, Nathan never was real good at taking orders. "What about Jamison's daughter?"

Her back became more rigid, and she swiveled to a stop. "Jessa's a clever one." Her clipped British tone became businesslike in an instant. "Much too curious for her own good."

"Then I'd be much obliged if you kept her home from now on. I don't need her snooping around and messing this up."

"We are the visitors here. Cimarron is Jessa's home. She's free to roam wherever she pleases." He didn't miss the caution in her voice. "You'll do well to remember your manners where she is concerned.

"In other words, none of the tom-foolery you're known for," Cade greeted them as soon as they entered the parlor.

How was it that he was *known for* so many things that were news to him?

At the Padre's nudge, Nathan conceded. "I'll be glad to avoid her every chance I get. Just keep her out of my way, and she'll be just fine." There. Manners with a spit shine.

Another woman entered the room with some kind of gray uniform on and a white apron tied around her thin waist. She carried a silver tray with glasses and a pitcher on top.

Lily claimed a seat on the leather sofa while Father Miguel and Nathan remained standing to acknowledge her presence.

Instead of offering them a lemonade, however, the tray suddenly crashed to the floor and the fool woman gaped at Nathan like she'd seen a ghost.

"Miss Ramsey!" Lily flew to the lady's side. "What on earth?"

"Swooning good looks?" Nathan bent to retrieve the fallen tray.

Lily patted the dazed woman's hand, sending Nathan an impatient glare. "While I'm glad to see you still possess a sense of humor, you pick a peculiar time to show it."

Miss Ramsey whispered an apology as she allowed Lily to lead her to a chair. Obviously still in a muddle, her eyes opened wide when she again spotted Nathan.

Father Miguel hovered by her side reaching for her hand. "There, now, dear one. No one is here to harm you."

Her gaze reluctantly left Nathan's face and centered on Father Miguel. The woman looked terrified.

Apparently, his reputation preceded him. The Ramsey woman must have recognized him and figured he'd shoot them all before the main course.

"I assure you, ma'am, you're safe enough. I try not to terrorize innocent women and children. At least not until after dessert." Though he spoke quietly, he couldn't hide the disgust in his voice at having to offer such a loathsome explanation.

"Oh goodness, no! I-I never thought that." She ducked her head as her face reddened. Nathan found it odd the way she averted her eyes from his view. "Excuse me. I'll fetch more drinks." With that she withdrew from the room, leaving a stunned silence in her wake.

Finally, Lily stepped around the mess of broken glass and lemonade pooled on the brick floor to reclaim her seat on the sofa. "You mustn't take it personally, Lobo. Miss Ramsey is a bit on the nervous side."

"The name's Nathan, remember?" He ran his hand over his hair, wishing he hadn't given up his Stetson. It grated on him to hear her address him as the outlaw she knew nothing about. They'd been through plenty as colleagues. The Rangers had worked hand in hand with the Pinkertons in the past. She needed to keep in mind he was the same man who'd helped them round up a band of cattle rustlers just a couple of years ago.

"All right, Nathan." Lily motioned for him to sit across from her in a matching leather chair. "You must try not to frown so. It is enough to frighten anyone."

"How did she know who I am? I could see if I had on my hat and guns, but not in this garb."

"Perhaps we should have warned her." Father Miguel spoke absently, his eyes still trained on the doorway where the woman disappeared. "I must go see about her. I will make certain she has recovered. Excuse me?"

"Certainly, Father." The answer didn't come from Lily, but from Jamison's daughter as he passed her inside the doorway.

Looking completely different in a swanky yellow dress rather than buckskin britches, he had to admit she was a sight to behold. Soft light from the pewter sconces on either side of the doorway reflected brightly in her golden eyes.

Nathan was immediately drawn to their warmth.

He was plenty of things, but delusional wasn't one of them—especially to himself.

Running a hand over his jaw, he peered at her like she was a pacing wildcat.

Jessa Jamison was more dangerous than any outlaw he'd ever encountered.

Chapter Nine

POLITE CONVERSATION FILLED the whitewashed dining room, yet Jessa barely noticed. Paying unusual attention to her meal, she swept lima beans into her mashed potatoes and made swirling designs in the hollandaise sauce.

Intent on figuring out the odd fascination she felt for the man sitting across the table from her, she silently prayed for guidance. Surely God, Himself, was trying to show her something. Otherwise, why would she be so awestruck by his every move?

All evening she'd watched Father Nathaniel as he talked with the others. His broad shoulders, his dark, longish hair, and even that small scar on his left ...

Jessa stole a peek at him as she brought her fork to her lips.

... no, it was his right eyebrow. The one he quirked when he said something offhanded. Which he did often. Mostly, she noticed, to get a shocked reaction from everyone else at the table. She'd had to keep herself from laughing more than once.

His bold profile and the strong set of his jaw looked like a drawing in her magazine ads. She could just imagine him in one of those fine evening jackets and silver brocade vest. Wouldn't that be a sight?

Just then he turned toward Lily, and Jessa marveled at

how the high angles of his cheeks lent a boyish quality to his face.

His attention swung over to her and too late she realized she was gawking. It was a good thing he didn't smile more often, she'd likely make an idiot of herself before the evening's end.

Splitting her sourdough biscuit in two, Jessa spread sweet butter on one half and strawberry jam on the other. What would cause a man like Nathaniel to give up his life to serve God so unselfishly? Only a most devoted man would contemplate such a sacrifice.

Absently, she brought the butter spreader to her lips, not wanting the slightest bit of jam to go to waste. All at once she felt his eyes on her, like a stolen kiss, warm and brief.

With a quick glance around the table, she lowered the spreader to her plate, and with a flick of her tongue, she removed the last of the jam from the corner of her mouth.

Bucky bounced in his seat, cackling like a laying hen. "I know something you don't know."

"Eat your dinner." Three voices spoke at once.

Father Miguel cleared his throat. "The children enjoyed your visit to our mission the other day, *Señorita* Jamison."

Jessa wiped her hand on the red linen napkin draped across her lap. "I loved spending time with them. They are so well-behaved." She shot a warning look at her brother.

"Now that the days grow warmer, it would be a fine time to take the *niños* for a picnic lunch, to play on the grassy banks of the river.

"Yes!" She answered so quickly everyone at the table took pause, but she didn't care. The thought of an entire afternoon of romping in the sunshine with nothing but rippling water, open space, and crisp, fresh air. No guests, no responsibilities, and even if it was just for one afternoon, not having to crack the whip to get Bucky to finish his schoolwork sounded wonderful.

"Is it safe?" Juliana's brows knit in concern. "What with all the disappearings going on? Augus may have been targeted, which would mean you and Bucky may not be safe. We're not sure if it's one acting alone, or there could even be a whole gang working together at this point."

"I'll bring my lasso." Jessa leveled a look at her new friend. They shouldn't be discussing the case in front of guests.

"No, now, Jules has a point. I'd feel better if you went along … Nathaniel." Cade directed his attention to the younger priest who looked like he didn't think much of the suggestion.

"Excellent." Father Miguel lifted his knife to make a thick cut in his steak. "Shall we say a week from today at about noon?"

Jessa felt her face warm when Father Nathaniel's gaze rested on her. She knew he had been hornswoggled into accompanying her, but she couldn't say she was sad about it. She was glad for a chance to get to know more about him. "That will be just fine."

After a full minute, Nathaniel surprised her when he responded with the slightest tug of a grin at the corner of his mouth. "On one condition. You leave the lasso home. The Padre tells me you're dangerous with that thing."

Laughter filtered around the table.

Jessa was mesmerized by the way his dark, stormy-gray eyes suddenly took on a roguish glint. He was much more playful tonight than he had been at the mission the other day. More relaxed. Less intense.

It wasn't like her to turn doe-eyed over a man. She wasn't sure what had gotten into her. With a deep breath, she squared her shoulders. Setting her napkin on the table next to her plate, she was determined to meet her fascination with this man head-on. "Father Nathaniel, tell me, how did you land in New Mexico? I mean, surely there are other places you could've gone to learn about priest … ly duties." The question didn't come out at all like she'd meant it, but she'd jumped in headlong now. Praying no one else found her question as silly as it had sounded to her, she charged on. She'd worry about *what* she'd said later. For now she was making progress just speaking at all. "I think maybe they need to order you a better robe, though. That one doesn't seem to fit."

Father Miguel choked into his water goblet and for a second time Jessa feared she had half killed the man. With Juliana's help he was quickly restored.

Jessa made another attempt at coherent conversation. "Where *do* you come from?" Steadily, she held his gaze. "You seem kind of young to be a priest. And why do you wear spurs beneath your robe?" Her heart was pounding until her breath caught in her throat. Still, she refused to look away, or to hush up apparently. The more she tried to ask a serious question the more ridiculous she sounded. "What I mean is, who, exactly, sent you here? To us—er, to New Mexico."

"I told you she was a curious one." Lily, too, set her napkin beside her plate and leaned back in her chair.

If Father Nathanial was taken aback by her interrogation, he didn't show it. Instead a slow grin crept up his lips. A bolt of sensation went clear through her as she fought to keep her composure. Despite her resolve to remain serious and detached, she couldn't help but smile back when he looked at her like that.

"I decided." His answer was just as direct. "I was raised in New Mexico. This was my home for eighteen years."

Interest got the best of her, and she instantly forgot her discomfort. Leaning forward, she rested her elbows on the table. "You were raised here? Where? I don't remember ever seeing you."

A deafening bang echoed through the dining room.

Jessa startled.

Father Nathaniel was out of his chair in an instant, crouched low with his hand poised at his side as if ready to draw.

Slowly, he straightened as the cause of all the excitement became clear.

Bucky was the only one laughing, but he laughed until he lost his breath. His hand still rested on the heavy pine shutter at Father Nathaniel's back. Evidence enough that he'd purposefully slammed the shutter against the solid adobe wall to cause a scare.

Why?

Even more intriguing was Father Nathaniel's swift reaction. Fierce, without a moment's hesitation. As he reclaimed his seat he looked like he wanted to throttle her brother. He obviously had a long way to go to become as docile and tolerant as Father Miguel.

Why was Bucky so intent on riling this man?

"Bucky." Jessa's patience had reached its limit. "That will cost you dessert, and if you argue, it'll cost you dessert for the rest of the week." She pointed to the stairway outside of the arched doorway. "Apologize, then head to your room for the night."

"Sorry, *Father*," Bucky snickered, not a bit upset that he'd just been denied pie. Something suspicious was going on.

"Please, *Señorita Jamison*, do not be too hard on the *niño*." Father Miguel looked over at his novice. "Some boys are just born high-spirited. Very much like another who used to amuse himself with such pranks."

"I was nothing compared to that kid." Father Nathaniel stirred his coffee then lifted the cup to his mouth.

"You and young Bucky were very much alike." The older priest chuckled. "As I recall, you missed plenty of desserts as well."

"You two knew each other back then?" Jessa was truly stunned.

"*Si*. Nathaniel was raised at our mission."

Jessa flopped back in her chair with her mouth gaping. Father Nathaniel—an orphan? "So you came back to the mission to repay Father Miguel by serving the community that took you in? How gracious!"

"It's not like that." Father Nathaniel shook his head.

"Yes, how incredibly gracious. Please continue, Father. Tell us what Saint Nathaniel was like as a child." Cade took a sip of his coffee.

Father Miguel was quick to take up the conversation. "As I said, he was very much like your Bucky."

"More coffee?" Miss Ramsey appeared at Father Nathaniel's side with a steaming pot. The usually shy housekeeper was pouring him a second cup before he'd even finished his first. He thanked her, and she scurried off to the kitchen, leaving Father Miguel still holding out his empty cup.

With a shrug, the small priest continued. "I recall the

time when a distinguished professor, Sir William Barret was visiting us from his home in Stockton. Highly dignified man. He was sent by The Royal College in Dublin, and the Society for Supernatural Research."

"I've heard of him, though never had the privilege of meeting him." Lily moved to the sideboard and took up the coffee pot to refill Father Miguel's cup herself.

"He came to investigate claims of strange phenomena in the new west. It was a very popular subject in upper circles in those days. The Natives are known for being superstitious and had reported sightings of a ghostly figure in a white flowing gown. The Acomas related their stories to the military that brings them supplies. One thing led to another and before we knew it this college across the ocean had decided to come write a book on the subject."

"My magazine says that the west is full of wild stories." Jessa nodded. "I think people are just afraid of what they're unfamiliar with. I've never experienced anything personally to be afraid of."

"What then, Father?" Juliana wanted to know.

"You must understand. Nathaniel, he was not at all pleased to have given up his bed for the week. I took Nathaniel's bed, you see, while Sir William slept in mine. This put Nathaniel in the floor on a pallet."

"How old were you?" Jessa asked Father Nathaniel.

"He had just taken Holy Communion, so he must have been about eight," Father Miguel answered.

"More biscuits?" Miss Ramsey was again at Father Nathaniel's side. Completely ignoring the hand he held up to decline, she plopped two fluffy biscuits onto his plate. By all appearances, she was as caught up in the story as the rest of them.

"After the third night, *mijo* decided that he had had enough of this sleeping on the hard floor. Everyone knew by that time the good professor was half frightened by all he had seen and heard. He was at a loss for a reasonable explanation. And because he was a skittish man, he was convinced the land was cursed."

"He'd probably never heard of such things in Stockholm." Juliana sat with her hands folded in her lap.

"Indeed, not," Lily agreed.

"So, on the fourth night," Father Miguel continued, "just as Sir William laid his head to his pillow, a small image in flowing white appeared in his room out of nowhere."

Jessa couldn't contain a giggle, pointing at Father Nathaniel. "You?"

He shrugged. A mischievous gleam in his eye was definitely reminiscent of her brother.

Adding a dramatic flair, Father Miguel spoke as if telling a story to the children. "Then, the *fantasma* spoke: 'Pack thy bags, Scallywag. Get thyself back to wherever you came from. Quit thy meddling where you have no business, or I shall cause the earth to open up and swallow ya whole!'"

Even Cade was laughing now.

"The poor professor left before the sun ever rose. Without even saying goodbye."

Jessa laughed so hard, she had tears in her eyes. She couldn't help but notice how much friendlier he appeared without his usual scowl.

"How did you figure out it was Nathan?" Juliana wanted to know.

"I had witnessed the entire encounter." Father Miguel

chuckled. "The next morning, after Sir William was gone, the nuns discovered the dossal curtain, which usually hung at the end of the clerestory, was missing. One of the sisters said she had seen Nathan lurking about earlier. It was not hard to figure he was the one who had sent the poor man running."

"Yes, but did he ever admit it?" Lily wrapped her hands around her coffee cup smiling at him.

Father Nathaniel spoke up in his own defense. "The Padre threatened to send the authorities out to arrest the professor for stealing the curtain. It had silver threads running through it and was considered valuable. Anyway, I ended up coming clean. I wanted the man gone, not strung up."

"I never had any doubt that you would, *mijo*." The wise priest looked up at him with something akin to pride beaming on his face. "So you see, *Senorita Jamison*, just like your brother, Nathaniel also had a wayward streak, but underneath..." He patted his chest. "...he has a heart of gold."

"Pie?" Sniffling into a hankie, Miss Ramsey scooped half of the apple pie onto Father Nathaniel's plate.

He didn't seem inclined to argue. Taking up his fork, he dug in. When he complimented her cooking, she was nearly beside herself. Jessa marveled at how quickly she'd recovered from her earlier episode.

Looking across the table, it occurred to her that when he wanted to, Father Nathaniel had the charm of a tipsy Irishman. Which led her to another conclusion—most of the time he just didn't want to.

"Miss Ramsey, love. May we also have some pie?" Lily sent a direct look at the housekeeper. Her point taken, the contrite woman hurried to the lady's side with pie plate in hand.

Jessa watched Father Nathaniel enjoying his dessert. Though admittedly defiant, it was still a brave thing for an eight-year-old to do.

As if sensing her high regard for him, Father Nathaniel grinned over his fork and sent her a wink.

Jessa looked over at Lily, certain she was wrong in what she had just seen.

Lily's frown said she wasn't.

Lord, have mercy. She'd just tempted a priest.

Chapter Ten

"YOU SURE?"

"Checked it out myself the day I got here." Nathan dropped into a leather chair set before a large oak desk. "The trail's just now thawed enough to pass."

Cade Matlock sat at the desk with a trail map open in front of him. "I'm sure up until a couple of weeks ago the ground was solid ice beneath a layer of snow."

"It would stand to reason the trail has been impassable since November when Augus disappeared." Lily pored over packets of papers stacked on a hand-carved credenza.

"Even if we could pinpoint where Augus left the trail, the woods are dense up that way. Plenty of wildlife up there to see that nothing's left of a man's body." Nathan glanced over at Father Miguel snoozing in an overstuffed chair in front of the fire. They needed to keep this meeting brief.

"And then there's the Indians." Cade continued to study the map. His time trying to keep peace with Texas renegade tribes had his suspicions pointing in the wrong direction.

"The Apache and Ute aren't interested in taking down a lone rider. Certainly not Augus Jamison. He was considered a friend."

Lily pulled open the top drawer, removing another leather folder. "Augus took a hard stand against this corporation of land grabbers. Families granted land from the Mexican government generations ago, and homesteaders who've since come to settle here. Being forced to vacate—at gunpoint."

"Jeb Hollinger's bank is authorized to expedite the takeover. He has his hand in every last bit of it." Cade leaned back. His gaze falling to where his wife had also fallen asleep in a chair beside the fire. "Conveniently, his bank holds the note on most every parcel of land in the county. A corporate lawyer named Johannsen just opened a slick new office in town."

"I can just about guarantee none of the tribes are involved." Nathan rested his elbows on the arms of the chair, his hands clasped across his middle.

"You and I both know there are always a few rogue Kiowa, and even one or two Apache, that can be coaxed into attacking for little to no reason. Desperate times. Much different now than when you worked the Territory before the war."

"Maybe, but the attack on Augus wasn't carried out by the natives." It was more than a gut feeling. Nathan had spent hours going over the details.

"Why do you say that, Nathan?" Lily asked without turning around.

"His horse and two pack mules came down from the pass without him. DeLaney says he was never without a small sack of gold in case he needed to negotiate with claimstakers along the way. That was gone. He had supplies and most likely a good amount of cash in his saddle packs, which also turned up empty. Even his saddle went missing."

"All consistent with robbery." Lily came to stand beside the desk, continuing to flip through the leather-bound folder in her hand.

"Maybe if your thief had an interest in white man's money, or gold, or camp supplies. Natives have no use for such things. They don't ride with saddles. They'd be more inclined to leave the bags and take his horse and mules. The Apache especially have a taste for mule meat."

"Which could have been staged for the right price," Cade pointed out.

"Paid or not, the Kiowa never do anything they don't take credit for. If Augus was targeted by them, they'd make sure everyone knew about it. What they lack for in numbers, they make up for in intimidation. He'd have come down from that mountain skewered to his horse by a spear trimmed with speckled feathers as fair warning to anyone else who might dare cross their land."

Cade had no choice but to agree.

"To our advantage, Augus kept meticulous notes." Lily placed several sheets of paper on top of the map. "He documented every meeting with the homesteaders including names, dates, and any perceived danger." Removing another bound set of papers, she laid them beside the others on the desk. "He also documented his meetings with the corporate investors. There are some impressive names mentioned in these notes. From Santa Fe to Washington and all points in between. The tone of these discussions leaves no doubt, multiple thousands of dollars are at stake. These men are willing to go to whatever lengths needed to see that their vision for this land is carried out."

"You think Augus was in on it?" Cade was the first to broach the question none of them wanted to ask.

"A couple of correspondences indicate his interest in investing. But his journal entries confirm it was merely a ruse to gain entrance to the meetings." Lily pointed to a handful of meeting notes. "But that was before his neighbors were served demand notices. After Hollinger became brutish, Augus quickly spoke out against him."

"Says here Augus was doing everything he could to sound the alarm." Cade pointed out a journal entry. "Sounds like he was able to get some attention, too."

"Attention has never been the issue." Lily seemed to be looking for something in particular. "Congress is fully aware of the corrupt dealings in Santa Fe as well as this group of investors. The question has always been, at what point do they decide it's time to do something about it?"

Lily laid her hand on Nathan's back as she passed behind him. "We have a month—possibly two—before interest wanes and we lose our support all over again. I don't intend to let that happen."

"Jules and I head out on Friday's stage. It will be up to you two."

Lily smiled. "I'll be sorry to see you go, Cade. You've been a tremendous help."

"I have every confidence in you both." Cade offered a smile and a hand to Nathan. His confidence wasn't easily won, but he did give it honestly. "You're on your own with Jessa, though. If you chose to take her on, Lord help us all."

"What does that mean?" Nathan had a bad feeling about where this was going.

Lily took her time answering. "You've developed a certain fondness for Augus's daughter. Am I right?"

Nathan was stunned silent.

Lily's perception was usually razor sharp, but this time she was way off track.

"No, you're not. I find her to be a distraction."

Cade cleared his throat. "You might as well get used to

having her around, Lobo. Whether she comes on as an additional operative in this case or not." Cade was at his side with a heavy hand on his shoulder, instantly reacting when Nathan bristled. "Yes, you heard me—operative. As in the two of you would be partners. That's for Lily and Pinkerton to decide."

Lily came around the desk to cross her arms in front of him. "Jessa has a distinct advantage here. Everyone already knows her. She can be as curious as she pleases. No one thinks a thing of it."

"And while you're at it, stop toying with her affections." Cade was getting hot under the collar for no reason. Nathan had no interest in Jessa Jamison. "I don't care what you do with other females. That's your business. But leave Jessa alone."

Confused, Nathan instantly reacted with a frown.

Cade waved off his irritation. "Don't act like you don't know what I'm talking about. The way you played footsies with her at dinner was bold, even for you. She's not some saloon girl to be cavorted with. Clearly, she didn't know what to do with your suave advances."

Suave advances? He was off his rocker.

"I don't cavort with saloon girls. Matter of fact, I make it a point not to cavort at all."

"Look, Lobo." Cade shut the leatherbound journal on the desk with a whack then slid it over to one side to prop a hip in its place. "You know I consider you more than just an ex-partner. I regard you as a brother. No better Ranger, present or past. But I owe this to Augus." Cade propped a fist on his thigh. "I aim to do everything I can to protect Jessa from your sort."

Impatience took over, like it always did with offhanded

comments like that. Considering it was Cade who'd made it, the sting went deep. "What sort would that be, Matlock? Cold-blooded killer? No name half-breed?"

"Heartbreaker," came the curt answer. "Jessa can take care of herself where the other kinds are concerned. But she's too trusting to defend herself against pretty words."

"And playful glances," Lily added.

Nathan gave an ugly laugh. "I wasn't aware I offered any pretty words or playful glances."

Jessa was neither too young nor too naïve to appreciate a man's attention. Looking like she did, she probably got plenty of it. Besides, he was only being friendly. If they misconstrued his intentions, it was their own mistake. He hadn't heard Jessa complain.

"If I remember, you weren't one to seek attention from the ladies." Lily stepped into the space between them. "But that never stopped them from trying. Perhaps, you don't know your own charm."

"So, we're calling it charm now?" Cade relaxed and swatted Nathan with a folded newspaper. "A good pair of spectacles could cure that."

Nathan grinned despite his soured mood.

"Nathan, I daresay there are times you seem to be your own worst enemy." Lily's voice had a candid tone that made him stop and listen. "You've a knack for drawing people, yet you keep them at bay, or push them away altogether. You seem determined to live your life alone, even if doing so makes you miserable."

"She speaks truth, *mijo*." Father Miguel spoke up from his seat by the fire. "Since you were a boy, you have the ability to get crossways with yourself. God blessed you with a good, kind heart. Others are drawn to this. Yet you do not allow them to come close."

"I see what you mean." Juliana was also awake now, looking him over like he was a prize hog. "Charming with a certain vulnerability."

"Vulnerable?" Now they were grasping at straws. "I stay alive by making sure I'm *not* caught vulnerable." Nathan took up his discarded cassock, intent on collecting the Padre to head back to the mission. "And if I offended anyone, my apologies."

"Stay focused, Lobo," Cade called after him. "You wouldn't want to be taken down while making eyes at Miss Jamison."

Chapter Eleven

THE EAST SIDE of the mountain showed signs of color. High in the sapphire sky, the sun blazed brightly and a cool mountain breeze felt good on her skin. Jessa lifted her face to the promise of warmer days ahead.

This winter had been an exceptionally harsh one.

On November 21st, Papa's horse appeared on the old Taos Trail without him. Every day since had been a struggle to keep those who'd depended on him at an even keel. The hotel staff, the ranch hands, the stage drivers, and Bucky.

By mid-December, Christmas decorations had been set out, gifts were exchanged, and a fat goose, trimmed with cranberries, was served to all the guests.

But still no Papa.

It was easier to convince herself that he was off on yet another wild escapade. Helping brand cattle in Wyoming or setting up trade in Colorado. More times than not, they'd spent Christmas Day without him. Not that anyone blamed him, Cimarron wasn't an easy place to get home to in the winter. From December through March, most routes in or out of town were closed down at some point in every direction. The stages slowed to one or two stops a week, and usually those had to be rerouted.

No one thought anything of it. He was Augus Jamison. Larger than life. Friend to all. Nothing could contain him.

No person or place could hold down a man like him for very long. No one, except their mother. He'd lived for the times he could be home with her. After she was taken from them, his trips away became more and more frequent, and he stayed gone longer.

Come spring every year, he'd show up again, riding in on the horizon with that big smile, big gifts for everyone, and even bigger tales to tell.

Jessa's gaze swept the distant mountain range in the direction where the high road split from the trail up to Elizabethtown. Part of her held on to hope that even death could not contain him. Whatever had happened out on that trail, he'd eventually conquer it like he always did. Any day now, he'd come sauntering back into town, declaring the pass was officially opened up again.

"What's got you a million miles away?" A deep voice beside her brought her back to where she sat on a quilt spread out on a grassy knoll.

The north bank of the Cimarron River was awash with sunlight glistening like stars in the shallow ripples of the water. Too early for much runoff, the river was the perfect depth for splashing and dipping your toes beneath its icy cold surface.

"About how glad I am that Father Miguel asked me to come here today. Watching the children play without a care in the world does my heart happy." She smiled over into the chiseled face of Nathaniel.

Father Nathaniel.

"Looks like they played themselves out."

All three of the children were scattered on blankets under the warm April sun, asleep with full bellies. The older boy had stayed behind at the mission tending to his lessons.

Father Miguel was a stickler for not missing. The nuns insisted that baby Nora was still too young for a picnic, so they had only the three six-year-olds with them today.

"You know, I've lived on instinct a long time. I know the difference between what a person says and what they mean." Nathaniel reclined on the blanket next to where she sat. His hands were clasped behind his head, and with one knee bent, his well-worn boots showed from beneath his robe. A long straw of grass stuck out from the side of his mouth as he spoke. A black hat shaded his eyes from the sun and from her view.

Thick muscle caused the robe to pull tight across his arms. His chest was broad and his stomach flat.

Turning her head away, Jessa desperately tried to rein in her thoughts. It was a good thing he couldn't truly read a person's mind.

"I'd say you aren't as undisturbed by all this as you try to make everyone believe. Your heart has taken quite a beating these last few months."

Jessa's turned back around. Had he truly read her thoughts?

"Augus was quite a man, don't get me wrong." He shrugged in answer to her questioning glare. "His passing is bound to hurt. Especially since he left you alone to look after that pain in the neck brother of yours."

"Bucky's been my responsibility for a very long time." She frowned. "He's a good kid."

"Mmm hmm." Father Nathaniel nodded in mock agreement. "I met him, remember?"

"He is good. For the most part. He is bright and can be very thoughtful. He usually tries to do what's right." That sounded hollow even to her own ears. "Most of the time."

Nathan pushed back his hat with a thumb and the heat of his direct stare prickled her conscience.

"Sometimes." The last came out as almost a whisper. "Once every blue moon."

He was certainly good at coaxing a confession out of someone.

"He's missing Papa and doesn't know how to show it, that's all."

"How about you?" Father Nathaniel rolled from his back to his side, propping up on an elbow. His dark features softened into a smile that Jessa immediately found appealing. "You must be missing him, too. No one could replace your papa."

"I do miss him. But he's not—" She caught herself just before she admitted her doubts about his demise.

Father Nathaniel shook his head slowly, moving the straw from one side of his mouth to the other. By the time she realized that she was staring at him like a loon, his grin told her he'd already noticed.

"Tell me what makes you think he's not."

Jessa pulled her knees up close to her chest, careful to make sure the skirt Lily talked her into wearing was sufficiently covering her legs. Father Nathaniel didn't need any more tempting. He was entirely too virile all on his own.

"Well, for one thing, they've never found him. If he fell off his horse, or if Indians got to him like some suspect, his body would be out there on the trail somewhere in plain view. Don't you think? DeLaney took a whole posse up there when his horse and mules were found. Papa was nowhere to be found."

"He could have fallen off a cliff or got bucked into the

brush."

"Not on the pinto he was riding. She's one of our best mares. Gentle as a lamb. If he'd been laying in the road somewhere, she would not have left him. She'd have stayed with him until they found them both up there."

He turned a hard focus on the lower mountain range. "Too many things don't add up." His voice was quiet but strong. "The Apache would have sent him back on his horse and taken his mules. The Ute are too few to cause a stir." He removed the straw and tossed it away. "And if robbery had been the intent, they would have taken his horse, too."

Discussing the circumstances of her father's disappearance caused a heaviness to form in the center of her chest. She'd done a fairly good job of avoiding the subject up until now. If she refused to think about it, hope was easier to keep alive. Listening to Father Nathaniel list the possibilities of what might have been Papa's last moments alive was almost too much to take in.

The novice priest seemed to sense her discomfort. Sitting up, he leaned in a little closer with a disarming grin. "Tell me more about these pintos Augus was so proud of."

Jessa still needed a moment to recover.

Her most cherished memories were when she and her father went chasing down pintos. Gradually, a smile formed on her lips. "Every spring, Papa and I camped out in his hunting cabin near the cascades over by Rayado Mesa. Just waiting for this wild herd of mustangs to come around that always roamed over that way."

"I've seen them. Big herd."

"They're perfect. Fast as lightning, too. If you catch one just right, you can cut him off from the others and rope him in without causing a stampede."

"Augus was quick with a rope."

"He was the best." A lump formed in her throat that made going on impossible.

"I hear you inherited his skills." Father Nathaniel nudged her shoulder with his. "For what it's worth, we all miss him. Augus was one of a kind. He took me under his wing and taught me to ride."

Jessa was astonished. From what she'd seen, he was a skilled rider, even in a robe.

"I was sixteen. I had no experience on the back of a horse. Anytime I went to town, I took that buckboard over there and handled the reins from a springboard seat. Kit Carson came to town one day and asked the Padre if he could borrow me to help scout. It was an honor to be chosen to ride with his company, but I was ashamed to admit I didn't know how to ride. Never an issue, though, because Augus Jamison stepped up and told Carson he needed me first. Promised to hand deliver me to Taos before the week was out. For three days, I lived in a saddle. Took my meals in a saddle and stayed there until I nearly fell off from exhaustion at night. By the end of that week, I was sore, but you can bet I had learned how to ride. Your papa even sent me off to meet Carson with a saddle and a horse of my own. I'll never forget it."

"Papa was always bringing someone new around." She glanced over. "But I'm sure I would have remembered you. Even if I was only about ten."

He smiled and she felt her face grow warmer. It hadn't taken much to figure their age difference of six years. If he was twenty-six now, and she'd just turned twenty, then it would only serve to reason that when he was sixteen, she would have been ten.

Why did she suddenly feel like her saying it revealed more than she'd intended?

"Anyway, Papa was always adding to our stables, mostly from the wild mustangs. We brought them in willful and untamed, but Papa managed to saddle break them. If he couldn't do it himself, he knew men who could. We sold the ponies for a premium, too. He was partial to the tricolored ones, so we became known for our pintos."

"You will miss going with him this year." His statement was quiet but firm, and it hung in the air between them.

Slowly, the importance of his words rolled over her like a mountain of hot lava, burning up the last of the innocent excuses for her father's vanishing.

Hot tears stung her eyes as she avoided looking in the direction of Rayado Mesa as fervently as she avoided the outright pity in his eyes. The truth was, she'd refused to think about this all Winter long, certain by now Papa would be back and there would be no reason to have ever been concerned.

But spring was here. And he was not.

She didn't know how to admit there would be no rounding up of wild ponies this year. No campfire stories. No two whole weeks of having Papa all to herself.

She'd never consider going out there without him. That would be downright dangerous. Without his stories, or competitions to see who could lasso the first, there would be no joy in going alone.

She could talk big about all the exciting things she had planned for the future, but admitting that she was destined to face them alone sent a shock of sorrow right down to her toes.

Chapter Twelve

JESSA SMELLED SWEET like wildflowers on a summer day. Fortunately, Nathan wasn't partial to wildflowers—or any other flowers for that matter.

He was more interested in hearing her take on what happened the night her father was killed. He would've happily bowed out except this picnic provided the perfect chance to ask her a few questions without Cade and Lily staring a hole through him.

So far, the day was pleasant enough. Jessa was friendly, likeable, actually, not pretentious or scheming like most women he knew. She spoke her mind—often—but with honesty and a certain thoughtfulness that revealed good inside of her.

Not that she wasn't full of pluck if given half a chance. When he came across too solemn for her liking, she was quick to tell him about it. Not mean-spirited, she just felt free to poke fun at him more than he was used to. Pretty soon, he began to read when she was getting ready to trim him down. She'd turn her head ever so slightly, shoot him a sideways glance, then grin that teasing grin that made him want to sidle up next to her and run for the hills all at the same time.

After a while, he eased up. No sense in fighting it, her teasing was harmless enough. He could see certain traits in her that was similar to her father. Good humor was second nature to her. She was a heap prettier than Jamison ever was, but the way her smile spread across her face to light up in her eyes mirrored her papa.

Nathan never met a man who truly cared about people like Augus Jamison did. Folks knew it, too. Everyone liked him, and his daughter was much the same. Watching her now, sitting cross-legged on a quilt in the grass beside him, she naturally drew a person in. Truthfully, he couldn't recall ever seeing anyone more naturally beautiful.

"What about you?" He figured he'd ask a few questions of his own. "What does the future hold for you?"

She answered without hesitation. "Well, I had planned on being a missionary. In an exotic location far, far away."

"Like a schoolteacher?" Nathan was surprised at her answer. She didn't seem the schoolteacher type.

"Well, I suppose sort of like a schoolteacher and Bible teacher combined. Like a Sunday School teacher, I guess. Except in a foreign land where there's a great need."

"I'd say there's a great need right here in your own backyard. Far as I can tell, there's no schoolhouse here either. And until they replace the circuit preacher, the kids in Colfax County don't have anyone but their mamas to give them Bible lessons."

He could feel her frustration, and it made him grin. She could use a good dose of truth. Talking about running off to who-knows-where, chasing some dream to save the world. The way he saw it, her world right here was in need and was as good a place to save as anywhere else.

"I've decided to join the Pinkerton's instead."

So Cade hadn't been joking. Had Lily made a final decision about this?

"I could still visit important places and help people, but this way I don't have to go alone. Lily and I can take cases together."

He happened to know Lily preferred to work alone, but he wasn't going to be the one to burst her bubble.

The more she talked, he realized she didn't have a good handle on what she wanted to do with her life. She hadn't mentioned getting married or having a houseful of kids. He had to assume she was more interested in escaping that kind of responsibility. Seems like she'd carried a heavy burden so long that she was ready to run off to experience everything she thought she'd been missing.

Thing was, life was just as hard and challenging out there in her faraway places as it was right here. Every place had its own set of problems. Learning to navigate and roll with the punches, that's what she really needed.

As the afternoon wore on, two things became clear. One, Jessa was a dreamer, every bit as much as her father had been. And two, wildflowers were entirely more appealing than he'd first given them credit for.

When he'd pressed her for answers concerning her father's disappearance, she'd sidestepped every question with the flash of a grin and an arsenal of useless information to fit every occasion. Only when he'd suggested that Augus's death might not have been an accident did she quiet down and stare off into the distance.

Plainly, she wasn't letting herself consider he was probably gone for good.

Nathan didn't believe in fostering a lie. Delusions never helped anyone. Life was full of unpleasant experiences, and no one could choose to live out only the good ones. A person had to learn to take the bad with the good, a lesson he'd learned early on. No matter how much you hope and pray for someone to come back, there's a fairly good chance they never will.

So, you move on. You learn from it. Let it make you stronger.

Pretending wasn't going to bring Augus back.

He tried to steer her toward the truth as gently as he could, but then without warning her eyes pooled up with the biggest tears he'd ever seen. Suddenly, he regretted ever saying anything at all.

"Look, if he's out there, Cade and Lily will find him." He fought the urge to put an arm over her shoulder. "But if he's not, you can't think on it too long. Thank the good Lord for the blessing that he was—then move on. That's how your papa would want it."

Jessa took a long time before agreeing.

As hard as he was trying to be gentle, he knew his efforts cut like a knife. He'd never concerned himself much with mincing words to spare a lady's feelings, but Jessa didn't deserve to be hurt. Even if it was for her own good to make her see the truth, he had to remind himself that she was more fragile than the saddle-worn drifters he spent most of his time with. She hadn't lived much life outside of Cimarron Canyon and it showed. He needed to cut her some slack.

She was exactly who Lily said she was. The sheltered daughter of Augus Jamison. She put up a fierce front, but her intentions were pure as the melting snow. She had yet to be burnt by careless people, wasn't familiar with the sting of rejection. Her heart was tender. She still felt things deeper than most.

An odd protectiveness settled over him. Something so

rare needed to be guarded, not thrown out to fend for itself. What was Augus thinking leaving her here to deal with everything he was unable to?

Glancing over, he watched her catch a tear against the sleeve of her pretty cotton dress which he was certain Lily insisted she wear.

Then, unexpectedly, a look of determination stole across her dainty features, and her back straightened. "If my father is actually gone—I'm not saying he is or isn't—why has no one come across his body? I know there are plenty of wild animals up there, but not so much as a drop of blood was found on the trail from E-town to the mining camps. You can't tell me he was mauled by a bear or skewered by Indians and didn't bleed even a little."

She may have been sheltered, but she had the fortitude of ten good men. He lowered his chin to hide a grin. "That's what Lily has come to figure out."

"And that's why I intend to help her." She flashed another big grin in spite of the dampness on her cheeks. Her wet eyelashes sort of stuck together, so long they nearly touched her eyebrows, giving her the look of a doe fresh from a dip in the river.

Something stirred down inside him. He'd never met anyone like her.

Even though she'd been left to her own for a good long while, she was doing just fine. The way he saw it, everyone should just leave her be. Let her live however she saw fit. If she wanted to wear buckskin britches and blaze across the mesa astride a half-wild pony, then he didn't see as how that hurt anyone. It certainly didn't bother him.

Nathan tossed a rock into the water.

To say nothing of the way she kept her half-wild brother

in line. Better than the kid's own father had.

He shook another rock in his hand a few times before tossing it as well.

The lady had a way with half-wild creatures.

Himself included.

Nathan swiped his hat off and ran a forearm across the sweat beading on his brow.

If she wanted to help the Pinkertons figure out what happened to her papa, there was no reason she shouldn't. Bringing in his killer might help her come to terms with losing him.

"The children love you." Jessa nodded to where the little Navajo girl was cradled up next to him, sound asleep with her little cornhusk doll clutched in her hand. Nellie Bradford was asleep on her other side.

He threw another rock, farther this time.

The corners of her mouth turned up in a natural grin. "They all love you." She flattered him with her pretty eyes. "Do you know what happened to their families?"

He followed her gaze to the boy laid out on a quilt. A touch of sadness sounded in her voice.

"The Bradfords were part of a wagon train headed west. They were set upon by Kiowa. The oldest boy, Jacob, kept his sisters tucked up under a buffalo hide until danger passed. Both of their parents were killed. After the dust cleared, a couple of mule drivers came across them and found the boy digging graves single-handed. They were brought into the mission about four months back."

"Only four months? No wonder Jacob hangs back from the rest. He's still grieving."

"Maybe. But he doesn't need your pity." Nathan's tone caused the little girl next to him to stir. Quieting his voice, he went on, "He's a sturdy kid. He'll land on his feet."

"I don't doubt that for a minute, but he's still a child. He *is* allowed to miss them, you know." Her indignant tone matched his own.

Pulling his hat lower on his forehead to block the afternoon sun, Nathan let the conversation rest. There was no sense in hashing it out.

"I know how he feels. I lost my own mother at a young age." Apparently, she was not of the same mind. "Bucky was just a baby when Mama was killed, and now that Papa's ... misplaced, I don't think he'll ever get over missing them."

Misplaced? That's the conclusion she'd come to? Like Augus's horse trotted back down the mountain because he couldn't remember where he'd left his rider?

Beneath the brim of his hat, Nathan narrowed an eye, watching her continue with her endless reflection on his calloused reasoning. As she spoke, she used her hands to make her point. Long graceful fingers. His attention was drawn to her hair which was alive with golden strands reflecting the sun every time she turned her head. More than once, he had to stop himself from reaching over to test the softness of it.

"... but then, you were raised at the mission, so you know how they feel. You lost your family, too."

His brows drew together as he caught the tail end of what she was saying. "I never lost a family because I never had one to begin with."

"Never?" Her question was barely above a whisper.

"My mother left me with the Padre right after I was born. The sisters saw to it that I was taken care of."

"No wonder." She dipped her head to peer under his

hat. "You've never missed or grieved over your folks because you can't miss what you've never had."

She may as well have peered straight into his soul. A familiar ache deep in his gut caused him to lean away from her. Anything to escape the regret of having spoken aloud his deepest thoughts. He'd spent a lifetime stuffing down feelings of rejection, deep down where they were no threat anymore.

But dinner at the Jamison ranch the other night reminded him he was alone in this world by no choice of his own.

Much the same as she was.

Just as he'd had to do, she would eventually come to the conclusion she didn't need anyone else. She'd make it on her own just fine, same as he had.

The Ramsey woman with her extra pieces of pie and special kindnesses got him thinking about things all over again. It hadn't escaped his notice that the housekeeper's last name was Ramsey. Same as the last initial on his handkerchief.

Out of sheer habit, he reached for the cloth in his left vest pocket.

As a kid he'd searched the face of every female passing on the street, hoping to see a glimmer of recognition in the lady's eye. There was always the possibility that the woman who gave him life could still be living somewhere around Cimarron. That very likelihood was what compelled him to leave this territory altogether at age seventeen, and he'd never come back.

For years, he'd put his past behind him. Like an old wound. Healed over, but prone to ache now and again.

"That's a nice handkerchief."

Nathan realized too late that she was still watching him.

"Hand-embroidered, it looks like."

He didn't answer. Let her think what she would. He didn't owe any explanations.

"Was it your mother's?" At that, Nathan rewarded her curiosity with a glare meant to silence her.

Instead, she leaned over for a better look. "Beautiful stitching. Who is A.R.?"

"I don't know her." Nathan stuffed it back in his pocket. "Time we get back to the mission."

"Was that your mama's initials?" Her softly spoken question felt like a kick in the ribs. "I think you carrying her handkerchief is sweet. Certainly nothing to be ashamed of."

She had more gumption than sense. Even his most intimidating scowl didn't faze her.

Jessa leaned over him to catch the girl's doll caught in a sudden gust of wind. Silky strands of hair escaped her long braid to caress his face.

The sweet smell of her skin, the soft feel of her hair, the warmth of her smile filled his senses, until before he could stop himself, he reached over to cup her cheek in his hand. Their faces a mere inch apart.

Jessa froze.

He was suddenly jolted by how quickly his thoughts had turned to kissing her. Lily's warning screamed in his head.

"Jessa is much too trusting to defend herself against your pretty words and skillful advances."

If he kissed her now, Cade would have every right to call him a heartbreaker. He had no intentions of sticking around Cimarron long enough to offer her anything other than a kiss.

"We should get back." Nathan's hand dropped to his side. Replacing the hat on his head, he stood to his feet and offered her a hand up.

"Wait." Jessa pulled back. "Did you …? Was that …? Did we …?"

"Almost." He shook his head. She needed to learn when to leave things alone.

As he started to go wake up the boy, he caught sight of her standing with a hand resting on her slender hip, looking annoyed. "I'm certain that's not allowed, *Father Nathaniel.*"

"You have no idea," he answered, as he continued to walk away.

Anymore days like today, and he really would be up for sainthood.

Chapter Thirteen

THE OLD BUCKBOARD creaked loudly in protest as Father Nathaniel guided the oxen over timeworn furrows along the old Santa Fe Trail. The children were in the back, all talking at once, excited over the shiny nuggets of fool's gold they'd found beside the river.

Jessa held tightly to the sidebar just to stay seated.

She could barely hear herself think, which was just as well. The shame she felt at having nearly kissed a holy man was only surpassed by her annoyance at him writing her off as unkissable. She'd never kissed a man before, but whenever she did, she'd like to think he'd be amenable to kissing her back.

Not that Father Nathaniel, or Student Cleric Nathaniel, or whatever he was called, was allowed such thoughts. Still, his intentions were plain enough. Then just as quickly, he obviously concluded that she wasn't capable of making it worth his while.

Jessa swiped grass from her skirt, wishing she'd ignored Lily and worn her britches instead. Some women weren't suited for calico and lace. At least not ones down here in charge of a small working ranch and busy stage depot. Plenty of rabble wandered in and around Cimarron—most up to no good. Anything in a dress was fair game as far as they were concerned. Growing up, her father had insisted she wear suspenders and trousers. She never even questioned it, until Lily came along.

When Papa was in town, no one dared look her way. When he wasn't, he made sure she had all the protection she needed. Every ranch hand and cowboy from here to Silver City knew Jessa was off-limits or they'd have Augus Jamison, Kit Carson, and the entire volunteer cavalry to answer to.

So, instead of dresses and high-button boots, Papa ordered her special-made britches in canvas and buckskin. Over time, she'd gotten spoiled to the ease of moving freely without having to fool with stiff lace and corsets.

Occasionally, she caused a stir when walking past a new batch of drovers and miners in town looking to pass some time. Eventually, though, they'd be directed by Papa's ranch hands to turn their attention elsewhere. Up until today she'd never thought twice about her ability to turn a man's head. Not that she'd been trying to turn Nathaniel's, but she'd felt just the same.

Refusing to look over at him, she wished for this eternal bumpy ride to be over. Her backside was taking quite a beating. Maybe the Lord's punishment for being such an unrefined heathen.

The wagon wheel hit a rut, and she gripped the side rail tighter to keep from falling out of her seat. The children, bouncing in the back, were utterly entertained by the wobbly ride.

Jessa threw a glare at the driver, suspicion narrowing her eyes. If she didn't know better, she'd say he'd hit that bump on purpose to shake her out of her musings.

His confident side-grin said she was exactly right.

As they pulled onto the narrow path leading to San

Gabriel Mission, she was grateful to see Father Miguel in the road up ahead with his hands clasped behind his back.

After the oxen came to a halt, Father Nathaniel jumped to the ground and lifted the children one at a time from the back of the wagon.

"Please, allow me." Father Miguel stepped forward to offer Jessa a hand. "I trust all went well?" He looked from Jessa to Nathaniel.

Jessa mumbled a quick greeting, then with a wave she headed for her horse. She didn't trust herself to talk right now. She needed to find Lily.

Lily had a way of making everything make sense.

Jessa spun her pony around and sent him off on the winds of a fast gallop.

Riding into town it suddenly occurred to her that Lily wasn't in Cimarron today. She'd gone to Elizabethtown to attend a Ladies' Society meeting. The wife of every prominent citizen in the surrounding area would be there, and she was hoping to glean more information about their husbands' land dealings.

Slowing her pace, Jessa tried to remember when Lily's stage was due to return. Not until half past four this afternoon. Juliana left this morning, so talking with her wasn't an option. Miss Ramsey, heaven help her, was as uninformed about men as she was.

Was there no one else she could have a good woman-to-woman talk with?

As Jessa rode into the edge of town, she tried to recall snippets of conversations she'd overheard at Phillips's General Store where most of the town's women gathered on Thursday afternoons to gossip. According to Maybelle Sutter, there were only two kinds of women: respectable, church-going ones fit for marriage, or shameless hussies who enjoyed kissing and such.

Jessa never paid much attention to them. Never had a reason to until today.

Her afternoon with Father Nathaniel and the children had been perfect. One of the most relaxing days she'd had in a long while. A natural friendliness flowed between them. But then, in the blink of an eye, things became heated.

All the way back to the mission, she'd thought hard about it. She couldn't put her finger on any one action or reaction that had caused the air around them to sizzle up like an August lightning storm. One minute they were smiling and laughing, and in the next she saw a flash in his eye so intense she forgot how to breathe.

His gaze had lowered to her lips, and she froze, shocked when she realized that he was on the verge of kissing her.

A shiver skittered up her spine at the memory of it.

Then, she was even more horrified when he didn't. Disappointment poured over her like a cold, soaking rain. The playfulness between them cooled to an odd indifference that made her want to take back whatever she'd done to prompt that beautiful, horrifying moment.

What side of Maybelle Sutter's fence would she fall on? The marrying side, or the seedy side with Miss Arlene's dance hall girls?

Jessa climbed down from her horse and tied him to the post outside of the Jamison Hotel. Smoothing his mane, she peered at the dance hall from over his graceful neck, pondering her options.

Suddenly, she made up her mind. With purpose in her stride, she crossed to the forbidden side of the road.

What better way to figure this out than to consult with

the head hussy, herself? Miss Arlene was snubbed by most of Cimarron's genteel population, but she seemed pleasant enough whenever their paths crossed. She always greeted Jessa with a respectful nod, and Jessa was quick to return the gesture. No one had ever chastised her for it.

Wheezer called out to her from the boardwalk in front of his father's store. She knew she was gathering curious stares but didn't have time to worry about it.

"Miss Jessa?" the barkeep of the Silver Spur Saloon called out as she passed the batwings of his establishment, bringing several of his patrons to the windows to gawk.

Jessa gave them a friendly wave but didn't slow her step.

A sleepy-eyed woman, half-dressed and spouting lewd suggestions to a pack of miners passing through town, turned from her resting place on the front steps of Miss Arlene's red-painted house. "Just where do you think you're going? Does your daddy know you've come across the street to play with the big girls?"

"I've come to speak with Miss Arlene." Jessa swatted dust from her calico skirt. "Would you know where I can find her?"

"Well, you might find her in her office, first door to the left. Just don't go lookin' around too close or you might see a whole lot more than you bargained for."

"I'll take my chances." Jessa caught up her skirt with one hand and headed for the large double doors. She'd almost kissed a man today. Nothing could shock her anymore.

"Suit yourself. But don't say I didn't warn you," the woman called after her.

A bell jingled when she opened the door, and a large woman with a brown braid wrapped several times around her head came bounding down the stairs to greet her. "Yah? Vot is it? We gave to the soldier's funds already."

"I need to see Miss Arlene." Jessa took in the lavish surroundings. Who would have guessed this place was so elegant on the inside? Just past a beaded doorway on the right, portions of a dance hall with a huge stage could be seen, complete with red velvet curtains.

"Miss Arlene is busy. Be a goot girl now and scoot!"

Undaunted, Jessa made her way down the hall to the first door on the left like the woman outside had directed. She passed a sitting room, impressed by the expensive carpet and high-quality furniture. A white marble fireplace with a brass screen nearly took up one entire wall.

"Vait!"

A deep laugh drifted from inside the parlor and Jessa couldn't resist pausing to take a peep inside. With no regard for the costly furniture, a painted lady with black-netted stockings sat on the arm of a chair with an arm slung around the new land surveyor.

"Oh!" Jessa stumbled backward and had to react fast to keep from knocking over a huge flower arrangement in a big brass vase.

"Here now!" The large woman was gaining on her so Jessa quickened her step.

Something on the wall, however, stopped her in her tracks. A small painting of a mission with its bell tower. San Gabriel, no doubt about it. In front of the church, a small dark-headed boy drew in the dirt with a long stick. The likeness was so clear and vivid that Jessa couldn't resist reaching out to touch him.

"I'm guessing Lily hasn't a clue that you're here. Am I right?"

Jessa whirled around, startled by the sound of Miss Arlene's rich, throaty voice.

"No, ma'am. I need to speak to you. Alone. Woman to woman." Her hand dropped from the painting.

Nodding, Miss Arlene took a long draw from a thinly rolled cigarette, eyeing Jessa before motioning her to follow. Blowing a puff of blue smoke from the side of her mouth, she opened the door to her office and waited for Jessa to enter ahead of her.

"Your place is very nice." Jessa tried not to cough as she passed through a cloud of smoke. Tufted satin armchairs with matching pillows were angled in front of her white desk.

"It serves a purpose," came the casual reply. "But you didn't come to admire the furnishings. What's on your mind?"

"Kissing," Jessa blurted, losing her battle to hold back a cough.

Miss Arlene lowered her cigarette to a painted china dish. The beginnings of a smile tugged at the corner of her mouth. Strangely familiar.

"Just why would a young woman such as yourself be interested in kissing?"

"I shouldn't be. Or should I? I was hoping you could help."

With a sweep of her polished fingers, Miss Arlene invited her to take a seat. Turning, the voluptuous lady walked to the other end of the room to peer out the window.

Jessa marveled at the easy way she swung her rounded hips in a dress clearly two sizes too small. The fine cut of her burgundy velvet gown suggested it came from a fashionable dress shop somewhere up north. Certainly nothing to compare it with from Phillips's store.

The older woman remained quiet, as if weighing her words carefully.

Beneath all that paint, Miss Arlene was a reasonably attractive woman. The bright red of her hair was unnatural, but her tall figure was enviable. Buxom, but with an impossibly small waist. Though her eyes were rimmed in kohl, they shone with intelligence.

Looking over her shoulder, it was as if she just realized someone else was in the room. She returned to her desk and chose to lean against it rather than sit in a chair. "You want to know if you are a proper lady or a two-bit floozie, all because some young buck caught your eye and made you think about kissing."

Jessa was amazed at her insight. "Yes! Except he's not a young buck. Well, he is young, but he's a priest."

For an instant, Miss Arlene was stunned, but quickly recovered. Jessa supposed she should have eased into revealing that bit of information.

Bringing her dish with her, Miss Arlene claimed the chair across from Jessa's. "You'd best start from the beginning. I have a feeling this could be interesting."

Taking a deep breath away from the smoke, Jessa began. "A couple of weeks back, I went out to the old mission to read to the children there. Father Miguel's place on the way to Rayado. You know the one?"

Closing her heavily made-up eyes, Miss Arlene nodded and brought the cigarette to her mouth.

"The last thing I expected to find that day was a tall, handsome-as-they-come stranger in a priest's robe, but there he was."

"I thought the devil had exclusive rights to men like

that."

"I found him intriguing from the very first time I saw him. Something about his stormy gray eyes and the way he watches me."

Miss Arlene's hand froze halfway to her lips, and she slowly replaced the glowing tip onto the dish. Her focus turned hard, and Jessa wondered what brought on the sudden change. "Go on."

Jessa decided it was time to get to the point of her visit. "Well, today we took the children on a picnic beside the river. We were having a wonderful time until one thing led to another and ..." She hoped Miss Arlene would catch on without her having to say it aloud, but the lady's expression didn't change. "Well, I guess he ... we ..."

"What's this priest's name?"

Jessa didn't know why that should matter. She really wasn't here to get him into any trouble. "I call him Father Nathaniel."

"Nathan." Miss Arlene looked a little pale as she sat back against the cushions of her chair. "So, he's back."

"You know him?" Maybe he had led the life of a scoundrel before he gave it all up for the church. Or maybe Miss Arlene knew him when he lived at the mission as a boy. "Tall? Dark, longish black hair that curls against his collar? With a sly grin?"

Miss Arlene nodded and sat forward once again, having regained her composure. "It's been a long while since I've seen him, but yes, I believe he's the man I'm thinking of."

An awkward silence fell between them.

Jessa looked down at her hands, trying not to let it bother her that a woman of Miss Arlene's profession would be on familiar terms with Father Nathaniel.

Then again, it was no business of hers. She was here to sort out her own moral fiber, not his. When she looked up again, she found Miss Arlene studying her intently with a hint of a smile on her powdered face.

"So, he kissed you, did he?"

"Almost."

"But you wanted him to?"

Jessa hesitated for a moment before slowly nodding in answer.

"Good for you, honey." Miss Arlene slapped the mahogany arm of her chair causing Jessa to jump.

Not sure how to take the encouragement, she felt a tinge of hope. "But he's a man of the cloth."

"Not yet, he's not." Smiling broadly, the older woman got up to fetch a brass box with a cameo on the lid. Opening it, she brought out another thin cigarette. "And from the sounds of it, he's a man who knows what he likes." She chuckled deeply, striking a matchstick.

"So what does that make me?" Jessa came to her feet to confront her qualms head-on, once and for all. "A lady or a floozie?"

"Because you wanted to kiss a handsome man?" Miss Arlene laid a bejeweled hand on Jessa's shoulder. "Honey, that makes you a natural-born lady."

Jessa relaxed, releasing a heavy breath.

"With the heart of a well-loved floozie." Miss Arlene's deep laugh filled the room. "Any gentleman worth his spit will appreciate that about you." She consoled the younger woman with a pat on her shoulder.

"But Mrs. Sutter said—"

"Ignore those old hens. They know nothing about their old roosters, or we wouldn't see any of them over here.

Believe me, your Papa never came around," she added with a stream of smoke.

What the woman said had some truth to it. Whenever Jessa did decide to take on a man, she'd make sure he spent his evenings at home. If kissing was what it took to keep him, then so be it.

"Things aren't always as they seem. Now go on back to the hotel and have a talk with Lily. She won't fault you for having these thoughts. Don't let a good man get by you. Fight for him if you have to. I wish I had."

Chapter Fourteen

NATHAN KEPT TO the shadows, standing in a corner of the Cimarron jail house beside the front window, watching the bank building across the street.

"You can't be serious!" DeLaney swung his feet from atop his broken-down desk. "Jessa has no business on this case. Hollinger and all who back him will skin her alive."

With arms crossed, Nathan leaned back against the cool brick wall.

Wanted posters faced every which direction, haphazardly tacked to a board hanging crooked on the wall next to him. Another heap was stacked on DeLaney's desk waiting to be sorted. Didn't appear he was much at keeping up with his own job, much less dictating who Allan Pinkerton should employ.

Back when they put DeLaney in as sheriff, Cimarron was nothing more than a dusty little dot on the map, a far cry from the busy crossroads it was today. With a main stage stop and rich veins of gold high in the rocky crags, Colfax County was a magnet for those up to no good.

The end of the war brought plenty of drifters to these foothills in search of gold. Men scarred with hate and bitterness, hoping to get rich after years of hardship on the battlefields. Easy prey for the swarm of outlaws hiding out, trying to stay a step ahead of the law.

Everyone knew DeLaney was in way over his head.

"You're confident Maxwell isn't in on all this?" Nathan wasn't here to discuss Jessa. "Lily says he's decided to sell off most of his land grant. Why all of a sudden?"

Lucien Maxwell was one of the biggest landowners—if not *the* biggest—in the entire United States.

"Rumor is he was on the verge of losing it all." DeLaney poured coffee into a dirty tin cup and offered it to Nathan. "Congress held a hearing to decide if that massive land grant of his is even legal."

Nathan waved off the offer. "Why would they question it?"

"Maxwell married a daughter of one of the original Mexican landholders. Got a good bit of land." Nathan kept an eye on the front window, ready to make an escape out back if anyone approached the front. As long as that warrant was out on him, he couldn't take any chances. "Not all that he owned, mind you, but with cash in his pocket and some fancy dealing, he bought out other landowners from Taos to Denver. He owned nearly all of the northeastern part of the Territory."

"Land worth millions."

"Or worth nothing. The Mexican government lost that war. US officials say those old land grants are null and void. They claim it's all US Territory now with full squatter's rights. Depends whether congress decides it's worth shaking up a hornet's nest in Santa Fe. I say, he's smart to sell off." DeLaney took a long sip then made a face. "We need some of that good coffee like they serve over at the hotel. Now, there's something you could have Jessa do. Bring over a pot of coffee."

Nathan chose to ignore the sheriff's comment. There'd

come a day when this town would thank Jessa properly for helping put an end to this ordeal. If he had to see to it personally. "Who did he get to buy his land? I don't imagine that was an easy sale."

"Never underestimate Maxwell."

Nathan kept an eye on a couple of high-dressed strangers paused at the bank entrance. Both scanned the boardwalk before talking something over as they watched the jail. When they finally entered the bank, two of Hollinger's gunmen followed them inside.

"Maxwell's shrewd when it comes to business. That's why him and Augus got along so well. They had a die-hard friendship. Did you know, he's the one who hired Pinkerton's Agency to come get to the bottom of Augus's death?"

Three more gunmen pulled up and disappeared into the bank building across the street, but not before looking up and down the street to make sure no one saw them going in. They were gearing up for something. There's a good likelihood that Hollinger was onto the fact that Lobo was in town. They'd wait it out and make their move when it best served their interests.

Nathan pushed off from the brick wall and stood in front of the window, no longer bothering to hide himself. He'd just as soon get this taken care of here and now.

DeLaney pulled in a shutter to conceal the front window. "You trying to get yourself killed?"

Nathan flung it back open. "Hollinger's well aware I'm in town. Besides, he can't make an arrest without you."

"Jeb Hollinger doesn't wait for the law to serve justice. You'd best keep that in mind if you plan on staying here long. If he takes a notion to act on that warrant, he and his men will be judge, jury, and executioner before you ever strap on your guns." DeLaney inspected the bank building with a cautious eye. "And there's nothing you or me either one can do to stop him."

Nathan was of a different opinion on that, but before he could say so, Hollinger and six of his gunmen exited the bank and started out across the street. The two in silk vests chose to wait on the other side.

Rushing toward the back, Nathan tucked himself behind the solid pine door that led to the prisoner's lockup just as the front door burst open.

Several sets of boots shuffled in. Nathan counted four.

"Afternoon, Jeb." DeLaney's voice came from the area where his desk was set. Nathan heard the squeak of his chair. "What can I do for you today?"

"Where is he?" He recognized Hollinger's cigar-raspy voice. "You said you'd made the arrest, so where is he?"

"I'm guessing you mean Lobo?"

Nathan couldn't get a good take on exactly where DeLaney's loyalties lie. From what he gathered, the sheriff was apt to go along with whoever he was with at the time. A man like that served only himself and could be easily bought off.

The double click of a revolver was DeLaney's answer.

"Careful now, Jeb. I have immunity, remember? Santa Fe gave me full authority to exercise law and order in Cimarron."

"Put the weapon down, Snake. I gave no order to shoot." Hollinger's heavy footfall crossed to where Nathan stood behind the door. "Except where landholdings are concerned. My bank has sole discretion in seeing to the interests of the new corporation." He stepped just inside the doorway to peer into the empty cell.

Nathan didn't breathe.

Through the crack in the door, he could see Hollinger's stocky profile barely a foot away. His droopy eyes, thick handlebar mustache, and slight underbite gave him the appearance of a bulldog.

A full minute passed before Hollinger rejoined his men.

"Now that Johannsen has set up office, his law firm will see that regulations always lineup with our objectives. So you can sit back and relax. My boys will take up the slack."

"I got your warrant for Lobo. Against my better judgement. But the agreement was, he is afforded full trial by his peers. You cannot take matters into your own hands with this one, Jeb. I won't let it happen. As long as I'm still law here, you'll abide by my decisions."

"Big talk for a man who owes the corporation more than he'll make in a lifetime."

Nathan's hunch had been on target. DeLaney had ties to the ring, but he was still fighting to keep his independence. A dangerous gamble.

"You're wasting your time and mine. Lobo's not here." The front door groaned on its hinges. "They brought him in then turned him over to the Texas Rangers until he stands trial. If you're still bound and determined to see for yourself that he's locked up, you'll have to hunt down Cade Matlock. They left yesterday morning. Probably to Amarillo by now."

Hollinger's curse filled the small room.

"What I can't understand is why you're in such an all-fired hurry to see Lobo hang for a crime we both know he didn't commit." The slow shuffle of boots told him Hollinger's men filed outside. "You have much more important things to be worrying about. Like why the newspapers up north are suddenly so interested in the corporation."

Nathan listened hard but Hollinger gave no response.

"Leave the outlaws to me. You just get the squatters off our land."

All at once, yelling could be heard from the street.

Nathan slipped from behind the door to better hear what the commotion was all about.

"The stage was robbed!"

Nathan snapped open his pocket watch. Earlier on the banks of the river, Jessa mentioned that Lily was due in on the four, ten.

Just about thirty minutes from now.

That meant Lily was on that stage.

Chapter Fifteen

J ESSA SPUN THE guest register around and around on its swiveled stand with her chin resting in the palm of her hand. After speaking with Miss Arlene, she had so many questions, but with Lily gone for the day, it would be nighttime before she could have a word with her.

The lobby bustled with activity around her.

The stage headed to San Francisco made its way through here every Tuesday morning and the Jamison Hotel was a popular resting stop for weary travelers. Sometimes they stayed a week, sometimes even longer until they felt rested enough or their funds ran out. Then they'd catch the same stage the next Tuesday and continue their journey.

A well-dressed man and woman, newly married from the looks of it, strolled arm-in-arm admiring various works of art hanging on the red-flocked walls of the lobby. The woman grabbed the man's arm tighter and buried her face in his shoulder every time they passed under one of Papa's prized heads of beasts that hung over the doorways and long windows.

The woman's flagrant excuse to sidle up next to her man was downright embarrassing.

Why did she have to act silly just to get her man to hold her? She should feel free to take his arm whenever the whim hit her. Why did everyone make the love between two people so complicated? What was the harm in showing the man you married a little affection? Surely the man in question didn't seem to mind.

Catching a glimpse of the enormous buffalo head over the doorway to the restaurant, Jessa smiled to herself. *Biggest buffalo to ever roam the earth*, her father used to say. If the silly lady played her cards right, she might get a real hug under that one.

A foursome of miners gathered around a piano in the corner, singing in off-key harmony about the loved ones they'd left behind, while a couple of Hollinger's regulators took turns peering from the lace-paneled windows.

Those two were up to something.

Most days, DeLaney would come move them along. Papa didn't tolerate trouble anywhere near the hotel, and neither would she. Experience told her that any man flaunting a fancy gun belt like that was nothing but trouble. They were either experienced bounty hunters looking to nab a reward, or inexperienced gunslingers seeking fame.

"Stage a-comin'!" The deep resonant voice of the hotel's stable keep sounded from outside, bringing Jessa's attention back to the printed schedule hanging on the wall next to the entrance. That stage heading west wasn't due in for another half hour.

"Miss Jessa, maybe you should go on out there and see what this is about." Harvey Chavez had been manager of the hotel for as long as she could remember. Polite to a fault, the thin, unassuming man would never come right out and say she was underfoot, but Jessa knew he liked things just so. "I have everything covered in here."

As if to prove the point, he carefully turned the guest register back around and situated the ink well exactly an inch to the upper right.

Jessa smiled. She needed some fresh air and should probably check on Bucky anyway. "All right, Harv. I'll go see about it."

Just as she opened the stately carved door, a rush of folks ran past her heading for the stage depot.

"The stage was robbed!"

"Stage was held up."

She could only catch bits and pieces of their hurried comments.

Lily was on that stage!

Lord, please let Lily and all the others be safe this time.

Before she could react, a strong hand reached out and latched onto her arm. "Act natural, Jessa. We need to talk."

If she hadn't immediately recognized Father Nathaniel's voice, she would have laid teeth marks into those bold fingers. With a quick assessment of their surroundings, Jessa led him around to the side of the hotel where a storage shed was tucked in back. The lock was easily sprung with a piece of wire kept on a ledge above the door.

With trembling fingers, she removed the latch and entered the musty storehouse.

He hastily shut the door behind them and moved her to where a thin shaft of light glimmered past a slat in the wall.

Pulling her to where he could see her better, he removed the cowled hood. Crystallized specks of dust stirred in the shimmering beam between them. Jessa searched his face trying to make sense of his odd behavior. She saw only concern shining in his gray gaze. "I need to see about the stage—"

"Where's Lily?" There was an urgency in his voice that instantly alarmed her.

"Coming from Fort Union."

He grasped her shoulders. For the second time today, their faces were inches apart. "When's her stage due in?"

"Quarter past four." The hair stood out on the back of her neck when his warm breath brushed against her lips. "Someone said it was held up. Lily's supposed to be on it."

He abruptly released her and started for the small door, but paused when he looked down realizing he was scaring the living daylights out of her. Cupping her cheek in his palm, he softened his tone considerably. "You go on home. See that Bucky stays with you. Wait for Lily there, and don't let anyone in until you hear from one of us."

"Nathaniel, what's this about? Do you think Lily was targeted?" She only meant to take a step forward, to implore him to tell her more about what was going on, but her foot caught on something in the dark, and she slammed into his chest instead. His arms came around her and she could feel the strong pounding of his heart against her temple.

"I didn't mean to scare you."

Squeezing her eyes shut, she ordered herself to snap out of it. He needed to go check on Lily, and she needed to find Bucky. But try as she might, she couldn't get her feet to move. She dared not lift her head for fear he would finish what he'd started this morning beside the river.

Nathan seemed to sense her dilemma and made the move for her, stepping back to find the door behind him with his hand, with one arm lingering around her waist.

Jessa squinted in the brightness when he pulled the door open. Then as quickly as he had appeared, he was gone again, leaving her to replace the lock in a daze.

"Miss Jessa." Harv Chavez was out of breath as he

bounded toward her. "Miss Valentine said to give you a message."

Jessa worked to calm the poor man down before he passed out from all the excitement.

"Is she all right? What did she say?"

"Said to tell you she is f-fine." He took in another gasp of breath. "Gone over to give her statement to the sheriff. Will meet you at home."

After encouraging him to take a few more deep breaths, Jessa was suddenly anxious to get home. Lily would be there soon, and she needed to know that she had come to no harm. She'd get Miss Ramsey to make a pot of her favorite tea. But first she needed to find Bucky.

The boardwalk was deserted. The good citizens of Cimarron had split into various groups to discuss the latest attack to affect their town.

As she approached Phillips General Store, she saw the boys standing next to the horse trough where Bucky squirted Wheezer with water he squeezed from his clasped hands.

"Hi, Jessa." Poor Wheezer needed rescuing from her brother yet again.

Reaching down, Jessa lifted a large rock and plopped it hard into the trough, giving Bucky a good spray.

He sprang backward with a squeal. "What'd you do that for?"

Jessa pulled a handkerchief out of the pocket of her skirt. With small circles, she cleared the lenses of Wheezer's round spectacles to reveal his large, unblinking eyes filled with adoration. "Better?"

He nodded vigorously.

"Good. One of these days, Bucky, Wheezer's going to

get enough of your shenanigans." Replacing the sodden cloth to her pocket, she unwrapped her pony's reins.

"He knows I'm just funning with him. Don't ya, Wheez?"

Wheezer gave a small shrug.

"See there? He likes it."

Jessa cast an empathetic look at Wheezer before turning her horse toward the stables. "Just the same, I want you home now." Not leaving any room for argument, she turned her back to him, preparing to mount up. "You can walk or ride with me, but you're coming home. Tell Wheezer bye."

With a mischievous grin, Bucky blocked her stirrup just as she lifted her foot. "What were you and Lo ... er, that preacher man doin' in the woodshed?"

Jessa prayed for grace not to strangle her papa's only son. "Talking. In private." She held up a hand before he could even ask. "None of your business."

"Maybe she needed to confess some sins." Wheezer thought he was helping her out. He wasn't.

"Have anything to do with why you went visitin' the red house today?"

Dear Lord in heaven, this child ....

"You two couldn't possibly understand, so I don't want to hear any more about it. Get yourself home, and I don't intend to say it again. Tomorrow, I'll see that you're occupied with a few extra chores to keep from having so much extra time to be spying on folks."

Bucky's smile dissolved.

Jessa lifted herself up into the saddle.

"Wait! We got something for ya. Go ahead, Wheez, give it to her."

Jessa folded her hands on the pommel and prepared to

be gifted. She'd gotten the best of him, so more than likely he had a dead spider or green grass snake to wave in her face.

Wheezer dug deep into the pocket of his suspendered britches and pulled out a piece of fuzzy taffy. With bumbling fingers, he pushed his glasses back on his nose and lifted the candy to her.

"Not that, Wheez. Your back pocket."

Momentarily at a loss, Wheezer looked around, unsure of what to do with his candy. Finally, he popped it into his mouth and pulled a small book from his back pocket.

Jessa winced. Thanking him politely, she accepted the book from his grimy hand.

"We figured you could use something new to read to them kids out at the mission besides baby books."

The boys grinned a little too wide.

"A dime novel?"

They nodded in unison.

"Not another gunfighter, I hope. Those stories aren't worth the paper they're printed on."

"Just read it. I hear tell there's boys out at the mission, too. I'm telling ya, they'll like this one. Right, Wheez?"

"A-And you, too," Wheezer said with a blush staining the apples of his cheeks.

Jessa turned the small book over and studied the picture of a wolf howling against the backdrop of a harvest moon.

What could possibly be different about this one?

"The Legend of El Lobo," she read aloud.

Chapter Sixteen

THE LEGEND OF EL LOBO
With cunning anticipation, he waits.
Dubbed dangerous by outlaw and lawman alike.
A foe to be reckoned with.
Never was there a more imposing figure to defend
the American Frontier than the gunslinger known far
and wide as
El Lobo – the lone wolf.

A shiver caused Jessa to pull the knitted throw from the back of her chair to cover her lap as she turned the page.

Deep in the wilds of our great West,
the wolf's prowess is legendary.
Quick to detect weakness,
Swift to use it to his advantage.
An elusive beast by nature, he travels alone.
A soulful cry on a distant hill, a fearsome reminder
of his presence.

"That and a couple of Wells Fargo stages stripped bare," Jessa muttered.

"Did you say something?" Miss Ramsey looked up from the book she held in her hands.

"No. Just trying to read this dime novel the boys thought I'd find interesting." Biting her lip, she turned another page.

> *Larger than the average mongrel and infinitely*
> *more instinctive,*
> *Always watching with gun-steel eyes of gray.*
> *Daring and proud.*
> *The beast serves a hard lesson to those*
> *who attempt to trap him unawares.*

Jessa smirked at the shameless propaganda. "If people like this stuff, snake oil peddlers must make a fortune up there." Rubbing at the gooseflesh on her arms, she noted the unseasonable chill in the air.

Whoever this trigger-happy renegade was, she didn't like Bucky idolizing him one bit.

> *Thus, with feral charm and a deadly aim,*
> *Nathaniel Wolfe leaves an unforgettable*
> *footprint everywhere his boot touches ground.*
> *So goes the legend of El Lobo.*

Jessa sprang upright in her chair.

Gray eyes? Feral charm? *Nathaniel* Wolfe?

Surely not!

Jessa flipped to the last page and gasped, dropping the book to the floor like it had just grown fangs and bitten her.

There on the last page was a photograph of Father Nathaniel in a black outfit with a cocksure expression on his face mocking all considered holy.

"Told ya you'd like it." Bucky's dimpled cheeks belied the devious little scamp he was.

"Jessa? Are you all right?" Miss Ramsey stood, wringing her hands. "Take a sip of your lemonade, dear. You're pale as a sheet."

Jessa reached for the dime novel at her feet and sent it hurling through the air with a loud thud against the opposite wall.

Miss Ramsey ducked.

"No wonder he didn't act like a priest is supposed to. He's not one!" Jessa cast the knitted covering aside and reached for an ugly vase papa purchased from a tinker's wagon.

Miss Ramsey saved the hideous vessel just before Jessa let it fly. "Who's not acting like a priest?"

"I tried to tell ya." Bucky held out another trinket for Jessa to smash.

"Where's Lily? She should be home by now." Jessa rubbed at her temples.

"Her note said as soon as she gave her account to Sheriff DeLaney, she'd come straight home." Miss Ramsey moved the lemonade glasses to the sideboard.

Jessa couldn't remember ever being so shaken. She had to warn Lily. As long as that canine pretender was out there none of them were safe. To think he'd been right here under their very noses the whole time. She'd taken him at face value, even confided in him. Had shameless thoughts about him in the woodshed, for pity's sake. She'd braved the seedy side of the street. All for a lie. Every bit of it, a foolish, good-for-nothing lie.

The sting of hot tears caused her to grab the figurine out of Bucky's hand, which Miss Ramsey promptly retrieved from her other side. "Nathaniel ... Lobo ... whoever he is! He came asking about Lily this afternoon. She must've caught on to him. We have to find her. He may have—"

"Found her. Brought her home safe and sound."

With icy dread, Jessa realized that someone had come in behind her. Spinning, she tried to make out a figure standing in the recessed shadows of the doorway.

"May as well show yourself, Nathan. She needs to hear the truth from your own lips." Lily entered in behind him and didn't seem the least upset. He obviously had her good and fooled.

As if stepping from a nightmare, the phantom took shape. Dressed in solid black, his head bowed low under the brim of a seven-dollar Stetson, he wore a gun belt slung low on his hip.

Jessa drew a sharp breath. Even without the benefit of seeing his face, she knew at once who he was. "You!" she rasped.

Ignoring Miss Ramsey's hand on her arm, she took a step toward him, but stopped short when he lifted his head and pierced her with an icy-gray stare. Her heart pounded in her head, but she refused to look away.

"Surely you don't believe everything you read, Miss Jamison." The sound of his voice pulled at her battered senses.

Balling her fists, she spoke, though barely controlled. "Lily, get my rope. I'm hauling this outlaw to jail, myself."

"Simmer down, love. Let's not be too hasty." Lily scanned the room, taking in the discarded book splayed against the floorboard.

Miss Ramsey took Bucky by the hand and scurried to the door. "Come, Bucky. You need some pie."

"Jessa's been dealt an awful shock." Lily came to Jessa's side and put an arm around her waist. "Nathan, please explain who you really are and why you're here."

With a couple more steps, he closed the gap between

them.

So much confusion caused her head to spin. Nathan reached out to steady her.

She immediately brushed off his assistance. "I need no help from a mangy gunfighter."

He lifted a dark brow, seemingly to weigh her bold statement for truth. After an eternal silence, he pushed back his hat with a thumb. "You afraid of wolves, Jessa?"

"Only lying, thieving ones wearing high-dollar boots." She held his gaze, heated by the challenge in his eyes.

Lily squeezed her waist, reminding her to remain calm.

Sheriff DeLaney entered the room and swiped his hat off. "The Ramsey woman let me in. What's all the ruckus?"

"He had us all fooled." Jessa took a deep breath to steady her nerves, her focus never leaving the beloved face she hardly recognized anymore. "This man is none other than the gunslinger they call, El Lobo. The one wanted for robbing our stages. And the man they say could be responsible for assaulting my father."

"So much for your cover." DeLaney cracked a pecan from a bowl on the side table and popped the nut into his mouth. "How'd she find out?"

"These infernal dime novels." Lily bent to retrieve the small book. "I suppose we have Bucky to thank for supplying the information."

"You knew?" Jessa's attention shifted to the other two in the room. "You all knew?"

She tried to make sense of their betrayal but found no viable reason they'd turn their backs on her father by welcoming his killer into their fold. Why was he still free with the county sheriff and a government agent standing right here?

"Jessa, you must calm down and listen." Lily removed her gloves. "Nathan did not kill your father. He was in Kansas at the time. He is here now at my request."

"Lobo's been undercover. Helping us look for the real killer." DeLaney helped himself to coffee on the sideboard. "Cade thought it best to keep it from you until they had a chance to gather some evidence. He's only agreed to help out for a couple of months."

"Why didn't you tell me?" Though she asked the question to no one in particular, her attention was centered on the man in black.

"Couldn't take any chances," DeLaney piped in. "The slightest slip could get him killed."

So, it had all been an act. A very well-played act on all of their parts.

Lobo stood stoic with arms crossed and no discernible expression.

"Initially, I'd hoped to spare you from this, but you're too bright by far." Lily gave her a half-hearted smile. "You don't need protecting, I know that now. But I'm afraid by doing so, we only managed to hurt you. I am truly sorry."

The ache in her chest was much more than wounded pride. She had failed to guard her heart, and the man who'd easily found a place there never even existed.

This man in his place was everything she detested.

How had she been so blind?

Chapter Seventeen

EMBERS OF MISTRUST smoldered between them every time her gaze lifted to his.

Before tonight, Nathan hadn't fully appreciated how comfortable things had become between them. Or what a loss it would be if Jessa ever shut him out.

But thanks to a heap of questionable choices, that's exactly what happened.

Lying to her had never been his choice. This was Lily's case. How she saw fit to run it was none of his business. If it had been up to him, he'd have ridden into town under no disguise at all and taken his chances with Hollinger's gang. Let the chips fall where they may.

He was done sneaking around in a cleric's getup. It was time Jessa and everyone else dealt with the man he was. He was accustomed to curious stares and mama's running off with their babies when he walked down the street. But Jessa's reaction cut like a knife. Worse than any snub of a stranger.

Truth be told, he was sick and tired of ignoring the feelings that flared up every time he was alone with Augus's daughter. Having to pretend they were strictly one-sided on her part wasn't entirely fair. They were not a figment of her imagination.

That had been the biggest lie of all.

Jessa made him feel—something he hadn't allowed for a good long while. He'd been lying to himself by trying to deny it. Getting things out in the open was best for everyone. One day soon, he'd have to walk away. He didn't want her hurt any more than she already was.

As it was now, she'd be glad to see him go.

Just as well. He didn't plan on staying in Cimarron. As soon as his name was cleared, he'd join back up with Hickok in Kansas, putting as much distance as he could between them.

"So you see, love, I take full responsibility for having kept it from you. I felt it was best for all involved." Lily untied the ribbon of her black feathered hat and removed it from her hair. "You understand, prior to now, you were merely a civilian that I'd sworn to protect. I couldn't chance losing you. However, you've proven your worth to this investigation. I've gotten full approval from Allan to extend an offer of employment as a Pinkerton agent, if you're still interested."

Jessa's steady regard of Nathan broke as she turned to her friend. "Are you serious?"

"Effective immediately."

He watched Jessa's expression soften as Lily pulled her goddaughter into an embrace. A shot of relief coursed through him as he watched her try to smile again.

"From what I hear, this was mostly Lobo's idea." DeLaney made himself at home in Augus's overstuffed chair.

"He did pull hard for you." Lily unfastened her gloves. "One by one we all came to see his reasoning. You have what it takes to be an excellent operative."

"Do your Papa proud, kid." DeLaney cracked another

pecan.

Finally, Jessa turned back to Nathan. She fought a noticeable battle to be civil. Clasping her fingers a good minute or two, she finally extended her hand. "Then I guess I have you to thank."

Nathan accepted her hand. A peace offering, he supposed. "Congratulations, Agent Jamison."

"You two will make excellent allies." Lily came up beside them both. "For what it's worth, love, Nathan also wanted to reveal his true identity long before today."

Nathan held onto her hand longer than necessary, forcing Jessa to look up at him. "I'm still the same man. Nothing's changed but the disguise."

Silence met his graceless explanation. At first, he thought she was going to argue, instead she reclaimed her hand, and turned away. But not before giving a good eye roll.

He had that coming.

"I came across some interesting information during my visit with the officers' wives out at Lucien Maxwell's place at Fort Sumner." Lily seemed to ignore the exchange as she settled into a green high-back chair, but Nathan watched her give a quick visual check to the door and windows before she sat down. "Congress agreed to keep the matter of Maxwell's land grant an open issue to be considered."

Jessa spoke up. "The government ruled in favor of Lucien Maxwell back when he held the land, I thought."

"The question has been reintroduced. I'm not sure Mr. Hollinger knows it. As usual, he's been too busy making mincemeat of the law to care. He has one objective and that's to see his interests are protected."

"The dangerous aspect to all of this is he's backed by

the ring, *that* he does know," Nathan provided. "Judges, politicians—even lawmen have a vested interest in that land. But in order to see a payoff they have to take it away from the hardworking families who have worked it for years to sell off to the highest bidder." He directed a hard look at DeLaney.

"Now that the railroads have an eye on it, that bid will go higher and higher." Jessa chose to stand rather than sit, so out of respect, Nathan stood, too. "Papa owns plenty of land up near Mt. Baldy where the gold stakes are being made. He bought it from Mr. Maxwell years ago. Do you think they will force him to give it up?"

Lily took a sip of her tea, nodding. "Maybe. If I were guessing, there is more to be made by leasing small claims out to prospective miners than from any actual gold being mined from the river and streams. It is possible, however, that Hollinger and his men were leaning on Augus to relinquish his rights to them. I certainly wouldn't put anything past them."

"I will help you look through Papa's records and journals. Maybe there's something in his papers about this."

DeLaney took notice of a crowd beginning to gather outside. Lily went to the window as well.

Jessa moved to her father's desk and pulled open the bottom drawer. Lifting a leather-bound volume, she flipped it open to the first page. "This was his latest journal. It was found in his saddlebag the night his horse came home without him."

Nathan hid a grin. The night he was *misplaced*.

"That will be helpful, love." Lily watched the road intently. "Nathan, this is not at all good."

He stepped to the window to see three of Hollinger's

most feared guns riding into town shooting into the air. Behind them, they towed another horse with a rider bound at the wrists. The moment he saw the Apache they brought in as prisoner, he started for the door.

"Hold up, Lobo. You can't just go strolling out there pretty as you please. You'll play right into their hands." DeLaney moved in front of him. "Hollinger has no idea you're here at the hotel. He thinks you're halfway to Ft. Worth. I'd like to keep it that way."

Lily pulled a tasseled cord to bring the heavy panels together in front of the window. "Poppycock! He knows you are here. This stunt is nothing more than another antic to smoke you out into the open. They'll have you captured and hanged before you step off the boardwalk."

"Is this why you were in disguise?" Jessa stepped in front of him to block his way. "Because Hollinger wants you dead?"

"He made Nathan a rather lucrative offer to head up his collection of gun men. Nathan of course refused. Hollinger's most likely under the assumption that Nathan has come to assist the opposition. I doubt he's clever enough to figure out the four of us are here to find Augus's killer. I trust he won't hear it from anyone in this room." Lily also pinned DeLaney with a look of warning.

"Just in case, Lobo, you need to lay low." DeLaney flipped open his revolver, checking to make sure it was fully loaded. "This is my town. I'll go out to see what this is about."

"That man they're dragging in is Apache." Nathan wound his way around the sofa and chairs to peer out the other window. "The lone red feather he's wearing in his hat means he was next in line under Gray Wolf. The black store-bought clothes means, for whatever reason, he has deserted his people."

"Some of these young warriors don't welcome the government's generous assistance to herd the tribes off to designated lands. Some fight it. Some join the opposition. Looks to me like Hollinger recruited himself one to pose as your imposter. Powerful likeness. Nice of them to haul him in for me."

"It makes no difference why he left. That's an eldest son of the chief of the Jicarilla. Hauling him in like a rabid jackal is a guaranteed invitation to war. I have to put a stop to this now before there's a whole lot of innocent bloodshed." Nathan brushed past DeLaney, but again Jessa blocked his way.

"The sheriff's right, you can't go out there like that. You're safer in your robe. At least that way, you have a chance to take them by surprise."

"I don't own a robe." Nathan settled his hat lower on his forehead. He would confront Hollinger's hired guns just the way he was. If they wanted to try and stop him, he was ready for that, too.

"I thought you were smarter than that." She again blocked his exit, continuing to hold her ground. "Going out there and getting shot won't prove anything except you're easily drawn into a fight."

"A minute ago, you were hoping I'd get shot." Nathan swiveled past her but she beat him to the doorway and pulled the pocket door shut, effectively cutting off his escape.

"That was before we were colleagues. Now I have a responsibility to see you finish out this assignment in one piece. If you go out there and blow our cover, I'll never convince Mr. Pinkerton to let me work for him again. I'll go. Hollinger's used to me asking questions." Jessa turned and started to reopen the door when Nathan's hand above her head prevented it from moving. "No one in this entire county would put up with them laying a finger on me."

"If Hollinger had any inkling you are working with the Pinkertons, he wouldn't hesitate to make sure you end up dead, too."

Jessa gave the door a good yank but Nathan still barred it from budging.

"You can both stay where you are." Lily reached behind Jessa and pulled open the door. "Sheriff, ride out to Fort Union for backup. Tell them it's on the order of Allan Pinkerton. Jessa, go to the hotel office and have Mr. Chavez wire Allan personally. We need a government-backed pardon for Lobo as soon as possible. I will go out and get some answers."

"I'll go with you." Jessa grabbed her lasso off of a hook on the wall.

"I'm giving you an order, love." Lily set her hat back on her head. "This is not negotiable. No argument."

Nathan refused to sit back and let Gray Wolf's offspring take a fall for another round of Hollinger's botched plans. It was one thing to intimidate defenseless farmers and ranchers, but this town had no idea what they were up against if they ever truly riled the Apache chief.

"From what I can see, the young warrior was not hurt." Lily tied her ribbons before checking her small derringer tucked inside her muff. "There is a slim chance he can be released unharmed. We must do all we can to avoid an all-out range war."

This dancing in the doorway was a waste of time. Gray

Wolf and his people deserved more respect than this. The chief had always treated him fairly. Nathan intended to return the favor. He moved forward, but this time it was Lily who stopped him.

"The order stands for you, too. I won't chance losing you. There's no point in you walking out there and getting shot. We both know it's a trap." Nathan started to argue but Lily's hand on his arm gave him pause. "Let me do my job. We are all working together." Her voice softened with her expression. "I promise to do all I can to see the prisoner is released."

NOT HALF AN hour passed before Lily swept back through the front entrance, unmistakably agitated. "That huge ignoramus with the shabby hat and hairy knuckles would benefit greatly from a lesson in manners."

Jessa quickly moved from her perch at the window to meet her friend in the adobe foyer. "It looked to me like you gave him one."

"He made a crude reference to my frilly drawers. I refuse to discuss lingerie with cretins who spit tobacco at my feet."

"So, you flipped him on his keister." Lobo laughed quietly from his position at the window watching the crowd quickly disperse.

Lily hooked an arm through Jessa's and led her back toward the drawing room. "I refuse to be manhandled."

"The big one's name is Snake Newcomb. Used to ride with the Musgrove gang. They're known for robbing wagon trains and laying blame on the natives."

"He's in charge of guarding the prisoner and isn't letting anyone into that jailhouse."

Miss Ramsey came in with a tray, offering pie and coffee.

As Lily accepted, Jessa took two cups and brought one over to Lobo. "With the sheriff gone, Hollinger has his men set on every side of the jailhouse. Surely, he doesn't expect his five ragged gunmen to hold off an entire war party should Gray Wolf hear about this." She took a long sip trying to make sense of the odd situation. "Why has the sheriff given them the right to guard the jail anyway? Most of their faces are on wanted posters hanging all over the walls of that office. You'd think they'd avoid the place at all costs." She watched two men on either side of the jail door kicking rocks into the street, making bets as to which of them could kick farther. "Then again, gunslingers aren't the brightest humans."

Casting a sly glance at the tall one standing next to her, she couldn't help but add, "No offense."

His slow grin struck her, causing that ache in her chest to flare up again.

Lily sat on the rolled arm of the sofa, clasping her hands on her crossed knees. "Apparently, DeLaney doesn't feel he has enough backing from the territorial judicial system to arrest Hollinger or his trigger-happy employees. Because of it, they define the law to their own liking."

"All well and good, but we're wasting time. As long as that Apache is held up in Cimarron, the town is vulnerable to a surprise attack."

"The man you call Snake was spouting off about how the warrior was caught working with Lobo to rob the stage today. Said he was skulking around in the brush. He's managed to cause quite an uproar among the townsfolk." The tone of Lily's voice dropped a tad causing both Lobo and Jessa to turn at her sudden seriousness. "Hollinger knows you didn't leave town with Cade. Everyone saw them leave on the stage to Amarillo. He is trying to lure you out into the open. But the moment you step outside that door, they will lynch you from the nearest tree."

A shiver ran up Jessa's spine that had nothing to do with the chilled night air. She took a step toward Nathaniel Wolfe. A hundred reasons ran through her mind why she shouldn't care, but she did. Pretending otherwise would get him killed. "What Lily says is true. You can't go out there. I will figure a way for you to get in to check on Gray Wolf's son."

"As honorable as that is, love, I'm afraid you'll not be able to gain entrance either. You, nor I, can stand up to five gun-happy killers, all well-paid to enforce Hollinger's wishes. At this point there's a town full of vigilantes who are prepared to help them if it means restoring order. We can't afford to have Hollinger's cohorts deem us a threat to their homegrown law enforcement or we become part of the problem in their eyes."

"So, we find a way around their set-up. Shouldn't be too difficult." Lobo tugged his gun from its holster and gave it a spin before setting it back in place.

Jessa was irritated by his arrogant trick, though grudgingly impressed. "Hopefully, we find a way that doesn't include shooting your foot off."

"Might I say something?" Miss Ramsey spoke up with a dust rag in her hand. "Whenever there is a prisoner taken into the jailhouse, the ladies from our prayer circle take turns bringing over meals. In turn, Sheriff DeLaney provides us safe escort from the church to our homes after we meet on Sunday evenings."

She still avoided direct eye contact with Lobo, looking half-terrified of him.

He never even noticed, however, because he was too busy staring out the window. Something needed to be done about his careless attitude. He had moments of true concern for others—she'd seen glimpses of it herself. It didn't matter if he was the fastest gun in all of the western hemisphere. If he didn't learn some humility, he'd never be the man God intended him to be.

"That's it! Miss Ramsey, you're brilliant." Jessa threw her arms around the woman's slim shoulders. "They have to let the prisoner eat, right?" Donning a bright smile, she turned to Lobo. "I know just the person to bring him breakfast first thing in the morning."

Chapter Eighteen

"You've all lost your minds!" Nathan pushed a pair of feminine hands aside as they came at him with a pot of goop. He'd have never shown up if he'd known her plan included painting him up like a clown.

"Nathan, calm down." Lily took on that high and mighty tone of hers. The other two hovering over him pushed him back down into his chair. "I know this isn't quite what you had in mind, but Jessa's idea makes perfect sense. You do want to get into the jail, don't you?"

"Not like this." He swatted again at the pesky fingers in his face, shooting Jessa a stern glare.

She smiled.

"Under any other circumstances, I'd agree wholeheartedly. But this time we've no other choice." Lily lifted the window enough to allow the fresh morning air to circulate around the room. "Jessa's on to something. When you work with Pinkertons, you never know what cloaking skills might become necessary."

"I brought Bucky over to Mr. Phillips' store first thing this morning, so we could get you in and out of that jailhouse before noon," Jessa announced. "Time's wasting."

Nathan continued to look past the brush-wielding women to focus on Jessa. She hung back from the group, leaning against her father's desk beaming like she swallowed a swarm of fireflies. No doubt about it, she was out to settle a score, and the twinkle in her eye said she was enjoying every moment.

"Sit still. If they recognize you, they'll shoot you on sight. You can do it this way, or the undertaker can do it for you later. Your choice." A woman with a top knot and flame-red hair poofing out at the sides held a powder puff on him like it was the business end of a Colt. "Surely, you're man enough to handle a little war paint. Because, darlin', this is war."

"Arlene, don't be so pushy." Miss Ramsey spoke up from her position at his left, waving the fancy hairbrush in her hand. Even the mousy housekeeper was party to this cockamamie scheme. "Nathaniel's merely expressing the same concerns that any other red-blooded man would in his predicament."

"Any other red-blooded man would have more sense than to walk right into the enemy's camp. This one's determined to rush in with guns blazing." He recognized the woman as owner of the brothel. Why Jessa chose to fetch her to help play dress-up, he couldn't tell. "No matter how sure of yourself you are, Lobo, you're only one gun against five. Pull his hair back away from his face. He has fabulous bone structure." She stood back to look him over with a critical eye. "You got some hairpins, Lily?"

They ignored his refusal.

"Wonderful idea, Arlene. I have some on my dressing table."

Lily winked at Jessa, who had the nerve to giggle.

"Now hold up!" Nathan grasped the cloth they had hanging around his neck and tossed it to the floor. His patience hit rock bottom. It was bad enough these females were bound and determined to color him up like a prized easter egg, but he didn't have to sit back and take it. "Save yourself a trip, Lily. I don't need face paint or hairpins or ridiculous clothes to get me inside that jail. I will handle this on my own."

"Oh, but you mustn't." Miss Ramsey ran the bristle brush through a handful of his hair. "I'm quite certain those men are waiting for you to show up, and you would be killed on the spot. No, hmm-umm. You must let us help."

"Sit still or you'll have lips clear to your ears." The Arlene woman waved a red-tipped brush in front of his nose.

Nathan rose to his feet, his temper at a slow boil. "Look. Ladies, I appreciate the concern, but the closest thing to a dress you'll ever see me in was that priest's get-up. *Comprendé?* And sure as the day is long, I'm not wearing any face paint."

He watched the redhead straighten to an impressive height. With a determined shrug of her shoulders, she took a step closer to him. "Care to make a wager on that?"

Nathan met her challenge with one of his own. "How much you lookin' to lose?"

The last thing he expected was to see amusement tug at her full red lips. She was a tall, solid woman and conveyed a certain confidence like one who knew she made more money than the rest of the town put together. She had no qualms about looking a man straight in the eye.

"Well, now ..." With a shrug, she pulled a shiny cigarette case from the side pocket of her scarlet gown. "I'd have thought a man of your profession would be used to doing whatever it takes to keep himself alive." She lit a matchstick and paused. "Surely you can tolerate a bit of theater paint if it means getting you where you want to be ... alive."

Nathan brought a thumb to his mouth, then reached over and squelched the flame between his fingers without saying a word. He wasn't in the mood for smoke in his face nor paint, neither one.

She gave a sideways glower at him through sooty black lashes. What he didn't expect was the unpredicted jolt that threw him off-center when he caught sight of soft gray-blue eyes studying him from beneath a layer of kohl.

Who was she? And why was she really here?

As his gaze intensified, she turned her head.

Staying silent, he turned his attention to Miss Ramsey who nervously chewed her bottom lip until she, too, averted her eyes. Surveying one, then the other, he was about to ask the one question burning in his mind, when Lily presented a dish of hairpins at his side.

Something in the way all three women snickered made him hold his tongue. He wasn't completely sure he wanted to know what they were hiding. Taking a good look at the gutsy redhead, it occurred to him that he might not care for the answer.

He spotted Jessa standing beside the window, hands clasped in front of her and sporting a contented smile. Despite this little attempt at payback, she was like a ray of sunlight breaking through a thick fog.

"You weren't exactly clear on why I needed to be back here bright and early this morning." He leveled a hard gaze at her. "You said you had a plan to get me into that jail. You said nothing about going in as a ..." He waved his hand at the table full of goop, unable to even bring himself to say it.

"Do you prefer your hairpins with or without pearls?" she asked slyly.

An outright dare sparkled in her eyes, and Nathan grinned despite the crazy predicament he found himself in. She was out to even the score, alright, and he couldn't say he blamed her. They'd all done her a disservice in keeping his identity from her.

"We have both," Jessa persisted.

Oddly enough, he understood exactly what she was doing. It was Jessa's way. She approached everything with passion and spirit and a whole lot of daring.

He'd lost that kind of excitement for life a long time ago.

When her question was again met with silence, she sauntered over, lifted two hairpins, and held them up next to his head, as if truly contemplating the difference. The warm glow of mischief in her gaze caused him to reach out and caress the soft flush of her cheek with the back of his hand.

Miss Ramsey stifled a gasp.

Let Jessa have her fun. He was curious to see just how far she was prepared to take this little game. Catching her off-guard, he slipped an arm around her slender waist and gently brought her in closer.

Collective gasps filled the room.

The hairpins fell forgotten from her hand. He could feel her heartbeat quicken against his chest.

"Mr. Wolfe!" Miss Ramsey was clearly shocked.

Nathan and Jessa locked gazes, as if they were the only two in the room. She was no coward. He liked that.

To his surprise, he felt her thumb caress his arm. Something akin to curiosity fluttered over her features as her attention roamed over the stubble on his jaw to settle on the curve of his lips.

"Don't even think about it," Lily warned.

"Too late." Arlene lit a cigarette before blowing out the flame at the end of her match. "Looks to me like they've both thought about it—and plenty."

The redhead was correct. He'd thought plenty about kissing Jessa lately. Problem was, he'd thought of little else.

"Unhand her, Nathan." Lily plucked the silver-handled brush from Miss Ramsey's hand and smacked his arm with it. "We have work to do."

Nathan released her.

Jessa hesitated before stepping out of his reach. "I'd say he's more the plain hairpin type. Nothing *too* girlie."

"I'm a no hairpin type." Nathan swept up his hat and placed it firmly over his brow. "Pardon me, ladies. Much as I appreciate a good tea party, I have an appointment to keep." With a nod he started for the door but came up against the woman in red, who moved a good bit faster than he would have given her credit for in that tight dress.

"You're not leaving. They'll recognize you in an instant. If I have to knock you senseless and let Jessa hogtie you to the chair, then so be it." He'd never seen a woman get riled so fast. "Don't think for a minute we won't do it."

"Oh, my!" Miss Ramsey dropped the trinket box to clatter noisily against the floor as she brought a hand up to her throat.

Arlene was good and mad as she rested a fist on her rounded hip. "If the world was a perfect place, we'd all sip champagne and eat bon-bons all day. Wouldn't have to worry about men like Hollinger taking over our towns and businesses. Running off every honest man from here to Denver. That includes Father Miguel, too. Don't think for one second Jeb will spare the mission if he thinks there's profit to be had. He won't hesitate to eliminate anyone who gets in his way. It's high time you do your part and put on that disguise. Do whatever it takes, Lobo. You three are our only hope of stopping him from ruining this town."

Her heated speech obviously came from experience with Hollinger and his men.

"She has a point, love." It was Lily who came to present a voice of reason. "If they riddle you with gunshot, that won't do any of us any good."

He studied the pine beams in the ceiling, then blew out an exasperated breath.

"If you try to get into the jail without our help, Mr. Wolfe, they will kill you." Miss Ramsey spoke quietly. "We are concerned for your safety."

"Why?" He glanced down at her and asked the first thing that came to mind. "Why do you care what happens to me?"

"Because you've been wronged. And the Apache in that jail has been wronged." Her weathered face was a picture of sincerity. "It's time to set things right."

"But we have to be smarter than Hollinger and his henchmen." Arlene held her ground between him and the door. "We can get you into the jailhouse, but you'll need to make sure no one around here halfway recognizes you in order to do it. It could turn deadly fast."

Lily joined the united effort. "Miss Ramsey will accompany you. She will introduce you as her Aunt Winnifred, from Ohio. The two of you will deliver a benevolent meal to the poor soul being kept in the jail." With a flourish of her hand, as if painting the masterpiece plan out of thin air, she turned and gave him a satisfied smile. "Once you're inside,

Jessa will retrieve Miss Ramsey, and you may do whatever you see fit to get both you and the Apache out alive."

"Fine," Nathan relented with a hand resting on the hilt of his gun, his head bowed to where none of them could see that he was genuinely questioning his sanity. "I'll do it on one condition: no face paint and no corsets. And you ..." His head rose as he pointed at Jessa. "... stay home."

"That's three conditions," came her reply. "I'll give you the first two as long as you wear a black veil to cover your face." She crossed her arms. "But I'm not staying home. I have a job to do and so do you. We'll just have to trust each other."

"Then it's agreed." Lily took his arm and pulled him back to the chair.

"We can use this hat." Arlene produced a small blue contraption that had a daisy thing springing from the top and black netting hanging off the front.

"Ooh, that's lovely," Miss Ramsey cooed. "Did that come from Phillips' store or did you have it special ordered?"

"Ladies, please. Can we get this over with? Nathan snapped. With every tick of the clock, the odds of Gray Wolf's son making it out alive became less in his favor.

The cathouse matron produced a couple of dresses that looked big enough to shelter two or three grown men in a rainstorm—with room to spare. She insisted they were the only ones available to accommodate his height on such short notice. From what he could gather, he had someone named Olga to thank for the contribution.

On a quick vote, in which he had no say, the blue dress was decided upon. Lily insisted it best matched the hat which Jessa claimed best suited his eyes.

"I believe we've done all we can, girls." Arlene turned her head to each side as if he might look more convincing from a different angle.

"Hmmm. I don't know. Needs something." Lily tapped a finger against her mouth.

"I know! A handbag." Miss Ramsey chimed in.

His well-behaved manners were stretched as thin as they could go. His spurs clanged underneath his skirt as he stood. "Forget the handbag. This is as good as it gets. Ladies," he tipped his veiled hat, "*adiós!*"

"Don't forget these."

Nathan reacted quickly as Jessa tossed over two large balls of yarn that hit him square in the chest. Her bright smile told him she savored the moment.

"Perfect!" The three women at his side were satisfied at last.

Chapter Nineteen

"*BELOVED, AVENGE NOT yourselves, for it is written, 'Vengeance is Mine,' saith the Lord.*"

Jessa had just read that passage in Romans last Sunday. However, Saint Paul would surely agree that Nathaniel Wolfe needed a good taste of humble pie a whole lot more than she needed a lecture on taking matters into her own hands.

Perched on the second-floor window seat overlooking the street, she raised her field glasses hoping to catch sight of Nathan crossing the road.

Frankly, she was surprised he hadn't kicked up more of a fuss.

Earlier, as the ladies coddled and cooed, she'd observed a battle raging inside him with the working of the muscle in his jaw. Submitting to their ridiculous attention went against everything in him.

And yet, he'd sat there.

After a bit she was forced to admit he had a moral fortitude that was enviable. Fierce determination to right the wrong being doled out on a stranger overruled his momentary discomfort. He willingly did whatever was required to get in there to free the man who he felt was being used unfairly. He didn't let a dress, or hairpins, or even a cute little hat keep him from his purpose.

A niggling twinge of guilt overshadowed her moment of satisfaction.

Jessa had been around plenty of arrogant gunfighters in her time. Most wound up dead. The ones left standing were feared and revered, strutting through town barking orders at those they considered lesser men.

She refused to allow Bucky to end up that way.

At first she'd wanted to make sure that Lobo was served his just desserts. But now, she could see a decent sort of compassion was behind what he was trying to do.

Jessa lowered the field glasses, staring at a faint reflection of her guilty expression in the upstairs window. Is that what she was doing? Making him pay for the fact that she'd essentially made a fool of herself?

She shook her head to clear her thoughts.

No, Nathan Wolfe had shamelessly encouraged her. Well, not exactly encouraged, but he hadn't discouraged her that's for sure.

Except the times when she'd gotten too close.

Oh, for heaven's sake, why was she questioning herself all of a sudden? This plan was a good one and had practically fallen into her lap. Not only would he get his chance to rescue the prisoner, but this was a good opportunity to remind him he wasn't as high and mighty as that dime novel made him out to be.

She'd seen glimpses of the man he was capable of being. She'd marveled at his quiet wisdom. He was insightful and thoughtful, and had a way of making a person want to confide in him.

But then, when he'd come swaggering in last night wearing that black leather vest and high-dollar Stetson, he looked every bit like the legend Easterners thought he was.

She'd panicked. This had been a chance to take him down a peg—remind him he was so much more than a two-bit gunslinger.

And at the same time, serve notice that Jessa Jamison was not one to be trifled with. This was all for his own good.

Wasn't it?

She would have laid odds that he wouldn't actually go through with it. She never thought in a million years he'd go so far as to walk down the center of town dressed like a church lady, but there he was, doing just that.

Jessa quickly lifted the lens up to her view.

Not bothering to lift the hem of his skirt, he ignored the steps leading to the street and swung down with all the finesse of an ape dropping from a tree. Stepping to the middle of the road, Nathan never broke stride, trudging purposefully through a mud puddle as Miss Ramsey scurried to keep up. The peculiar pair marched down the center of the road with woven baskets in hand.

She couldn't see Nathan's face because of the lacy black veil, but she imagined his frown was intense. Moving the lens, she watched Arlene slowly taking the backway to her establishment, discreetly keeping an eye on him.

No doubt, Lily watched from a window down below.

Jessa's heartbeat stampeded in her chest as she fought to contain her nerves. What if they got to the door and that big Snake man refused to let them in? Would Nathan shoot his way in? Or what if someone were to recognize him? He and Miss Ramsey both would be in danger.

Suddenly, her neat little plan felt more like the worst idea she'd ever thought up.

Dropping the field glasses, she ran for the stairs.

If anything happened to Nathan or Miss Ramsey because her pride had been stung, she'd never forgive herself.

"Lily!" Not bothering to take the steps, she hopped up on the bannister and slid to the bottom level. Throwing the door open, she ran the short distance to a side door of the restaurant. Disregarding stares from curious guests, she burst through the dining room into the hotel lobby where she found Lily casually seated in a corner seat facing the window. "Lily, we have to stop them!"

With a careful hand, Lily folded her napkin and set it next to her cup. Coming to her feet, she placed an arm around Jessa. "What has that darling brother of yours gotten himself into this time?" The warning in her eye reminded Jessa that they weren't alone.

"Oh, uh, he and his ... friend ... are poking sticks at Snakes. It's all my fault, Lily, I practically dared him to do it. We have to stop them."

Snickers passed around the room. While not untrue, she had stopped Bucky from that very thing last month. She needed Lily to understand the dire position she'd put their other *friends* in.

"Let's go have a look, shall we? Surely, it's not as bad as all that." Lily led her toward the front doors, greeting an interested couple along the way. "They are out on the side of the jailhouse, you say? We'll see to it right away."

Once outside, Lily loosened her hold, but kept her arm around Jessa's shoulder as they walked. "While I'm glad to see your conscience finally getting the best of you, love, you must remember to stay with the plan."

"If anything happens to them—"

"Shhh. What did I teach you about trusting your fellow operatives?" They picked up their pace to keep Nathan and

Miss Ramsey in their sight. "Your partner is shrewd. No one is making him do anything he isn't willing to do. Rest assured in that."

"Hey, Jessa!" Wheezer Phillips waved from in front of his father's store ahead of them. "Wanna come see how many boiled eggs Bucky can fit in his mouth?"

Miss Ramsey turned back to glance at them, but Nathan kept right on walking.

"Thank you, Wheezer. Maybe another time," Jessa called back.

"Why, yes, we would love to," Lily quickened her step guiding Jessa to do the same. "So convenient of Mr. Phillips to place his establishment directly across from the jailhouse, wouldn't you say?"

The perfect place to help if need be. Jessa presented Lily an apologetic face as the pounding in her chest kept time with the urgency in their steps.

"Now, who'd you suppose that is?" Newt Ferrell's voice could be heard from where he sat behind the big checkerboard outside of Phillips General Store. His grizzled jaw hung agape as he watched Nathan go by.

"Cain't say as I've had the pleasure." The other oldtimer across the board slowly shook his head, following the two ladies bearing baskets with open-eyed curiosity. "One thing's for certain, though. I reckon that's the handsomest hunk o' female I ever laid eyes on." With that, he released a brown stream of tobacco, missing the tarnished spittoon by a good foot.

"What are you staring at?" Nathan barked at a young miner who stopped to gawk as he passed.

The man was so startled, he turned and ran smack into a display of yams, causing an avalanche of rolling cans.

The old-timers nodded their approval of the old girl's grit.

"Aunt Winnie, let's remember our mission." Miss Ramsey managed to keep her focus on the gathering of gunmen outside the jail. Clearly, she struggled to maintain her nerve.

With a toss of his head and a shrug of his broad shoulders, Nathan shook his small hat askew. It bobbled against the side of his head with the veil flapping precariously, exposing one side of his face.

"Land o'goshen!" the old codger at the checkerboard cackled.

"Oh, my." Miss Ramsey froze, looking aghast at the stubble along his jaw.

Jessa jumped into action. Running ahead into the road, she grabbed Nathan's thick arm to spin him away from Hollinger's guards. "Might I say, what you dear ladies do for the prisoners is a true labor of love." She needed to keep talking to divert their attention. Unfortunately, nothing readily came to mind except figuring a way to recover his face. "I pray blessings on you both. Showers and showers of blessing. Sent from the Savior above."

Nathan narrowed his eyes.

"Merciful drops." She tugged on his arm again to keep him from turning around. "Round us are falling."

"But for the showers we plead," Miss Ramsey finished for her.

"We plead," Jessa echoed.

She had no idea what scripture that was from, but she'd heard it somewhere before. It fit the bill, that's all that mattered. She was fairly sure the heathens standing outside of the jail didn't know the difference anyway. "May the Lord bestow unto you amazing grace." She reached up and gently yanked his hat back into place, pulling the veil down to fully cover his features, disregarding his ominous glare. "How sweet the sound ... for such a worm ... and all that."

Nathan stepped around her just as Father Miguel was leaving Mrs. Apodaca's Pastry Shoppe with a bundle of baked goods in hand. Spotting his former charge, the priest's kindly smile melted.

"Father Miguel." Lily rushed to his side to soften the shock. She lowered her voice to keep from being heard across the street. "You mustn't give any indication to the gunmen that you know the visitors headed for the jail. As far as we are concerned they are simply angels of mercy from the church bringing food to the prisoner."

"This angel, she is reckless, no?"

"Yes, well, *she* had a bit of help." Lily inclined her head toward Jessa, who met his troubled eyes with a tentative smile.

Lily pulled the three of them into Phillips Store and immediately moved to the window where they had full view of the rock-style stockade that served as Cimarron's jail. The solid pine door was flanked on either side by Hollinger's enforcers who didn't seem inclined to let them by.

"Whatcha doin'?" Bucky came to look out the window to see what was so interesting.

"Appreciating the fine act of service Miss Ramsey provides for those less fortunate. Something we could all learn from." Lily had a way of making things sound much more important than they were. To boys like Bucky and Wheezer, important sounded boring.

"C'mon, Wheez. I'll race ya to the orchard. Last one there has to eat a rotten apple."

Too distracted to bother getting on to her brother, Jessa

watched the gunmen look over the mammoth-sized woman standing before them.

One shook his head, but the other moved out of Nathan's way.

Nathan pushed open the door.

"Ma'am, we have orders!" The guard followed him inside.

Jessa heard the other guard call for support to two more down the road.

Father Miguel started for the door, but Lily stopped him. "If they see you, Father, they will put two and two together. Nathan won't have a chance."

"We are from the church. I come every week to deliver food to the prisoners." Miss Ramsey was fairly screaming at the man trying to block her entrance. "We are here to feed the prisoner. He has to eat."

"Ain't no one said nothing about no goodwill visit. I have my orders. No one goes inside." The man continued to hold her back. "Now soon as we fetch the other lady there, you two can be on your way."

"That's our cue, love." Lily was outside in an instant with Jessa close beside her.

"My, what a comfort it is to know you have such competent men watching over your township. Wouldn't you agree, Miss Ramsey?" As they approached the men stood a bit taller. Lily had that effect. She didn't slow her stride but walked right past the dumfounded guard though the doorway and into the sheriff's office.

Jessa followed suit.

"O-Oh, yes!" Miss Ramsey scurried in behind them.

"Go get Hollinger," the Snake man hollered to the other two.

"Mr. Hollinger from the bank? His wife is such a dear. Had tea with her not two days back. I do hope she has come to town with him." Lily kept talking as she looked around for any sign of Nathan.

The harried guard was beside himself and was getting no help from the others outside. "You can't go in there, lady!" He clearly didn't know whether to shoot them or wait for his boss, considering she claimed to be a friend of his wife's.

Jessa squinted into the darkened room. An overpowering odor of human waste, combined with the damp, musty smell of sodden earth, met her as soon as she entered the building. She fought the urge to gag.

Lily struck a matchstick to light a rusted lantern. A dilapidated desk came into view as the flickering light illuminated the decrepit condition of the jail. Years of neglect was evident in the fetid dirt built up in every corner of the room. Didn't DeLaney own a broom?

Nathan had helped himself to the key ring, and Jessa decided to follow him when she heard the squeaky iron door pull open from the jail's only cell.

Slowly, she approached as he knelt on one knee beside a straw mat in the corner. A form lay still in the dark. Apprehension prickled her senses as she inched closer.

"He's dead." Nathan's low announcement brought Lily in as well.

Chapter Twenty

HE TURNED THE man over, and Jessa bit the inside of her cheek to keep from crying out. Beneath his shredded black shirt, a gaping wound covered the left side of his chest. His dark sightless eyes were fixed eerily on the ceiling.

It was not unthinkable that this man might pass for Lobo. There was a stark resemblance. Though his complexion was deeper, reddened from the sun, he had the same strong jawline, same thin, straight nose, and same full, sculpted mouth.

Jeb Hollinger's graveled voice could be heard demanding answers in the front office.

Lily acted quickly to intercept his progress. "Mr. Hollinger. Who, may I ask, has neglected to see to this man's burial?"

"In case you didn't notice, Miss Valentine, he is Apache. As such, he does not merit the same consideration as you or I." Hollinger cast a large shadow in the lantern light. "I'll only hold his body a few more hours until I order it to be thrown out to the vultures. If the savages choose to come claim it, they can have it."

Jessa's stomach turned as she became horribly aware that they were penned into the small, windowless space with no other way out besides the way they'd come in.

"This is outrageous." Lily sounded furious and Jessa knew it was no act. "Has his family been notified?"

"You want me to lock her up, too, Boss?"

"That won't be necessary. As far as I can tell, the ladies have done nothing wrong."

Obviously, he'd thought twice before riling Allan Pinkerton.

Snake spoke up, "They say the big one took down the keys after she was told to leave. That don't look too good. Folks'll get to thinkin' they can come in and do as they please. No regard for authority."

"On whose authority might that be?" Lily was having none of the banker's vigilante justice. "Sheriff DeLaney is the only one authorized to take such action, and he is occupied elsewhere."

"Yes, and he's the one who gave us permission to feed the prisoner." Bless her soul, Miss Ramsey sounded mortified.

"Where's that other women who came with you?" Hollinger's voice grew louder as he neared the back portion of the jailhouse.

Panic surged through Jessa. Reaching out, she gripped Nathan's arm to stop him from going out there. If he was discovered, there would be no escape.

Looking up, she could barely see his eyes through the dark veil. Something about the intensity of his gaze calmed her racing pulse.

"Don't worry." With a squeeze to her hand, Nathan strode straight back into the fray.

As they rounded the corner of the sheriff's office, Jessa saw Father Miguel peeking in from the front door.

Hollinger rushed at Nathan, and Miss Ramsey took an

audible breath. "What were you after in there?"

With a sneer, Hollinger's prize gunman grew bolder at Nathan's silence. "Is she ignorant as she is homely?"

Lily tilted her head. "The boorish behavior of your men leaves no question about who called for this horrific murder. Even if pooled together, they wouldn't possess enough sense to come in out of the rain."

Hollinger moved around Nathan, looking him over. "I gladly put an end to another thieving Indian, once again restoring safety to our stage line. You, Miss Jamison, owe me a debt of gratitude."

"Your tactics turn my stomach." Jessa took a step forward to put herself between Nathan and the banker.

"I'll tell ya what's unacceptable. Letting a hideous critter like that out in public." The obnoxious gunman adjusted his holster, apparently just realizing he'd been insulted.

"Quiet!" Hollinger's grating voice echoed off the thick brown walls.

Miss Ramsey took a step closer to Lily.

"Madam, would you kindly remove your hat? I don't recall seeing you before." His request was directed at Nathan.

"No!" Miss Ramsey made a desperate attempt to save him. "My aunt isn't well. S-She really shouldn't be out among people. I believe she may be contagious."

"Take it off, Lobo," Hollinger ordered.

Amid gasps from the onlookers gathered in the doorway, Miss Ramsey broke into tears.

Without hesitation, Nathan snatched off the hat revealing a deadly scowl.

"Well, well. None other than Cimarron's favorite outlaw bandit, *El Lobo*." Hollinger extended his ringed hand toward the cell block. "Good of you to make this easy."

With a shake of his head, Nathan sent hairpins flying about the small room. Hollinger's gunman backed up, hands on his gun.

Nathan's gaze was hooded with anger. He yanked the bodice of the dress, and the material ripped as small buttons sprinkled to the floor.

Father Miguel couldn't get past the gunmen blocking the door. "*Señor* Hollinger, please. There has been a terrible mistake."

"Yes, and your choir boy, here, made it."

Jessa noticed that Hollinger kept his distance from Nathan. Though he was full of hot air, he made certain his hired hand was placed between himself and the notorious gunman at all times.

"Lock him up!"

Jessa was shoved aside as the man made his move.

In the blink of an eye, he was thrown to the ground with an uppercut to his midsection when he tried to take a swing.

Hollinger yelled for the others to attack.

Fury consumed Jessa at the unfair advantage they took against yet another innocent man. Hollinger would have him hanged before the circuit judge ever heard the case. She had to do something. Anything. Scanning the room for anything to use as a weapon, she couldn't sit back and watch Nathan pay for something he had not done.

Lily gave her a sharp look of warning.

How could she remain so calm? With arms crossed, she gave no indication that she was even concerned.

Jessa made her decision in an instant.

Lily may not care, but Jessa did. Reaching over, she snatched a gun from the holster of Hollinger's big gunman.

Calling to Nathan, she tossed it to him. As he caught it, Hollinger's men scattered back outside like scared roaches.

Miss Ramsey wailed loudly, and Lily wisely chose to see the woman outside.

Father Miguel remained where he stood in the doorway. The furious gleam in Nathan's eyes seemed to cause him great concern. "*Mijo*, you must show restraint. God will reveal the truth. As long as you do not kill this man, all can be righted."

Slowly and with careful precision, Nathan cocked the gun and centered the barrel at the banker's wide chest. The sound two more guns readying for fire echoed through the stone room.

"Of course, he will kill again. Savage by nature. No better than the dead Apache on the floor in there," Hollinger goaded him. "Gray Wolf can come collect both of his worthless offspring."

Something flickered across Nathan's features at the mention of the Apache chief.

Jessa's heart stopped when she watched his finger move over the trigger of the gun.

"Stop! Let me by!" a woman's voice shrieked just outside the door. "Nathan, don't shoot!" Arlene elbowed the men who grabbed her. "DeLaney was seen heading toward town. He brought soldiers from Fort Union."

Jessa whispered a grateful prayer.

"Nothing changes!" Hollinger barked over the din of the excited crowd.

"You're wrong. This changes everything." With a quick flick of his wrist, Nathan spun the cylinder and emptied the silver cartridges into his palm.

"There's still a warrant for Lobo's arrest. I'm here to see

it carried out." A rise of panic defused Hollinger's threat, leaving his words hanging in the air. His men would be fools to carry out an execution with the law and Union soldiers on the way.

"Capture him! That's an order!" Hollinger's voice practically screeched as all but one gunman reholstered his weapon.

The one left came at Nathan in a half-crouch.

Easily side-stepping the man's awkward grapple, Nathan led him face-first onto the squalid floor.

"*Aye que mi.*" The gentle priest was clearly distraught. He silently crossed himself in prayer.

With one hand, Nathan retrieved the man's gun and emptied it as well. In two strides, he approached Hollinger and shoved the useless firearms into the man's chest. "I suggest you keep these locked up until your boys are capable of hanging onto them."

The dazed banker had to keep himself from falling backward into the wall. He pulled a revolver from inside his waistcoat. The crowd immediately grew silent. "Fortunately, I know how to hang on to mine. At the risk of repeating myself, you are under arrest." In his slick city suit with gold initials at his cuffs, he took aim.

"You have no business holding him, Jeb," Arlene called out. "It's over. We both know what this is about, and it has nothing to do with those stage robberies. Let him go."

"Before this day ends, justice will be served. I'll have the pleasure of watching the fearsome Lobo dangle from the end of a rope."

Jessa drew a sharp breath, stunned by the man's utter contempt for a man he hardly knew. Hatred oozed from every pore.

Why?

She searched Nathan's face for any clue to the bad blood between them.

His expression gave nothing away as he continued to stare the man down.

"You heard the boss, move it." The big gunman had a rifle, motioning toward the cell.

Nathan still didn't move.

Horses clamored to a halt outside. Gunmen, looming in the doorway, parted as Lily pushed her way through. "Drop your weapons, immediately!"

Jessa's attention snapped to where both Hollinger and Snake held their aim at Nathan. One tiny twitch from either of them, and it wouldn't matter a hill of beans what DeLaney had to say.

"No!" Jessa launched herself between Nathan and the guns aimed at his chest.

Just as quickly, Nathan grabbed her around the waist and pitched her behind him, shielding her with his body.

"Drop the gun, Jeb. You too," DeLaney commanded from the entrance. He burst into the room with three soldiers holding firearms. "You'd best have a look at these papers before you boast about hangin' an innocent man."

"I have a warrant. That's all the paper I need." Hollinger fired and Jessa heard herself scream as Nathan pulled her down with him, hitting the ground hard.

Fast as lightning, Lily drew her derringer on Jeb Hollinger. "I believe the sheriff has asked you to drop your weapon."

Lifting his hands, the banker recognized when he was outnumbered.

DeLaney slapped the papers on his desk. "Lobo's

cleared of all charges. He's in with the US Government. Has full pardon."

Hollinger snatched up the documents that DeLaney laid out. After scanning each page, he glanced around, until his hateful gaze settled on Nathan. "The US Government does not run this Territory."

"However, we do have a right to protect our valued operatives." Lily kept him at gunpoint. "And to protect the Indian tribes with whom we've struck a treaty. Therefore, the man in that cell, killed under your heavy-handed order, will be returned to his people at once. And you, Mr. Hollinger, will be held accountable to both the Apache chief and to the Bureau of Indian Affairs. I assure you, before this is over, you'll wish the US Government was on your side."

Hollinger's handgun dropped to the floor, and the big man put down his rifle.

At DeLaney's directive, the soldiers steered them from the jail.

Jessa clung to Nathan. From now on, she vowed to leave vengeance in the hands of the Lord.

Chapter Twenty-One

NATHAN KNELT TO cup a cold drink in his hands from a brisk mountain stream. The sound of water burbling over the rocks soothed his tattered nerves. Resting an arm on his bent knee, he paused to soak it all in.

He'd escaped to this spot often as a kid. Here, high in the mountainside above Rayado, he'd distanced himself from things he had no control over. Brooding was what the padre used to call it.

No matter, when he needed to get away, the mountains beckoned him. Some things never changed. The soft crunch of pine needles beneath his boot scared off a couple of squirrels that were flirting with a patch of sunshine as it came and went beneath a cover of clouds.

A few more weeks and all this greenery would ignite into a blaze of color.

A few more weeks after that, this entire area would be blanketed in snow and only the south side of these curving banks would see any sunshine at all.

For the first time in years, he just wanted to stay put awhile. He was in no hurry to get back to Kansas. Hickok was doing fine without him. Pinkerton had cleared his name and, for the time being, he was free to revisit the old places around the mission where he'd once found solace as a kid.

He had a good view of the palisades. Cliffs of sheer rock

that held a bevy of craggy characters in its drop.

Nathan straightened and readjusted his hat to better shade his eyes.

One formation in particular always sparked his imagination. A face nestled about halfway down with elf-like features. He'd spent many afternoons resting back against the smooth bark of an aspen making up stories in his head about how that elf had come to live in those rocks.

Still there, the boulder smiled down at him with the same weathered grin as it had back then. Except now, it looked more like a goat. Nathan studied it a moment longer waiting for the old magic to happen, but the more he stared the less special it was. Just a wall of distorted rock.

Shaking his head, he slapped a leather glove against his thigh. Childhood daydreams were a thing of the past. What was that Bible verse the padre was always quoting when the boys got too rambunctious? Something about to become a man you must put away childish things.

He never put much stock in dreams. Life had taken him in a direction he'd never figured on. The day he'd ridden out of here, with the sun in his face and Cimarron at his back, he'd given up in believing such foolishness. He'd set out to earn the respect of every man he encountered.

Men like Augus Jamison and Kit Carson. Bold and self-made. Men who looked out for themselves and looked nothing like the poor, meek religious community where he was raised. Father Miguel could talk about love all day long, but respect was what made a man. Love was fickle. No disrespect to the Bible's teachings, but love was all risk with no guaranteed payoff.

Whereas a man like himself didn't even need to be *liked* in order to be respected.

The only ones who went out of their way to seek him out wanted to put a bullet between his eyes. The stint in Kansas had been the longest he had stayed in one place in a long while. Yet, the familiar restlessness had begun to creep in. He knew the time was coming to move on.

Pulling on his black gloves, he climbed the bank to where his horse was tethered in the shade. Eight years ago seemed like an eternity. He'd left here half-cocked and determined to shake the New Mexican dust from his boots. Set on making a name for himself.

Now he was a man known throughout the country. Respected, yet reviled. Envied, yet despised.

And lonely as a man could be.

Soon enough, that familiar feeling would hit again and he'd be looking for a change of scenery. He'd leave these crazy notions behind all over again.

Unwrapping the horse's reins, Nathan faced the animal toward the road and hauled himself up into the saddle. He had done what he'd set out to do that morning. The body of Gray Wolf's son had been delivered back to his people. The solemn expression on the face of the proud chief as his wayward heir had come home draped across the back of a horse was an image Nathan would never be able to forget.

He took his time going back down the foothills, winding through dense, pine-filled terrain. Slowing his horse, he had one more look back at the land of his youth. The mountains were bathed in the deep pastels of sunset. Leaves glittered above like gold coins in the setting sun.

He'd seen Jessa's eyes turn that same color in the afternoon sunlight.

Nudging his horse to continue on, he couldn't help but admit she was another obstacle altogether. She was every bit as feisty and determined as her father had been. A rare combination of sass and innocence. But she wasn't for him. If he'd entertained any doubts before, yesterday in the jailhouse it was made abundantly clear.

He could still see her there, with an arm around Father Miguel, her eyes wide with terror, quietly begging him not to shoot Hollinger in his tracks.

He'd never had any intention of killing him, but the fact was crystal clear that she was convinced that he would. Any delusions that she had feelings for him shattered in that moment. She was incapable of seeing past the gun in his hand.

Nathan flicked up his collar against the cool mountain breeze and continued down the sloping trail.

Just ahead, a rider approached, kicking up dust like the devil was on their tail. As she neared, a chill of apprehension coursed up his spine when he realized it was Jessa riding recklessly toward him.

His horse fought against its bit as Nathan reined him in to an abrupt stop.

As her pony slid to a halt, Jessa called out to him. "They sent ... a warning." She could hardly get the words out as she gasped for breath. "The mission ... Father Miguel ..."

Panic threatened to take hold of him. "Is he all right?"

Jessa nodded emphatically. "Yes, yes. The children, too."

He urged his horse up closer beside hers. "Who sent a warning?"

"Whoever sent a rock with a note crashing through the mission's window."

Windows could be fixed easily enough. "What else?"

"They..." Jessa squeezed her eyes shut for a second then

and shook her head. "They set off a blast dangerously close to the sanctuary." When she reopened her eyes, her golden gaze was filled with tears. "The children could have been killed."

The news slammed into his gut. A blatant attack on all that was holy was beyond his comprehension. He needed to get back to Rayado. If Hollinger and his men had so little reverence for a church, they'd have no regard for a priest and his defenseless passel of orphans.

"Let's go."

"Wait. They aren't at the mission. The note demanded that you to leave the Territory, or next time it will be the mission. Lily convinced Father Miguel it was safer to bring the children to stay at the hotel for a few days." Jessa's pony skittered, reacting to her tense hold on the reins. "The landowners heard about it and they're furious, Nathan. There's a meeting at the grist mill in half an hour."

A threat to the mission was just that—a threat. If they'd seriously wanted to claim the land it sat upon, that blast would have blown the small adobe building sky high.

This was more personal than that.

As long as the landowners were convinced Hollinger had the upper hand, they would continue to feel helpless against him. And as long as high profile lawmakers had a stake in his profits, he was free to do whatever he saw fit to make sure those profits came through for them.

It was time someone put an end to all the high-handed regulation around here. The law states that settlers have a right to raise their families and work the land they spent lifetimes cultivating. They may not have the means or brute force to stand their ground for long, but Nathan had one advantage that they did not.

Thanks to Pinkerton's order, Hollinger and his pack of hired guns couldn't touch him. They were running scared and were beginning to make desperate mistakes. Ultimately, Hollinger would trip up.

As long as they had nothing on him, Nathan could move about freely, gathering as much evidence as needed to put Hollinger away for good.

❦

As they pulled up to the back door of the Jamison ranch, Jessa heard Miss Ramsey through the screen door as she called out to someone inside. "He's here! Thanks be to heaven he's alive and safe!"

The door swung open, and children spilled out all talking at once.

Bucky pushed through to meet Nathan as soon as he set foot on the ground. "You shoot any bad guys on your way in, Lobo? I figured that was probably what kept you." His blatant awe of someone right out of a dime novel made Jessa cringe.

"Two or three," Nathan commented, tossing the kid his reins. "Can you see to the horses for me? Make sure they get plenty of water."

"Yes, sir!"

Astonished, Jessa couldn't help but marvel at how quickly her brother moved and with no argument whatsoever.

"Lightning hit beside the church and it was so loud." Nellie intercepted Nathan on his way to the porch.

"It wasn't lightning. Wasn't even raining," Jacob spoke up. "It was blasting powder. I saw 'em clear a mountain once laying tracks for the railroad. It sounded just like that. Smelled like it, too."

"It hurt my ears." The little Navajo girl spoke quietly with her hands over her ears.

"It hurt Sister Helena worse than that. She fell and had to go to the doctor to get a plaster sock for her leg." Nellie walked purposefully up the steps. "Father Miguel said we should all be thankful that by God's mercy we were kept safe."

"Amen." Jessa followed closely behind. She could see by the way he put a protective arm around her, he was thinking much the same whether he said so or not.

Inside the door, Miss Ramsey held a handkerchief to her nose and made an attempt at gathering herself. Looking Nathan over from head to toe, she visibly relaxed once she saw that he was indeed all right. "I'll see to dinner." Catching Jessa's eye, she looked a bit embarrassed at having become so distraught.

"Children, go to your rooms now. Help the sisters unpack our things." Father Miguel stood beside the large wood cook table with the sleeves of his robe covering his clasped hands. The lines on his face and the tired look dulling his eyes were testament to the weight he carried for them all.

"Please sit, Father. Let Miss Ramsey pour you some tea." Lily held out a seat for him.

Nathan removed his gloves as he made his way over to the man who raised him. "Padre, how are you doing?" Concern shone on his face as he laid a hand on the older man's shoulder. "I should have been there."

"Nonsense, Nathaniel. There was nothing you, nor any of us, could have done. We were spared our lives. For that I am eternally grateful."

Jessa noticed that Nathan refrained from questioning him further. The father had already experienced enough trauma today. Still, he needed to know the entire town was standing with him.

"You and the children are precious to our community, Father. Hollinger won't get away with this." Jessa came to lay her hand over Nathan's on Father Miguel's shoulder. "Papa tried to stop them, but he couldn't do it by himself. It'll take the whole community coming together." She shifted to rest on a short footstool in front of him. "The other day at the jailhouse, they watched a man they know as Lobo refuse to back down. Even forced Jeb Hollinger to take a step back. He sparked a wave of courage among the homesteaders like they've never shown before. They're finally ready to take action to fight for their homes. Every one of them have been fed up for two years by Hollinger's constant browbeating. Today, when they heard he'd even gone so far as to attack the most vulnerable among us, they made a pledge to stop him."

As she spoke, she felt Nathan watching her. Lifting her eyes to meet his, she was struck by the appreciation she saw there.

"We've much to discuss." Lily took up her teacup and saucer. "We know who is behind the senseless killings, now we need proof that he is responsible for Augus's disappearance so that we can formally file charges. I've sent my report to include the unprovoked killing of an Apache. Even if Santa Fe chooses to look the other way, we may sway Washington to allow the Rangers to take action. If we present enough evidence that this shareholder corporation is a present danger to American settlers, using known outlaws to enforce their own brand of justice. I believe we might entice the Federal government to step in."

"We'll need proof that they pose a bigger threat than to just a few lowly farmers and an Indian or two." Nathan sounded unconvinced as he leaned against the counter and politely refused Miss Ramsey's offer of blueberry pie. "The murder of a Federal operative would get the ball rolling, but it will take hard evidence against him."

"Last night, I found something interesting in Papa's journal. He was onto something there's no doubt about it. He wasn't having any luck stirring up concern for Colfax County among the state officials. So, he began writing informant articles in detail. He sent them to newspapers all across the northern United States. I found at least four that featured his articles under an anonymous byline."

"That's remarkable!" Lily set her cup on the table showing more enthusiasm than she had in days. "How did we miss this? I'm certain Allan has heard nothing about these articles. You say he mentioned Colfax County in particular?"

"Knowing Augus, he named names and left no stone unturned." Nathan refused an offer of coffee.

"He named every one he knew about." Jessa was inspired by their interest. She'd meant to share the information with them this morning, but with all the excitement at the mission, she hadn't had a chance. "He provided proof of a coverup involving the preacher who turned up dead after crossing Hollinger on behalf of his congregation. Told of a judge who was hung by Hollinger's men after ruling against him. His descriptions were very engaging and very dramatic. He cited that none of the officials he'd contacted in Santa Fe chose to comment. His journal said that the newspaper readers had taken exceptional interest and were beginning to kick up quite a fuss."

"I must wire Allan right away. If he can strike while the iron is still hot from Chicago, perhaps he can speak directly with the editors of those newspapers. Get me their names, love." Lily disappeared down the hall.

Jessa glanced at Nathan before hurrying off to gather what Lily had asked for.

He was doing it again, giving her that slow appreciative grin.

On impulse, she hurled a crocheted potholder at him on her way out.

If he had doubts that she could pull off being a first-rate investigator, that ought to show him.

His laughter followed her all the way up the stairs.

Chapter Twenty-Two

By the time she rejoined the others downstairs, an inviting fire crackled in the kiva fireplace. Days were warmer in the high mountain plains, but once the sun disappeared the air quickly chilled.

Lily summoned Jessa inside. "Now that Nathan has returned from his trip to the Apache camp this morning, we have several items to go over."

Jessa laid the bulk in her arms on the desk before sinking into a large leather chair. "You went all the way out to the Apache lands?"

"He delivered the Apache man's body back to Gray Wolf. I'm sure I mentioned it."

She hadn't.

Nathan read from a Record of Survey from her papa's notes. "A man deserves to be laid to rest with his people."

"Nathan took it upon himself to deliver the body personally. I commend you." Lily raised her teacup in salute. "Few men I know would care enough, nor would they be bold enough to hand deliver the dead son of a powerful chief. Quite admirable."

"I have to agree." Jessa spoke her honest opinion. The soldiers could have made the delivery, but the sympathetic gesture of another person who simply cared made a much greater statement. "I'm sure Gray Wolf and his people were grateful for your kindness."

"It was a matter of doing what's right. Nothing more."

His thoughtfulness was so much more, and they all three knew it. She couldn't help but wonder what his dime novel admirers would think of their favorite gunslinger now. If they ever had a glimpse at who Nathan Wolfe really was, they would see that he was more than a man with a fast gun. He was kind and compassionate. A man who rarely acknowledged such traits in himself. He needed a good woman to point them out.

Jessa quickly looked away and shook the silly thought out of her head.

Too bad her father wasn't here. He could inform his newspaper readers and set them straight about this man they called Lobo. Showing his tender side would surely sell a few newspapers.

"It's a shame Papa couldn't finish what he started." Jessa lifted a newspaper and scanned the page for her father's article. "His readers haven't been updated since his last installment. Looks like it came out last December."

"Wouldn't they be especially interested to find out that the anonymous contributor who they'd grown so fond of had turned up missing." Lily flipped through one of Augus's journals. "Then to discover that *El Lobo*, himself, rode into town to avenge his supposed death could cause a mass run at the newsstand."

A thrill of excitement coursed through Jessa just thinking of the commotion that might cause.

Lounging in the chair beside her, Nathan pulled up one boot to rest over his other knee. Narrowing an eye, he watched her cautiously. "What are you thinking? Dare I even ask?"

"I've just had the most wonderful idea." She opened her father's latest journal to the place she'd bookmarked with a purple hair ribbon last night and handed it over the desk to Lily. She then passed a newspaper over to Nathan. "I believe I'll take up writing."

Lily read silently but Nathan just stared at her. "Writing?" His somber tone was decidedly doubtful.

Jessa opened the newspaper for him. Scanning for the anonymous entry, she pointed to the place on the page where the article began. "Starting here, read this."

With a bit of encouragement, he finally obliged.

"And look at this. I found a note scribbled on brown wrapping paper in Papa's journal directing him to examine the National Attorney General's interest in the land corporation. It cited a conflict of interest in a recent decision made in favor of the new corporate holders. The note isn't signed, and I don't recognize the handwriting. But Papa must have had an outside informant." She handed the note over to Lily. "Papa's journal says that after a bit of investigation, he indeed turned up the fact that the Attorney General was a principal of that partnership."

Jessa emphasized her point with a nod.

"I can see the wisdom in Augus holding onto that bit of information. It wouldn't do to publicly accuse a high-ranking government official on hearsay alone. However, without a viable witness to come forward, willing to be named …" Lily tugged at a fancy earring like the ones Jessa saw in last month's Harper's Bazaar. "However, we need solid evidence to prove these rather lofty allegations. Without it, our hands are tied." She laid the journal aside. "I'd like to hear more about this bright idea you've dreamed up. Are you thinking of finishing these articles Augus began with the newspaper?"

It was no wonder Lady Lily Valentine was considered one of the country's top-secret agents. She *knew* things.

Jessa rose and began to pace in front of the desk as she pulled her thoughts together. "Like you said, Lily, we aren't getting anywhere as long as the powers that be are the ones calling the shots." She paused in front of Nathan, who half-smirked at her beneath his black hat. With arms crossed over his broad chest, he made it clear what he thought of her plan.

Jessa knocked his foot off his knee with her hand then continued to pace. "You can't deny that Papa was clever. His only hope of getting Washington's attention was to find a way to bypass the Santa Fe ring. He took it straight to the ones who elect the United States Congress to their positions. He was well on his way to creating a public outcry. That kind of fuss refuses to be ignored. Washington had no choice but to listen."

Though he remained quiet, Nathan sat forward in his chair with arms leaning on his knees making it impossible for Jessa to determine his reaction. At least he was no longer staring at her like she'd lost her head.

"By his journals, we know that Augus did not act alone. He had an informant from within that fed him information to include in his exposé articles." Lily settled back in an overstuffed chair. "Unfortunately, he did not confide the name of his informant in his journal entries." With a heavy sigh, she shook her head, her focus centered on the portrait painting of Augus Jamison hanging on the red-flocked wall. "I can't understand what he was thinking going rogue. If he had only passed this information on to the agency, we would have backed his informant and this information would have real clout. We could be arranging for arrests right now rather than trying to piece together his case."

Jessa couldn't argue.

The question of why Papa had left the protection and influence of the Pinkertons had bothered her all night. "All I can figure is, he didn't know who to trust." Both of the others looked puzzled at her quiet observation. "Since the end of the war, there have been so many changes in government that even the Pinkerton Agency isn't sure which side the chips have fallen. This kind of information is life-threatening to our neighbors here in the Territory. The very lives of their families depend on trusting the right people. Most of their options have turned on them, killing their livestock, ruining their crops—some families have been shot dead on their own doorsteps. As long as Hollinger and his men have free rein, these folks have no recourse. Papa was determined to sift out and expose the ones calling the shots from the top down. I'm sure in his mind, no one, even Allan Pinkerton, was beyond suspicion until he had proof otherwise."

"That's a rather bold assessment." At first she thought Lily was angry, but when she looked up from the journal, there was no animosity. "A fair deduction, however."

"So, he went outside the due process and took matters straight to the people." Nathan laid the newspaper open on the desk. "Just when he got everyone good and worked up over it, the articles ceased."

Lily turned the newspaper to where she could read the article. "No doubt, the Times's readers are at a loss. They're open to speculation as to whether the anonymous contributor was silenced for presenting lies, or if he was caught in the same trap as those he wrote about."

"Exactly." Jessa removed a couple of envelopes from the pocket in her skirt and added to the pile of papers on her father's desk. "This morning, I found a couple of letters addressed to 'anonymous' from an editor begging for another installment. Miss Ramsey doesn't recall picking them up from the postmaster, and the postmaster doesn't recall where they were delivered. It looks to me like his informant may have picked them up then left them here to be found. If so, whoever he is may be open to providing more information for our cause. We should give the readers what they want. Otherwise, we're tossing out our best option for forcing Washington's hand."

"Problem is, none of us know who this informant is," Lobo stated flatly. "And another important detail you're forgetting, none of us are writers."

"I keep a journal." Jessa averted her eyes from his mocking stare. His lack of enthusiasm worked on her nerves. "Maybe not as consistently as Papa did, but I certainly could if I wanted to. I may be as good a writer as Mark Twain. You never know until you try."

"If Allan Pinkerton has a lick of sense, he won't let you try. Not on this case anyway." Rarely had she heard Nathan raise his voice, but for some reason he felt he needed to now. "Have you forgotten that these anonymous articles are likely what got your papa killed?"

"You don't know he was killed. Besides, Papa didn't have you and Lily here for protection. He went traipsing off alone like he always did and made himself an easy target. I won't go anywhere without you." Jessa moved to stand next to him. She caught the worry in his eye for just a second before he again lowered his head. Without hesitation, she slipped an arm around his broad shoulder and lifted his hat higher on his brow. "I promise."

Frown lines furrowed his brow. The need to reassure him that she had thought this through nearly overwhelmed her. The only weakness she'd ever seen in this man was when he was concerned for those he cared about. She knew Nathan cared about her, but until now, in this moment, she had no idea to what depth.

He leaned forward, away from her embrace.

Heaviness settled in her chest as she thought about the many times in his life he'd likely craved a bit of comfort but none ever came. Until he eventually convinced himself he had no need for it. Her touch was a searing reminder that he had feelings, and he had no idea what to do with them.

She'd give him the courtesy of helping him sort it out some other time. Sometime when they were alone.

Lily watched them from the other side of the desk. "I say let her have a go at it. At least send in one more article to keep interest up while we work to find this informant. We have no one else willing to take such a project on. I don't want to risk losing public interest."

"You forget, Hollinger doesn't know I'm helping you two with this case." Jessa leaned against the heavy pine desk. "He thinks he's silenced the anonymous reporter. So he'll be as surprised as everyone else when that paper hits the newsstands. We can use his confusion to our advantage. Hopefully, this will turn his attention away from you for a while."

"I do like the way she thinks, Nathan." Lily barely gave him a glance as she stood. "I will go and see to this at once. I'll have a confidential wire sent to Allan through our man in the telegraph office. In the meantime, go ahead and write your article, love. We'll have it wired and in print before week's end." She lifted the white panama hat, with black-striped ribbon to secure at a perfect angle over her ebony tresses. "I trust you two will take this opportunity to iron out your feelings toward one another before I get back."

Chapter Twenty-Three

WITH A CINNAMON bun between his teeth, Nathan stepped off the porch and unwrapped his horse's reins from the front post. There was a storm blowing in from the north. The twilight sky turned dark with dappled clouds rumbling ominously overhead.

He'd get the animal settled into a stall before the brunt of it hit, then find the Padre to make sure he and the kids were hunkered down for the night.

The blast out by the mission had been a warning, no question there. The townsfolk were none too happy about it either. They'd bombarded DeLaney's office demanding that something be done. Each of them scared to death that their place would be next.

Apparently no one was safe in this county, even the church.

The barn door rattled against the wind and the sides of the barn shook as Nathan led his horse to an empty stall. Shadows lengthened into the farthest corners of the stable as he lifted a lantern to a peg on the wall.

The first drops of rain pinged against the sides of the barn until the roar of a steady downpour drowned out all other sound.

Barn doors flung open at the other end.

Head down against the pelting wind, Jessa steered two

mares inside from the corral. The same sodden shawl covering her head uselessly draped over her shoulders. He could easily see she fought a good case of the shivers as she threw the dripping wool onto the hay.

Friendly whickering between the horses, about six in all, was lost in the noise of the storm. Jessa quickly made her way to deposit her two ponies in an adjoining stall.

Nathan unlatched his gear, keeping an eye on her as she filled feedbags with shaking fingers. With the help of an overturned bucket, she boosted herself up to hang her rope on an iron hook before grabbing an armful of towels to dry her horses. She shook the excess droplets from her hair which fell in drenched waves down her back.

He'd watched from the upstairs window of his room as she'd worked with her mustangs all afternoon in the corral. She had a natural way with them. Though neither pony was ready to be saddle broke yet, they let her lead them around the yard on the end of her rope. He knew from experience, she'd had to work hard to train them to accept her lead. She'd stroked their forelocks until she had them eating apples out of her hand.

"Is something on your mind, Nathan?" Jessa asked without turning around.

"Nope." He continued to unfasten his horse, trying to gauge her unusually quiet mood.

Lily's last edict had them both a little off kilter.

"Good. Then hear me out." Jessa tossed the wet towels into a bin then strode over to his stall. "I studied Papa's articles, the words and layout. I wrote it in the same way he did. Used just as many paragraphs. I wrote all about what's happened since his disappearance. I even mentioned what they did out at San Gabriel Mission. I'd like you to read it over before I give it to Lily."

For what it was worth, his approval seemed to matter to her.

Thing was, his opinion hadn't changed. Taking on the burden of Augus's news stories was an invitation for trouble. Not that he was one to shy away from danger, but he'd do all he could to keep Jessa out of harm's way.

"I'll read it." His concession brought a relieved look to her face. "But I make no promises about liking it."

"Fair enough." She smiled like she'd already won the battle. "As long as the newspaper readers like it enough to write to their congressmen."

She shivered, trying to rub warmth into her arms.

Nathan reached into his saddlebag, removing the blanket he used for cold nights under the stars. Stepping around, he gave the thin cover a shake before placing it around her. Gathering the edges, he brought them together in front of her, holding it there until he felt her quivering subside.

Whether intentional or simply seeking warmth, Jessa leaned in against him.

He held her, enjoying her nearness, absorbing the unexpected comfort of her embrace. Almost as if something crucial pulled them together like a whirlwind in the storm.

He brushed wet curls from her eyes with a finger, then traced the fine lines of her cheek to the delicate cleft of her chin. The wide cupid bow of her smile began to fade.

He was certain Jessa had never been kissed. She was not opposed to it, though. Proving his point, she lifted her face. He barely brushed his lips against hers until she pressed in to deepen the kiss. Her lips were soft and sweet. There was a caring that came with her kiss that he wasn't used to. Not just about a physical need, but loving and thoughtful with tender caresses that sent his head spinning.

For a matter of moments, the storm was forgotten and they were the only two in the world caught up in a tempest all their own. Something sparked inside him, something he'd thought long dead suddenly came alive as Jessa gently poured everything her heart felt into that one magical kiss.

A bright flash of lightning lit up the stables followed by a crack of thunder so loud it spooked the horses. The blanket fluttered to the ground as Jessa buried her face in his chest.

How was it that she, who fearlessly tamed wild broncos without batting an eye, was scared of a little thunder? It suddenly occurred to him that she had probably shivered through many a stormy night as a young girl wondering if her father was out there somewhere safe.

He cupped her head against his chest, breathing in the smell of her, wildflowers and sunshine. More intoxicating than Hickok's famous medicinal tonic.

They held each other in a comfortable silence until the rain tapered to a steady shower and the thunder rolled off to a distant rumble. The feel of her next to him warmed him clear to his soul.

For once, he was content to just let things be.

Finally, Jessa took a step back and swept her damp hair to one side over her shoulder. "That's a beautiful horse. I've never seen one like him."

"Cross-bred," he answered, returning to the stall. "I got him from a stockman up in Illinois. Part Arabian and part Perch."

"Perch?"

Nathan lifted his saddle from the horse's thick back. "From somewhere in France. Some long fancy name no one can pronounce. Folks over here just started calling them Perch. Strongest horse I've ever owned, but agile and quick on his feet. They're perfect mountain horses."

Jessa sat on a tack table, obviously intent on staying out here awhile. "We could use horses like that. You should breed them."

Nathan digested her casual comment for a minute before refolding his saddle blanket. With the life he led, there was no place for settling down. When his work was done here, he'd move on. A muscle worked in his jaw as he brushed the horse's sleek back and down his flank.

They were both quiet, each lost in their own thoughts.

He was here for a reason and needed to stay focused.

Hollinger and this greedy corporation of his was intent on destroying this land they called home. Power and greed were like pouring fuel over a fire already consuming everything in its path. Stopping them seemed like a futile attempt. Still, he had to try. What was it the Padre always said? Do not be overcome by evil, but overcome evil with good.

He sure hoped good could hold out. Evil had a mighty strong hold on this territory.

"Mind if I ask you something?"

He glanced back at Jessa who watched him with tilted head.

"Ask anything you want."

"How do you know Chief Gray Wolf?"

Her question took him completely off guard.

"It's obvious you didn't care for the way Hollinger disrespected the chief's son. I can't help but wonder how you know him. And why he seems to trust you."

Nathan's hand stilled. A breach of time passed before he heaved a long sigh and rested his arm over the horse's back. "I'm told the man fathered me."

Chapter Twenty-Four

THE FLICKERING LANTERN brought out proud angles in his face. Jessa wondered how on earth she could have missed it.

"Don't worry, you're safe." Nathan must have sensed her surprise. With a pat to his horse's flank, he stepped around the animal to return the brush to its place on the pegboard.

"That's not what I was thinking."

He must have mistaken her shock for disgust. She pushed herself off the table to follow him back to the stall. As soon as her foot hit the ground, she drew a sharp breath when her ankle buckled under her. Sudden pain caused her words to take on a sharp edge. "It makes no difference to me if you're part Apache. You'd be just as brooding and cantankerous if you were the king of France!"

He paused for a moment and barely turned to look at her.

Awkwardly balancing on one foot, she tried to appear as if nothing was wrong, but when she nearly toppled over, a grimace immediately gave her away.

In two strides, he returned to her, lifting her back onto the tabletop. Swiping off his hat, he tossed it onto a bench along the wall. Pushing her hands aside, he removed her boot and rested her foot against his thigh. His hands moved over the tender area until he could pinpoint where her ankle was hurt.

To her own amazement, she didn't refuse his help.

Nothing about Nathan felt threatening. The same gentle concern he was showing for her right now was the same she'd noticed countless times as he'd cared for the children. Even when he tended to his horse, he took extra care to see that the animal had his full attention. Or the way he'd defied Hollinger to kneel before a lifeless Apache to check for a pulse.

Looking down at the top of his dark head, she had the strangest urge to smooth down those wayward curls that usually peeked out from under the back of his hat.

His kiss had been more thrilling than anything she'd ever experienced. She couldn't wait to write down every detail in her journal, so she could relive it over and over again.

"Nothing's broken. You just gave it enough of a wallop to make it good and sore for a couple of days."

Jessa nodded, not trusting herself to speak.

Her papa had always called her the caretaker, but Nathan's heart for other folks put her own to shame. Why couldn't he see these things in himself?

All at once another question begged to be asked. "Do you ever wish you'd known your mama?"

At first, she thought he hadn't heard her above the sound of the rain, but when his hand stilled, and he raised his face to her, she saw traces of torment in his eyes. Straightening, he retrieved his hat, carefully schooling his expression once again as he placed it on his head.

She held a tactful silence, afraid she'd already asked too much. But just when she was sure this was something he didn't intend to discuss, he came back over to where she sat on the worktable and rested a hip beside her.

A gust of wind howled up near the hayloft and the horse barn groaned at the imposition. With the mountain rain came a sharp nip in the air. Leaning into the warmth of his shoulder, she merely smiled when his eyes met hers.

Reaching into the top pocket of his leather vest, he removed a small handkerchief. For a brief moment, he caressed the smooth cloth before handing it to her.

Jessa cautiously unfolded the thin handkerchief that he had shown her the day of the picnic. Faded with time, the pink set of initials were still intact and sewn with a careful hand.

"This is all I know about her." He took the handkerchief back and absently ran his thumb across the threaded letters before folding it back the way he'd had it. Then he placed the cloth back into his vest pocket. "She wrote a letter and said I was Gray Wolf's offspring. Said he didn't know about me. Her papa did, however, but wanted nothing to do with me." He pushed off from the table. "And that's about all there is to tell."

"That was it?" As unexpected as the turbulent wind shaking the walls of the barn, her ire was stirred at the thought of this unknown woman abandoning her precious child with nothing but a lady's hankie to know her by. Unless ... "Was she sick?

"Could've been, but the Padre never mentioned it. Matter of fact, the few times he's ever referred to her, he says she still asks about me. So I'm guessing if she was sick, she got over it."

"Father Miguel never told you who she is? Never mentioned a name?"

Nathan shook his head. "She's taken great pains to distance herself from the mistake she made. It's the way she wants it and that's fine by me."

"So you'd never even know her if you were to see her on the street." Jessa couldn't imagine the heartache he must have gone through wondering why she hadn't chosen to keep him with her. What could have been so disheartening that a woman would choose to leave her child behind?

"No, I've never seen her. Not that I could swear to, anyway."

Moved by the travesty of it all, Jessa suddenly had another undertaking to endeavor. "I'll find her."

Nathan gave her that scoffing side-glance of his that wasn't nearly as chilling as it used to be.

"I mean we. *We* will find her. I'll help you." Before he could completely destroy her gracious offer, she nudged his shoulder with her own, then continued, "We already know her initials, A.R. And there are plenty of folks in town that lived here thirty some years ago."

"Twenty-six."

She smiled. "Twenty-six. I'll bet if we asked around, someone could tell us about her. And what one doesn't know, maybe another one will. We'll just keep asking until the puzzle all falls in place." She had ventured this far, she may as well go ahead and present all their options. "And since you and Gray Wolf are on friendly terms, what would be the harm in just asking him?"

The way he pulled away told her she had just lost his cooperation.

"The woman made it clear she doesn't want to be found."

"She has no idea what she's missing out on. One day she

will thank me for—"

"Don't make me regret telling you about this, Jessa. Not sure why I did." He swiveled and planted his hands on either side of her and bent low to meet her eye-to-eye. "I've come this far without knowing her, and I figure I'll do just fine without her from here on out."

"Surely, you're at least curious." She was too caught up in the possibility of finding the woman to simply let the matter drop. Placing a gentle hand on the side of his face, she waited for the fire in his eyes to die down. "Who do we know with the initials A.R.?"

He cast her a testy frown, but she knew he wasn't mad. If he'd just give her a chance to help, he'd see that finding this person would be the best thing for them both.

All at once, Jessa's jaw dropped and her eyes widened.

The first A name that came to mind brought with it a picture of a small boy playing outside of a mission.

Her gaze snapped to Nathan who watched her with gathered brows.

"You're right. If she wants her privacy, who are we to horn in?"

"Jessa." The warning in his voice was impossible to miss.

"It's just a suspicion. Could be that it means nothing at all."

He straightened and rested an arm over the top of the stall. Clearly, he was torn. He didn't really want to know but couldn't help himself for wondering.

"The other day I was over at the dance hall."

Again, that side glance.

"Don't ask. Anyhow, while I was there I saw a painting of a small boy. He was drawing in the dirt with a long stick."

Nathan shrugged and scooped up a bridle that had fallen onto the hay-strewn floor. "Don't see as how that has anything to do with me. Kids play in the dirt all the time."

"Not black-headed little boys, playing in the courtyard of Mission San Gabriel."

Waiting for the importance of what she was trying to say to finally sink in, she gave him a minute before going on. She didn't have to wait long. After he hung the bridle on a peg, he turned to give her a pointed look. "Go on."

"Arlene." The rain had quieted to a drizzle. "Arlene starts with A."

"I've already thought of that." He nuzzled his horse before tossing in some fresh hay. "No one I've talked to seems to ever recall hearing her last name. So, short of coming right out and asking her, I'm good with not knowing."

"I can ask her. She doesn't need to know why I'm asking."

"No." No other explanation was needed. His answer was final, and she knew it.

She'd pushed him as far as she dared. Ultimately, this was his cross to bear. What he needed most from her was support no matter what his decision. He'd spent many years convincing himself he didn't want to know the woman. All because he felt powerless to make her care.

Nathan retrieved his blanket and pitched it over to her. "Bundle up, Jessa. We'd best head for the house before another round of storms moves through."

"I'll need my boot." She wrapped the blanket around her shoulders, but before she could jump down Nathan hauled her up over his shoulder like a sack of potatoes.

"Nathan!" Laughter bubbled up from deep in her belly.

"Hold still, you don't want to fall." He bent to pick up her boot, and she squealed when he nearly dumped her into the hay.

His chest rumbled when he laughed.

A fit of giggling overtook her when he lifted the lantern and kicked open the barn door.

Raindrops hit her face and the flame from the lantern was immediately extinguished. His quick steps caused her to bobble on his shoulder making her laugh even harder. Despite his extra load, he took the steps up to the porch two at a time.

He came to an abrupt halt, and the rumble in his chest ceased.

Jessa stiffened, trying to look behind her to see what had caused his sudden change of heart. There in the window, she saw the sheer curtain flutter closed, and Miss Ramsey slowly move away. Had she been watching them?

Nathan shifted her so that she tumbled down into his arms, yet his eyes never left the window. "What's the Ramsey woman's given name?"

She felt his arms tighten around her as she rested a hand against his chest. His heartbeat pounded steadily as she thought about his question.

"Alice."

Chapter Twenty-Five

NATHAN DREW MORE attention than a one-man circus. Jessa huffed on the outside pane of the lobby window then wiped it with a cleaning rag, the whole while keeping her attention fixed on Nathan and Lily outside of Phillips General Store two doors down. Now that he was free to walk the streets, he caused quite a stir. Some folks were clearly awed by him, some merely curious. Others, acted half scared to death, making a wide circle to avoid any unnecessary contact.

Word spread like a ragweed wildfire that Cimarron's most illustrious son had returned. With each retelling of the incident at the jailhouse, the story became more and more absurd until the last she heard, he'd single-handedly taken on fourteen, maybe fifteen, of the meanest, ugliest outlaws ever to step foot in Colfax County. By the time the smoke cleared, he was the only one left standing. Even managed to save a kitten from a tree and walk an old lady across the street before returning to Mission San Gabriel to lead evening vespers.

Jessa made a face at her reflection.

What people didn't know or understand, they simply made up in their own heads. This was why honest newspapers were essential. The only reason folks made up what they didn't know is because they lacked facts. Hard, unrelenting facts. No one could argue with the truth. Even the Bible said as much.

Glancing over at Nathan's innate swagger, she couldn't help admiring what a fine figure of a man he was. No one, it seemed, within a four-block range was immune to his dangerous allure. Oddly enough, he appeared indifferent to all the staring.

Lily caught sight of Jessa and offered a quick wave.

Jessa returned the gesture then continued to clean the same spot, giving special attention to an imaginary speck of dirt. She had no cause to follow them down to the general store other than to ask what Nathan might have found while scouting up near Bobcat Pass for the past two days. He'd been especially interested in looking around the area where her father had last been seen.

The three of them had come to an agreement. It was best for Jessa to distance herself from Nathan for the time being. Most everyone in town knew of the connection between Augus and Nathan, though she doubted anyone ever fully realized the depth of their friendship.

As far as they knew, he and Jessa were only casual acquaintances and had never met before. In order to remain unsuspected of any involvement with the Pinkertons, especially now that her father's anonymous newspaper articles had resumed, it was crucial that she go about quietly taking care of business as usual. To the casual observer, she had merely offered him and Father Miguel a place to stay when the mission was damaged.

For Bucky's sake, and her own, she needed to keep her distance.

They'd all meet up again this evening in her father's study. She could ask him about it then. In the meantime, it didn't hurt to do a little eavesdropping.

"Been meaning to thank you, sir, for promising my little Herbert Jr. riding lessons." Wheezer's father was the only one who called him by his rightful name. "Why, the boy's been so excited, he can barely sleep. Mighty obliged."

He set two mugs of sarsaparilla on the upside-down pickle barrel for the two old codgers playing checkers outside his store.

"He's a good kid. About time he learns to sit in a saddle." Nathan dipped his hat to a couple of young women strolling by, causing them to giggle behind their hands.

Jessa happened to know at least one of them was betrothed. Shameless. Some females were just plain silly.

She noticed that Nathan hadn't shaved for a few days. But from what she could tell, he had trimmed his stubbled jaw into crisp lines which added to his appeal.

"Miss Lily, I'm gonna let you accompany me to the Harvest Fair. What you say?" Newt Ferrell grinned with a toothless smack of his lips.

"Purty, purty. Too purty for the like of you," the other old doffer added before lifting a mug to his mouth.

"Lessin', you were of a mind to be askin' her, Lobo." Newt held up his gaunt hands. "Don't want no quarrel with no gunfighter fella."

"I do believe I would be safer with him than with either of you two scoundrels." Lily lifted a large red apple from a display by the door. "These look scrumptious, Mr. Phillips. I'll take a bag if you'd be so kind."

"I reckon you'd be right about that," Newt agreed, mischief lighting up his weathered eyes. "But tell me this, which one of you two's gonna be wearin' the dress? You or Ol' Auntie Whoozy Doodle, there?"

The other old man cackled, spewing sarsaparilla all over the checkerboard.

Jessa turned her back to them, biting her bottom lip to avoid laughing herself.

"If memory serves, Mr. Ferrell, you were quite smitten with dear Aunt Winnie. Were you not?" Lily wasn't one to disregard an opportunity to set a man straight.

Newt grinned widely showing all three of his teeth. He loved attention any way he could get it, especially from beautiful women. "When a body gets to be my age, eyesight's the first to go."

Jessa cleared her throat and barely glanced over at them, interested to see Nathan's face.

He leaned against the thick pine column and observed a pack of rowdy miners outside of the saloon across the street. Whether he'd heard the conversation around him or not was anybody's guess.

Mr. Phillips returned with a sack of apples for Lily. She removed coins from the reticule at her wrist and paid the man then said something to Nathan and they began to walk toward the hotel.

"You two behave yourselves," she called back to the two playing checkers.

"Ain't promisin' nothin'," Newt returned.

Jessa turned back to the window and rubbed at the same spot.

"Good morning, Miss Valentine."

Jessa swiveled so that she could see who had approached them.

"Good morning, Miss Valentine," a younger voice parroted.

To her surprise, the greeting came from Mrs. Hollinger

and her daughter, Violet. Standing outside of the bakery, they seemed awfully friendly to Jeb Hollinger's greatest adversaries. Their conversation wasn't as loud as it had been with the hard-of-hearing checker players. Try as she might, Jessa could only make out a few words here and there.

Lily and Hollinger's wife exchanged pleasantries. From what Jessa could gather, Hollinger had been released on his own recognizance by the district judge. He'd likely paid for the privilege. So until someone showed up with a Federal warrant—and someone trustworthy enough to enforce it—he was right back at the bank causing havoc as usual.

Jessa couldn't help but notice Violet practically standing on her head, trying to gain Nathan's attention. To his credit, he neither encouraged her, nor was he outright rude. Although, she wouldn't blame him if he'd just walk off and leave her standing there.

Violet Hollinger was a menace.

There wasn't a man from here to Fort Union she hadn't tried to entice only to toss them out like dirty bathwater once they became interested. As far as Jessa knew, she'd never been allowed to have an actual suitor. Her father wouldn't allow it. But it sure didn't stop her from collecting hearts just the same.

Watching her turning her head this way and that with her simpering grin, trying to add Nathan's heart to her collection made Jessa's stomach turn.

Shaking out her cleaning cloth, she averted her gaze from the four of them simply because she didn't trust herself to look.

"I'm so glad to have bumped into you this morning." Mrs. Hollinger was cordial, although she was known to be selective with her friends. Understandable, given no one in town trusted the Hollinger name. Apparently, Lily Valentine made the list. "I brought the fashion magazine I promised you at our luncheon last month. There is a lovely gown on page one thirty-six that would look exquisite on you."

Lily accepted the magazine without hesitation with a gracious smile. Odd. Lily already had that magazine upstairs in her room. She'd had it delivered to her by mail three weeks ago.

"We were just about to have lunch at the hotel," she heard Lily say. "Would you care to join us?"

"We'd love to," Violet answered for the both of them. "But only if Mr. Lobo agrees to sit beside me."

That was all she could take. Jessa turned the knob and escaped inside to the lobby before she did something that would blow her cover to smithereens.

Chapter Twenty-Six

NATHAN HUNG HIS hat on a hall tree made of antlers. The hotel's waitress, Conchita, showed them to a table next to the window. Wiping her pudgy hands on a towel hanging from the waistband of her apron, she spoke to only him. "I have your favorite spot all ready for your lunch. I know how you like the corner, so I saved it just for you."

Nathan thanked her. He'd never be accused of biting a hand that fed him. At Miss Ramsey's instruction, staff had taken special care to see that he always had everything he needed.

Settling into his usual seat, the Hollinger girl raced her mother to claim the seat next to him. She was the spitting image of her father with the droopy brown eyes, thick nose, and thin lips. And from what he'd seen of her so far, she tended to act like him, too. Bound and determined to have her way.

He caught Lily's eye, and she stepped in front of the girl. "Violet, love, I wonder if you'd mind if I took this chair. The way the sun shines on that side of the table catches the silvery blonde strands in your hair to perfection. Would be such a shame to banish such beauty to a dark corner."

The girl's pout reversed immediately. She swept her immense skirt around her and sank into the seat across from

Nathan.

Conchita filled their water goblets from a copper pitcher, making meaningless conversation with the ladies while a movement near the kitchen doors drew his attention.

Jessa flicked a feather duster over everything in sight, all the while watching their table from mirrors set around the dining room. She might've convinced herself she had a real knack for investigation, but truth was, she made a frightful spy. She lived her life out in the open with no secrets and no pretenses. Unfortunately, she was just as apt to take everyone else at face value, too. The world was a whole lot harsher than she knew.

She leaned across the table next them, making sure the vase of flowers got a good dusting. He half expected her to come dust off their silverware just to have a closer listen. At this rate, she may as well come pull up a chair.

Lily followed his gaze and smiled down into her lap as she spread a napkin over her skirt.

She knew it, too.

Nathan supposed he couldn't blame Lily for wanting to humor her. Jessa had been through the ringer these past few months, with so much uncertainty still hanging over her head. If she wanted to get in on finding her father's murderer, the least they could do is let her fumble her way through searching for clues.

Honest truth was, she wasn't too bad to have around. In fact, he'd had to caution himself not to get comfortable spending time with her. Jessa was the type of woman he could get way too comfortable with.

The two-room dining area smelled of cedarwood as a split log sizzled in the fireplace. Nathan took in a sweeping glance. Most of the lunch crowd had already cleared out.

Only a couple of tables were occupied by folks who he assumed were hotel guests given their city attire.

The restaurant, like the hotel, was impressive. He could only imagine back in its day, this would have been considered the Grand Dame of the Santa Fe Trail. Jessa said her mother had spared no expense and it showed. Besides large mirrors bordered by hammered silver, red chile ristras hung from iron sconces on the white-washed walls along with hand-painted mountain scenes in heavy wooden frames. Large pottery pots, filled with colorful flowers, took up every corner, and the tables were covered in costly Talavera tile.

Violet prattled on. Something about some soldier who'd had the nerve to whistle at her on the street and her daddy's man had shoved him clear into the alley.

Nathan gave Conchita his order then once again felt eyes on him.

Jessa peeked at them in the large, mirrored inset of the massive Hepplewhite china cabinet. Startled at being caught, she feathered a little too convincingly, sending a delicate crystal cup crashing to the wood floor.

Jessa stood frozen as everyone in both dining rooms craned their necks to see what had made such a clatter.

"Why, look. It's Jessa Jamison." Whether Violet meant for her loud observation to sound as nasty as it did wasn't immediately clear. "Mother, do call her over so we can be sure she's all right. She looks a tad sickly, don't you think?" She directed her question to Nathan, who easily ignored her. "But then Jessa always looks sickly to me. Wouldn't you agree, Mother? The way she rides all over creation in the sun with no bonnet makes her look jaundiced and eman … emanctipated."

"Good for you, love. I see you've been studying your vocabulary words this week. Keep it up. You'll no doubt get it right eventually." Lily was having none of it. Few things riled her, but downright meanness was apparently one of them.

Nathan pushed away from the table and went to where Jessa knelt, frantically picking up pieces of broken crystal with her bare fingers. Calling for Mr. Chavez to bring in a broom, he helped Jessa to her feet.

"Conchita, mind if we borrow your towel?"

The waitress was quick to oblige, concern marring her brow.

Nathan dampened the cloth and pressed it lightly against her hands, removing the tiny shards as best he could. Small traces of blood stained the towel, still she pushed away his hands and forced a wobbly smile.

"I'm all right. Really."

He led her over to his table where he could keep a better eye on her, and she wouldn't feel the need to knock anything else over trying to listen in on their conversation.

"Jessa, it's nice to see you again." Mrs. Hollinger smiled. As far as he could tell, she held none of the animosity that her daughter did. "How is Miss Ramsey?"

"Doing well, thank you. She's gone down to the market just now, but I'll tell her you asked."

"Jessa, really. I took you for a delivery boy in those god-awful britches." Violet again looked the room over, pausing to assess every man present. "Isn't she the most independent thing, Mother? I'd never have the nerve to go about showing off my backside like that."

And nerve it would take too, Nathan mused, remembering the girl's bustled rump.

"I rather commend Jessa's boldness." Lily gave her goddaughter a wink.

"She's a mite more comfortable, I'd imagine," Mrs. Hollinger responded kindly. "Sarah Jamison was one of my dearest friends. Jessa, you look more and more like her every day."

Jessa smiled at the lady.

The Hollinger woman was thoughtful for being married to one of the Territory's most diabolical men. Although she had plenty of money, she didn't lord it over anyone. She seemed at peace with herself. No matter what her husband was capable of, she didn't strike him as a lady who took her self-worth from hiding behind a powerful man.

She'd been nothing but cordial since they'd met. Surprising considering Hollinger's open contempt for him. For the life of him, however, he couldn't figure why she coddled that spoiled daughter of hers.

He pulled over a chair for Jessa, before taking his own.

"Mother, can you believe we're dining with *the* El Lobo?" Violet couldn't contain her excitement. "Did you have any idea, Jessa, that such a famous killer was staying right here at your little hotel?"

Nathan would lay odds that the Hollinger girl didn't attract many friends.

"Nathaniel Wolfe is the most skilled shot I've ever had the privilege of knowing." Lily sipped her tea while Conchita placed bowls steaming with chile stew in front of them. "Isn't it strange how a man can become famous, as you say, simply by defending himself?"

"No matter what made him that way, I've been dying to meet him." Violet bit into a chunk of potato and had to spit it back into the spoon.

"It's hot, dear." Mrs. Hollinger seemed a bit uneasy as she gave Nathan an apologetic glance. "Besides, we have yet to say grace."

Out of respect, they all bowed their heads as Mrs. Hollinger offered thanks.

Nathan made a mental note to ask Lily what she knew about the woman. She was fairly attractive for her age, certainly more so than her daughter. If he were guessing, she was from up north somewhere. She didn't have a southern accent. Her manner and deportment were far more refined than the locals. Where had Hollinger found her?

Obviously put out, Violet gave up and dropped her spoon onto the table. "Jessa, go tell that cook of yours that the food here is entirely uneatable. And get some fresh flowers, for heaven's sake. These on the table are half dead." Her frown switched to a toothy smile so fast Nathan had to look twice. "I feel it's important to surround oneself with beautiful things, don't you, Mr. Lobo?"

He smoothed the scruff on his jaw to cover a grin when Jessa rolled her eyes.

"Indeed, I do," he answered. "Like wildflowers in sunshine."

"Exactly!"

Nathan was fairly sure she had no idea what "exactly" she agreed to.

"Did I mention that I leave for New York in two weeks?" Violet bit into a buttered roll, chewing like it was cud while she continued to talk. "I will be attending a highly prestigious college. Elmira College for Women. Daddy arranged for me to stay with cousins who are very well-to-do."

"Would you like me to bring you something, Jessa?"

Conchita made the rounds refilling their cups. "How about a cup of coffee?"

"I should get back to—"

"Do say you'll stay, Jessa." Mrs. Hollinger patted her lips with a napkin. We so rarely get to visit. I've thought about you and your brother often since Augus ... well, since we heard that the two of you are alone now."

Jessa looked over at Lily, confusion evident on her face. "I didn't realize you and Papa knew each other. I mean, I'm sure you knew him, but given that your husband and Papa were at odds most of the time, I guess I didn't realize you cared."

Jessa reddened at her weak explanation.

"As I said, Sarah was a dear friend. Back when friends were very hard to come by. It never mattered to Augus who I was married to. Friend or foe. He was kind and always stood by his values. I respected that. We became friends simply because we chose to be. We had a high regard for one another. I was truly sad to hear of his passing."

"That's very kind of you, Mrs. Hollinger." Lily took a long sip of her tea, watching Hollinger's wife over the rim. "Augus was a friend to many. As you can well imagine, we are rather anxious to discover who might have had reason to do him harm. Perhaps, they were simply interested in shutting him up."

Leave it to Lily. She was never one to pull punches.

The two ladies studied one another for a good minute before Violet began to whine about being hungry and wanting to find some real food.

Mrs. Hollinger signed for the check, and they gathered their things to be on their way.

"I have an appointment with Mrs. Salas at two." Violet

stood and smoothed down her wide skirt. "She's making me a new dress for the big dance. You are going to the dance, aren't you, Mr. Lobo? Everyone will be there. I've received dozens of invitations, but I haven't accepted any yet." She tilted her head and twirled her straight blonde hair.

"Violet, your father has already arranged an escort for you. I'm certain Mr. Wolfe has better things to do with his time." Mrs. Hollinger sounded irritated. She evidently didn't want her daughter seen with a "famous killer."

Nathan stood out of respect for the ladies, blocking Jessa from making a quick escape. "As a matter of fact, I already have someone else in mind to take to the dance. If she'll do me the honor."

"Who?" Jessa crossed her arms.

"You," he answered tossing an extra coin on the table for Conchita.

"Jessa? You can't be serious," Violet spat. "I doubt she even owns a dress."

"Of course, she does." Lily added another coin for the waitress. "As I recall, she has a lovely turquoise gown that I brought to her straight from London."

"Hrrph." Violet obviously wasn't ready to let it go. "How lovely will it be when she lassoes the first man who asks her to dance and wrestles him to the ground?"

Nathan watched Jessa wince. "I wasn't planning on going to the dance."

"You see, Mother? Jessa's not only independent, she's practical, too." Violet took up her parasol. "None of Papa's men ever take her seriously. It's probably best she stay home and save herself the humiliation."

"Nonsense." Lily pinned on a wide-brimmed hat with plumed feathers. A perfect match to her royal purple outfit.

Nothing like that was made anywhere in the Territory, you could bank on that. When she stood, she squared her shoulders and the Hollinger girl took a step back. Lily had a commanding presence and knew just when to use it. "You certainly will go, love, and you will outshine every other unfortunate creature there. It was a pleasure to see you again, Mrs. Hollinger. Give my regards to your husband."

With that, she strolled out the door without so much as a backward glance.

Chapter Twenty-Seven

"Jessa, I didn't hear you come in." Miss Ramsey looked up from where she kneaded a lump of dough. The boys will be disappointed to see you. They were hoping you'd forgotten their arithmetic lesson today."

Jessa closed the screen door behind her. "I rode out to Hasler's Pond." With a heavy sigh, she sank onto a stool and absently rolled a little ball of dough between her fingers.

"That can only mean something's troubling you." Miss Ramsey buttered a bowl and placed the mound inside, covering it with a dish towel. "What is it, dear?"

Jessa looked over the white adobe walls of the kitchen. There was really no explanation for her melancholy mood. Since lunch, her insides felt twisted up in knots.

Rinsing flour from her hands in a washbowl by the basin, Miss Ramsey let Jessa sort through her thoughts. The sound of boys' laughter wafted in on a breeze that ruffled the curtains over the sink.

"You were never married, am I right?"

A frown fluttered over the housekeeper's face as she took a damp rag over to wipe down the table. "No. I never was."

"Maybe that's just the way God intended it. Some women are called to other things, bigger things." Miss

Ramsey never reprimanded her for her unconventional questions, but it wasn't hard to tell when she disagreed. She paused, tilted her head ever so slightly, and twisted her lips to one side before carrying on with what she was doing. "Well, there certainly has to be more important things than just playing helpmate to a man."

"You make the sacred bond between man and woman sound so dismal." The older woman swept flour scraps into her cupped hand, then deposited them into a trash bowl. "I believe the good Lord has every intention for us to do big things, and sometimes hard things. But I don't believe we were ever meant to do it all alone."

Jessa paced the smooth brick floor. This seemed odd advice coming from a woman who'd chosen to never marry.

"Where one is strong, the other can be tender. One may know exactly what he wants, while the other needs a bit of persuading when it comes to affairs of the heart." She brought over a woven basket filled with sun-dried laundry. Lifting a towel, she seemed to pick her words carefully. "I find it often takes a woman's sensibilities to temper most men. They don't easily express what they feel inside. But once the two find an agreeable rapport, that is where they can face just about anything—as long as they face it together."

How did she know these things? Jessa decided to simply keep quiet and allow Miss Ramsey to talk, hoping to glean a bit more information about the housekeeper's past.

"You were very blessed to have the papa you did. He and your mama made quite the pair. Traveled from way up north to fulfill a dream God put in both their hearts. Together they put up the finest hotel and stage depot the west had ever seen." Miss Ramsey's hand stilled, and her smile faded. "My father didn't have the love of a woman to temper his rough edges. We lost Mama early on, and as the years went by, he sank deeper and deeper into a pit of bitterness. He never showed us any form of endearment. Not that he disapproved of sentiment of any kind, just the demonstration of it. Made him uncomfortable and even angry at times."

"How horrible for you." Jessa took the stool next to her and began to fold a towel. "You never speak of him. I had no idea."

"Oh, I'm sure I've mentioned him. He died eleven years back. You were most likely too young to remember."

Jessa ran her hand over the thick cotton material. Her thoughts went back to the conversation she and Nathan had shared in the barn. Looking over, she studied the housekeeper for any signs of resemblance to Nathan's strong features. None immediately stood out. "Was your home around here? In Cimarron, I mean."

"All my life. Forty-some-odd years." Miss Ramsey laid one towel neatly upon another. "Do you recall hearing of Judge Franklin K. Ramsey?"

"*He* was your father?" Everyone in these parts had heard of the old judge.

"The very same. He was a caring father, but like I said, he preferred not to show it."

"How did he die?"

"Goodness me. You're never at a loss for questions." A faraway look stole over her face as a distinct sadness tugged at her mouth. "Let me think. The doctor had a long name for it, that I don't recall just now. But his heart finally gave out."

"If I know you, you cared for him right up to the end."

"Yes, certainly. He had no one else. Papa needed me." As if realizing where she was, she gave Jessa an embarrassed smile. "Listen to me going on ..."

"Is that why you never married? Because you felt like your papa needed you?"

Miss Ramsey looked so forlorn that Jessa almost wished she hadn't asked. "I'm sorry. I've gone to meddling again."

The housekeeper brushed a hand over her graying hair that was neatly braided into a bun at her nape. Her skin was smooth and clear. In her day, she might have been considered decently attractive. Her eyes had faded into a greenish-blueish color. Jessa supposed in a certain light they might be seen as having a gray tint, but even that was a bit of a stretch.

"No need to be sorry." Miss Ramsey waved off the apology with a snap of another towel before she carefully folded it in half. "What's done is done. I have no regrets. Nothing was ever changed by worrying over it."

A man like old judge Ramsey would have had plenty to say about serving as father-in-law to an Apache. That might explain why a young woman would feel desperate enough to leave her baby in the care of the church.

"Would you mind my asking just one thing more?" Jessa knew she was pushing her luck. The housekeeper could refuse to answer anything else at any given moment. "Do you like to embroider?"

"Embroider?" Miss Ramsey was clearly confused. "Not a stitch, dear. Why do you ask?"

Jessa shrugged and gave her a sheepish grin. "No reason."

Lifting stacks of folded sheets and towels, Miss Ramsey started for the back stairs. "Father Miguel and the little ones won't be eating with us tonight. The Methodist church is serving them dinner. We must see that the Presbyterian church organizes something similar. It will be wonderful exposure for the children. Perhaps we can find them homes after all. The Lord always works things out for good."

The screen door clattered. Bucky and Wheezer blew in like a couple of tumbleweeds in a whirlwind. Stopping at a platterful of fresh cookies set out on the counter, they each grabbed as many as their grimy fingers could hold.

"Hold it right there, you two."

They froze in their tracks as soon as they heard Jessa's voice.

"We are going over your sums this afternoon, remember?"

"Aww, Jessa. We ain't got time for that today." Bucky's cookie-garbled words were barely understandable.

Nodding in agreement, Wheezer hitched up his britches and stuffed another oatmeal cookie in his mouth with crumbs speckling his chin.

"*Haven't* got time for it today," she corrected.

"See there? You're too busy, too. We'll catch up tomorrow." Bucky started to leave the same way he'd come in, but Jessa beat him to the door.

"Go get your slates." Every day this week, he'd had a different excuse. Last week their entire brood of hens had been let loose onto the street. It took all afternoon to round them up and settle them back into the coop.

"My brain's tired of learnin' numbers." Bucky flopped into a chair. "It's almost as bad as studyin' a bunch of dead folks."

"You'll be doing a history lesson as well."

Just yesterday when it came time to "study a bunch of

dead folks," Wheezer suddenly came down with a monstrous stomachache. Writhing and moaning until Jessa, nearly beside herself with worry, had to send for his father.

Thank goodness Miss Ramsey stepped in with a good dose of caster oil.

Come to find out he'd consumed a half dozen crabapples on a spit-shake bet. Wheezer lost. And Bucky's recompense would be to study the Roman Empire twice as long this evening.

"No more play until you've each written out your table of nines, one through twelve." She was convinced the only way Bucky Jamison would ever amount to anything was if he was dragged there kicking and screaming. And she was responsible for seeing to it.

"I'd listen to the lady if I were you. I hear she has a mean temper."

The hair stood up on the back of her neck as she recognized the smooth voice behind her.

"That's what I been tryin' to tell ya." Bucky stood and dusted off his hands on his pant legs. "We got business to tend to. Lobo's gonna show us how to ride. Ain't ya, Lobo?"

Squeezing her eyes shut for a minute to gather herself before turning around, she prayed for patience. The moment she turned, a movement behind Nathan caught her eye.

The young orphan, Jacob, stepped into the open as Nathan prodded him with a nod.

"Hello, Jacob." Her heart went out to the sullen child from the mission. He always looked so misplaced, seemingly lost wherever he went.

Again, Nathan urged the boy to respond. "Ma'am."

All three boys stood rigid as they looked each other

over. Each recognized in the others the prospect of a friend. Or the potential of a foe.

Wheezer swiped his sleeve across his nose and looked to Bucky for confirmation whether the newcomer was welcome or not.

Bucky narrowed his eye. "Who're you?"

Jacob didn't answer but bowed his chest out a tad bit more.

Jessa felt a wave of protectiveness wash over her for the boy, but Nathan laid a black-gloved hand against her arm to prevent her from stepping in between them.

"Who's askin'?" Jacob gave a side glance with his own eye narrowed a degree.

The miniature showdown lasted a full sixty seconds until Bucky finally shrugged and offered him a cookie. Apparently, that was how long it took to glean all they needed to know about one another.

Amazed, Jessa watched the three boys disappear together out the back door.

"If it'll help, I can divide the horses by nine and have them count 'em up." Nathan offered a mocking grin.

"Truly? You can count that high?" she tossed back.

Crossing the kitchen, she ignored his low laugh. Foregoing the boy's lessons yet again left her with the rest of the afternoon free. Maybe she would take tea up to Lily.

"Listen, Jessa." She turned to find him paused at the back doorway. "What I said at lunch about taking you to the dance …"

Her back stiffened, half-prepared for him to recant his offer. The truth of Violet's cutting prediction still stung her pride. "You don't have to—"

"Wear the turquoise dress."

Next thing she knew, the screen door slammed shut and he was gone.

※

Lily watched from her window high above the corral as Lobo worked with each of the three boys in the yard, showing them how to handle a set of reins and sit astride a horse without toppling off at every turn.

And the boys were enthralled.

Especially Bucky. He clearly missed having a strong male influence to guide him through his ever-changing world. Losing Augus had been difficult for them all, but most of all, she would imagine, for a frightened ten-year-old boy who had lost his anchor and was desperately trying to regain his footing.

To her amazement, Lobo was infinitely more patient with him than Cade had chosen to be. Astounding, considering he was usually the last one to tolerate ill-mannered behavior out of anyone. Heaven could attest, Bucky was nothing if not mischievous to the core.

Perhaps they'd both done a bit of settling down these past few months.

In a way, they were both products of Augus Jamison. He had practically raised both young men from an early age. And in doing so, she knew he had to have instilled kindness, tenacity, determination, and his unique ability to sway every person he met to a better way of seeing things. It was his gift. A true innovator.

So very much like his daughter.

If Jessa could just harness the wild, wonderful visionary inside her. That same drive that caused her to crave making a world of difference on a large scale. If she could ever learn to be content simply by making small differences right where she was, she would be a true force of nature.

Despise not the small beginnings, for in due time ...

Lily straightened and leaned forward to better see down below.

Oh, no! No, no, no!

Bracing herself for the storm to come, she watched Nathan draw quick as lightning, sending a can into the air from thirty yards away.

All three boys whooped and hollered in riotous appreciation.

Just as she had predicted, the screen door flew open, and Jessa barreled toward them at full speed. "Bucky Jamison, drop the gun this instant!"

"It ain't real." He held it up to show her his whittled replica. "Lobo was doin' the shooting. He's showing us how to win the trick shot contest at the fair tomorrow."

"I said drop it!" Though Jessa spoke to her brother, the fire in her eye was directed at Lobo.

"I suppose you'd rather he never learn the proper way to handle a weapon. Shoot his fool leg every time he tries to clear his holster?" Lobo matched her fire and raised the ante with a helping of sound reasoning.

"I'd rather he never lay hands on a real gun at all." She left her brother to take two steps closer to Lobo, crossing her arms for good measure.

Careful, love. A man like Lobo can only be pushed so far.

"Papa had one," Bucky spoke up in his own defense.

"For all the good it did him," she answered without turning around.

The two of them locked stares and neither was giving in.

Lobo stood completely unruffled. He was used to being called out.

However, Jessa, with long golden hair whipping in the breeze and that beautiful gaze of hers set dead center on him, was unlike any foe he had ever faced down. One could be certain of that.

Slowly, he pulled his hat a bit lower over his brow and took a step toward her.

Steady, Lobo.

He was like a bull, raking the ground in preparation to charge.

The tension positively crackled between them. All three boys now watched from between the slats of the corral, none willing to enter the ring.

Like waving a red cape, Jessa challenged him by taking one more step forward, tossing her head with a defiant glare.

Jessa, Jessa, Jessa.

Lily let the curtain fall into place and lifted a teacup to her lips.

Her headstrong goddaughter had more than a thing or two to learn about men. Men like Lobo anyway.

Lily shook her head and took another sip.

To openly challenge him, in front of the boys who idolized the very ground he walked on. A man will only take so much provocation before he takes matters into his own hands.

An indignant scream filled the air as Lily stirred a spoonful of honey into her tepid tea.

"Put ... me ... down!"

A solid splash sounded from down in the yard, accompanied by elated whooping from the boys.

Lily made a mental note to remind Bucky to refill the water trough after dinner.

"Oh, my!" Miss Ramsey's voice came from outside her door, where she no doubt watched the goings on in the yard from the window at the end of the hall. "Oh, my!"

The house rattled its rafters as Jessa slammed the screen door below and attacked the stairs two at a time, sloshing past Lily's door without a word.

Chapter Twenty-Eight

RED, WHITE, AND blue pendants rippled over the entrance to the Colfax County Fair. Pleated banners with matching streamers fanned out over the center of the town plaza. An enormous, blue-striped canopy with table after table full of homemade delicacies was set to one side of the square while elaborate handiwork was displayed beneath the shade of another.

Nathan hoisted the baby up from the back of the mission's wagon. Excitement radiated from her cherubic face as she clung to him.

"Now get me." Six-year-old Nellie Bradford stood at the edge of the wagon bed holding her arms out to him. "You can be next, Kai."

The shy Navajo girl smiled.

Feeling chivalrous, Nathan grabbed them both, one under each arm, and swung them to the ground. Surprised squeals dissolved into fits of giggling as onlookers slowed to enjoy the sound of the little girl's laughter.

"Hey, Lobo!" Bucky Jamison and Wheezer Phillips made a mad dash across the crowded road to leap onto the wagon, then over to the other side landing atop one another.

"Get off, Wheez." Bucky shoved the dazed boy. "Where's Jacob? And what're you doing with them goobers?" His nose wrinkled up as if Nathan stood beside a couple of little skunks.

"We are not goobers. We are girls," Nellie answered for herself, swiping hair from her eyes. "Nathaniel gave us a twirl."

"Nathaniel?" Bucky's brows drew together while Wheezer looked around for someone else. "Well, the way you was squealing, I thought you was a couple of little piglets."

Wheezer snorted.

"Lookie here. This one even gots piggy tails." Bucky tugged at one side of Kai's braids.

The quiver in her chin sparked blue fire in Nellie's eyes. Snapping her hands onto her small waist, she took three deliberate stomps toward their mockers.

Nathan smiled as the boy's bluster fizzled with each step.

The fact that Bucky was a good head taller didn't faze Nellie one bit. She didn't pause until they stood toe-to-toe, wagging her petite finger in his face.

"You take that back, Mister, or I'll wallop you clear to next week!"

Bucky's baffled expression suggested he couldn't decide whether she was dangerous or just plain looney. Catching the curious stares of Jacob and Wheezer, he cast a frown at her. "You couldn't beat butter." He looked to Nathan for confirmation. "Could she?"

"I believe I'd listen if I were you." He decided to help the little lady out before she made good on her threat. "Ol' Deadleg Pete made the mistake of underestimating her once. Back when he had two good limbs."

"J-Jee hoshaphat!" Wheezer grabbed ahold of Bucky's

shirt to pull him away, eyeing the little girl like she was a stick of dynamite. "Take it back, quick!"

Bucky still looked doubtful, but a hint of respect for her daring caused him to reach over and muss her curly hair. "Don't get your hackles up. I was just funnin'."

He started to walk away, but Nellie ran forward to block his path once again. "Don't tell me, tell *her*." She pointed back at Kai, who chewed her lip nervously.

Nathan smooth a hand over his jaw to cover a grin.

With an exasperated huff, Bucky offered the girl a quiet, "Sorry."

Nellie's face broke out into a satisfied grin. "See there, Kai. They weren't being mean, they can't help it. They're just dumb ol' boys."

Both girls took out running, screaming, and giggling with the boys in hot pursuit.

Grinning, Nathan leaned back against a cottonwood, hands in his front pockets and a knee bent to rest his heel against the trunk. He imagined Nellie Bradford would outrun plenty of fellas before she let herself get caught.

Like someone else he knew.

A sense of excitement ran through the square as voices—young and old—mingled with the live music coming from under the gazebo set to one side. Whistles blew, signaling the commencement of various games, while noisy animals waited their turn to trot out in front of the judges.

It was clear the annual festival was still a highlight of the county. Countless hours had been spent in preparation to bring in the harvest and declare the season of labor had come to an end. The fruit of a year's worth of hard work was gathered, prepared, blessed, and ready to be enjoyed by one and all.

Nathan lifted his head to take in the smells of hot buttered corn on the cob, Indian fry bread from a kiva oven, and fresh apple cider floating through the crowd like silent fingers enticing hungry visitors to come have a taste.

Medicine shows were set at either end of town, toting miracle cures by the dozen. Rehearsed pitches by slick barkers filled the air, while various games dotted the plaza.

A rivalry of another kind went on under the tents where ladies from miles around waited with bated breath for the judges to hand out the coveted county fair ribbons.

Nathan scanned the fairgrounds with a discerning eye.

This patchwork of folks was bound by the common thread of land they called home. Their subtle differences made them all the more appealing as a whole. Northerners, Southerners, Mexicans, or Indians. Quakers, Catholics, Baptists or even those who hadn't darkened the door of a church for as long as they could remember. Today, everyone was a neighbor.

The one time of year when the inhabitants of the right side of the road allowed themselves to associate with the heathens on the other side. Arlene's soiled doves were tolerated at fair time, as long as they stayed in plain sight and kept their hands to themselves. Miners were on their best behavior greeting free-spending gamblers who'd likely cleaned them out of a full week's pay the night before.

Cattlemen teamed up with sheep ranchers to toss a few horseshoes, while homesteaders and farmers took part in the sack races. *Vaqueros* rode up from Santa Fe on tasseled horses showing off their rope tricks and riding skills, accompanied by Mexican ladies in colorful skirts and silver jewelry.

Even Hollinger, surrounded by his gun-toting posse, sat

at a table under the overhang of the Wells Fargo Bank building sipping hard cider with a couple of fur traders passing through town. His attention settled on Nathan as he lifted his mug and held it up long enough to convey an unspoken warning. Business between them was far from over.

Jessa's laughter beckoned him from across the plaza like the sound of church bells on a crisp Sunday morning. She wasn't hard to spot in the crowd, looking radiant in yellow calico. Her shining mane was woven into a heavy braid that hung down her back. Her smile beamed as she led a lively game of apple-bobbing. She had grown men kneeling beside wash bins, hands tied behind their backs, dunking themselves like a bunch of ducks for a chance at winning a kid's whirley toy.

His lip turned up in a grin.

When Jessa smiled, she lit up the entire countryside, and she certainly was in fine humor today. He watched her reward the winner with a kiss to his dripping cheek. The man blushed like a bashful bride, looking like he was ready to turn flips in the dung heap for more of the same.

She was something, all right.

Full of flash and thunder one minute, then sweeter than sugar cream pie the next. There was no guessing what Jessa was thinking. She lived her convictions out loud and made no apologies for standing up for what she believed. The Territory needed more folks like her if they ever hoped to take back their land once and for all.

Nathan readjusted his hat lower over his eyes.

Even with all the gumption in the world, the good folks of Colfax County were likely in for a long, ugly battle. What they needed to decide was whether this patch of land where the plains meet mountains was worth the fight. If yes, then it would take every able-bodied citizen with a gun to defend their rights. If Jessa was somehow able to attract attention to their cause from Washington, they just might have a chance at bringing down Hollinger's corporation.

If not, they'd all die trying.

"Good morning, Mr. Lobo." Looking up, he found a pack of matronly women bounding toward him, waving miniature flags. He recognized a couple of them. They'd stopped by the hotel to introduce themselves a couple of days back. Members of the Woman's Aid Society or League or something.

"Morning, ladies." He touched his hat, hoping they'd walk on by.

No such luck.

"Mrs. Apodaca and I were just saying how utterly spectacular the fair is this year. Wouldn't you agree?"

"It most certainly is, Mrs. Peterson." The small, bonneted lady spoke up before Nathan had a chance. "A spectacular undertaking, to be sure."

"Mr. Lobo." Mrs. Peterson rested a hand over her swelled bosom, trying to recover her breath. "As we spoke about at the hotel, you are our most notorious attendee this year. We simply must have you judge our jams, jellies, and preserves."

Nathan had been accused of a lot of things, but being crazy wasn't one of them. He certainly knew enough not to get himself caught in the big middle of competing women. Stealing a glance in Jessa's direction, he noticed she had stopped what she was doing to crane her neck his way.

"I appreciate the offer, ladies, but I'm no cooking expert." Nathan pushed off from the tree, intent on making a fast retreat until two other women came over to join the appeal.

"Oh, but you must!"

"We aren't asking you to judge the sewing exhibits. That would be ludicrous," Mrs. Peterson persisted. "But, surely you can tell whether something tastes good or not. I've always said the cooking contest is best judged by a man."

The other ladies offered their agreement.

Mrs. Apodaca put a hand on his arm and batted her wide brown eyes. "Father Miguel has agreed. He's judging the pickles, beets, and okra this very minute. And a parson from the Methodist church came all the way down from Pueblo to judge the pie and cake table. That leaves the jams, jellies, and preserves with no one to declare a winner. Dear, oh, dear."

"You're forgetting someone." Nathan nodded toward Hollinger, seated across the way. "Jeb Hollinger would be downright offended if he wasn't asked to officiate over something at this *spectacular* event."

"He gets to give a speech and strike up the band for the dance tonight. That's plenty enough out of him for one day," Mrs. Apodaca huffed.

"To be sure," Mrs. Peterson agreed.

Jessa approached the gathering, lifting her skirt and hopping over an edging of flowers.

"Maybe you can convince him, Jessa." Mrs. Apodaca waved her flag toward Nathan. "He's being contrary."

"Mr. Lobo? Contrary?" Jessa feigned disbelief. "Surely not."

He had to smile. The impish grin on her face was irresistible. "Fine, ladies, count me in."

"Thank you, Jessa. Have him there at 1:30 sharp."

"Did you hear that *she* is expected to take the blue ribbon again this year in both embroidery and needlepoint?" Another woman Nathan didn't know took over the conversation as the ladies turned to leave. "Every year it's the same. Time comes to hand out the prizes and you just know her stitchery will turn up the winner. Happens every time."

"Well, you must admit, she is the best embroiderer in the county. Probably in the state if we're being fair."

Nathan listened closer. Who was the best embroiderer in the county?

"It's getting so a person hesitates to even turn in an entry anymore."

Jessa took his hand. "Let's go have a look at the sewing entries." Her golden eyes shone bright with curiosity.

Before he could stop himself, Nathan brushed a fallen leaf from her hair with his other hand, pausing for a moment to caress the softness of her cheek. Instead of pulling away, her black lashes fluttered shut, and she leaned into the warmth of his hand. The honesty of her response humbled him.

"Come on." He gave her hand a squeeze and pulled her along toward the sewing tent.

Just before they crossed the road to the plaza, they ran into Lily and Mrs. Hollinger talking to a man Nathan didn't immediately recognize.

"Just wave and keep going. Lily says we shouldn't seem overly interested in him." Jessa spoke quietly beneath a friendly smile. Lifting the hem of her skirt, she quickened her pace, looking both ways as she crossed the road. Her heavy braid, whipping Nathan in the chest.

"Who is he?"

"A newspaper reporter from up north." She side-glanced him with a serious nod. "Sent down here to personally interview the anonymous contributor who's causing such a stir."

Nathan stopped in mid-stride, causing Jessa to grab onto him to keep from falling. "You aren't giving any interview, Jessa."

"No, but you are." Composing herself, she smiled in greeting to a couple passing by. "At four o'clock."

"Neither one of us are." He lowered his voice to barely above a whisper. "Even if he keeps your name anonymous. The ring cannot find out you're the one working with an informant to expose them, or they'll come after you just like they did Augus."

"We can't send him home empty-handed. The readers are already enamored with you, just give an interview about my father and how you've come to Cimarron to avenge his … whatever … and tell them you don't know who the informant is."

"That's a lie."

"Just because we saw Mrs. Hollinger give Lily a magazine she already had doesn't mean she's turning on her husband. We don't dare name her without hard evidence. Certainly not without her permission."

They were beginning to gather curious stares.

Nathan swiped the hat off his head and drove fingers through his hair before replacing it. He'd have to let this go for now. They couldn't risk being overheard or even risk stirring up any suspicions at this point. He'd get her alone somewhere later, and they'd finish this. Preferably with Lily there to talk some sense into her.

Clearing his throat, he was suddenly aware of how susceptible he'd let himself become concerning Jessa Jamison. She was a liability for sure. He had a hard enough time keeping himself alive, much less worrying all the time about keeping her out of trouble, too.

One more thing he intended to discuss with Lily.

"We have to hurry." Again, she took his hand and half-dragged him toward a tent. "We'll miss them handing out the sewing ribbons. I already looked over the entries. There's a pillowcase that has identical flowers on it as on your handkerchief. They won't reveal the names on the entries until the prizes are given out."

"You kids, git!" Bucky and his two friends were chased out from under the other tent. No doubt sampling the sweets exhibits.

A flood of memories came to mind as Nathan remembered snatching himself a prize cookie or two way back when. The Harvest Fair was one of the few outings where they were allowed to venture outside of the mission's walls. The older boys had dared him, and he'd been quick to take them up on it. Not to impress them, but to take charge of his own destiny. Having one small ounce of control in a world where he was given no say at all.

Running with one eye over his shoulder was no better than being holed up in a tiny mission out in the middle of nowhere. He still lacked the freedom to do whatever he wanted to do, or to even stay in one place long enough to call it home.

But the only person who could put Lobo to rest once and for all was Nathaniel Wolfe.

That thought was immediately sobering.

Ducking under the canopy he stepped inside and was

met with delicious smells of times gone by. Cinnamon, ginger, and all the spices that reminded him of fall.

Women wandered the aisles of tables all glancing curiously at him as they passed, exchanging pleasantries with Jessa.

"Are you Lobo?"

Looking down, Nathan saw a scrawny kid shaking in his boots.

"Pleasure to meet you." Nathan extended his hand to the runt whose eyes darted from Nathan back to his mother.

"Shake the man's hand," his mother prompted.

The youngster offered his hand then quick as lightning disappeared out the front of the tent.

"Didn't I tell you, you have a way with children?" Jessa grinned.

"The kid was terrified." Nathan shook his head. "Pretty sure he soiled himself."

"That's the one there." Jessa pointed to a rectangular piece of cloth with pink and red flowers decorating one edge.

Without thinking, Nathan stepped closer. It was fancier than the stitching on his handkerchief, but the general pattern and technique was the same.

Staring down at the entry, Nathan fought a wave of grief. His time-yellowed handkerchief had been made years ago by a girl he wasn't even sure existed anymore. Looking now at the brand new cloth with identical markings in fresh clean thread, he had no choice but admit the very same hand had probably created them both. Not a ghost from his past, a living breathing woman who still existed today. Who could be watching him look over her handiwork this very moment.

Nathan straightened and glanced around.

Instantly, like a rope reeling in a wayward steer, Jessa's arm hooked around his. Softly rubbing his forearm, she tried to calm the sudden tension in his muscles.

"Ladies and gentlemen, may I have your attention, please. We will now announce our winners in the needlework division."

A hush fell under the canopy.

"In the quilting category, the grand prize ribbon goes to Miss Cecelia Klein for her exquisite wedding ring coverlet."

An excited squeal came from the front as a mousy lady stepped up to accept her ribbon amidst polite applause.

"Our knitting and tatting winner is Mrs. Horacio Gomez."

A woman in matching red dress and bonnet claimed her ribbon with a shy smile.

"I'm so glad Mrs. Gomez won," Jessa said with her face lifted toward Nathan's ear. "She has nine children. I don't know how she finds time to knit at all."

At Nathan's raised brow, she lifted nine fingers to stress her point.

"And last of all, this year's winner for exceptional stitchery ..."

Nathan's heart began to pound in his ears. This was it.

"... goes to the unquestionable best in show for the flawless set of pillowcases ..."

Jessa squeezed his arm.

"... sewn by ..." Mrs. Peterson paused and swallowed hard as if the name was painful to say. "Arlene Calhoun."

Chapter Twenty-Nine

THE CHICKEN WAS undeniably purple.
Frankly, Jessa was glad for the distraction.
Following the announcement that Arlene was the one who'd crafted the pillowcases, Nathan suddenly pushed his way back through the crowd and was outside the canopy before she could find a way to go after him.

Running to keep up with his long strides, she finally cornered him down by the stockyards. In his usual fashion, whenever he was highly annoyed, he snatched off his hat and drove a hand through his thick black hair.

"Nothing is for certain." She could barely get the words out for trying to catch a good breath. "It just means Arlene can sew like whoever left your handkerchief. I think you should go have a talk with her—and bring the Father with you."

"There's nothing to talk about, Jessa." He spoke in a tone scarcely controlled. "I told you to leave it alone. I don't care. I am fine not knowing."

She wasn't going to let him avoid this now. They were so close to discovering the truth. "Of course you want to know. Doesn't mean you have to like what you find, but you *do* want to know."

For a split second, he looked every bit as dangerous as the papers made him out to be. One hand resting on the hilt of his gun, and his black hat low across his brow, barely shading the gray sparks of fury flashing in his eyes. "Leave it be, Jessa."

And that's when a commotion broke loose in the stock pens.

The sound of Doc Jennings' voice rose above the ruckus, capturing her full attention. "Someone fetch Jessa Jamison! At once!"

Taking up her skirt, she made quick tracks in the direction of the doctor's cry, praying fervently that Bucky had not been hurt. Curious folks blocked the entrance where the pens were set up holding the show stock. She tried to get through, but no one would budge.

"This way." Nathan grabbed her hand. He led her to a side door and pulled her in beside him.

A crowd was gathered near the judging podium. As they neared, it struck her as odd that most folks smiled broadly as she approached. Some laughed openly. That's when she saw Bucky standing at the podium next to Doc Jenkins with his pitiful purple chicken.

"Jessa, they won't give me my ribbon!" he hollered down to her as soon as he spotted her in the crowd. "The rules say the ribbon goes to the most outstanding entry. Dixie's the most outstanding chicken here. Ain't no one has one like her. I want my ribbon!"

Jessa crossed her arms over her midriff. "How did Dixie get to be purple?"

The crowd erupted in laughter all around her.

"Blackberries," he answered, proud as can be. "Me and Wheez dunked her in blackberry juice to make her more outstanding. It didn't hurt her none. She liked it."

Doc Jenkins wiped his brow and shook his head. "Now,

Jessa, you know we can't be giving our prize ribbon to a boy with a chicken looking like that."

"They didn't say nothing about what color it had to be. Look, I got the rules right here." Bucky pulled a tattered piece of paper, folded in fourths, from his back pocket. "Says, 'the most outstanding entry in each division.'" He implored her, desperately brandishing the squawking fowl at arm's length in front of him. "They're trying to give my ribbon to the ol' Harper woman for her expensive white one. That thing ain't half as purty as Carlotta."

"Doc, the rules don't specifically disqualify dyed poultry." Jessa tilted her head with a thoughtful look. "And Bucky's chicken is very festive, wouldn't you say?"

Again, the crowd guffawed.

"Yes, yes. But there are other qualities we must consider." The doctor eyed her wearily. "Naturally, we favor animals appearing as God intended. However, Mrs. Harper's White Java also laid bigger eggs and twice as many."

Bucky was still determined to argue. "Aww. She can't help it if that's all she's got today. Some days she can leave about six ... no, ten eggs in her nesting box. I bet they'll be purple now, and we'll be rich!"

"Mrs. Harper won fair and square," Jessa conceded. "Congratulate her and take Carlotta home." To his credit, he turned to shake the lady's hand before jumping off the makeshift platform.

"I think your chicken is pretty." Nellie met him as soon as he hit the ground. "If I was the judge, I would give you the ribbon because your chicken deserves it more than that silly white one."

Bucky's chest puffed out as gallantly as the roosters in a

pen next to him. The open adoration on her face seemed to be all he needed to sate his constant craving for attention. "C'mon. I'll show you how we did it. We got lots more chickens."

"I believe you've done enough damage to our henhouse for one afternoon." Jessa stopped him with a hand to his chest.

Nathan reached inside the front pocket of his vest and pulled out some coins. "Go put Carlotta up, then take your friends over to the games. Show them what a good sportsman you are." He placed a couple of coins in each of their hands, which caused a wave of excitement to run through their small group. "Be sure you get candy apples, too."

"Thanks!" The boys raced to the door.

"Thank you, Nathaniel." Nellie smiled sweetly while Kai nodded in agreement.

The moment they stepped out into the sunshine, Lily found them from across the road. Her broad-striped taffeta swished elegantly with every step. "There you are. Don't forget, Lobo, you have an appointment at four." She addressed him from under her matching parasol which to Jessa's eye appeared the height of sophistication. With a wave, she stopped to accept a glass of cider from Miss Ramsey while they chatted with Wheezer's father, Mr. Phillips.

"Doc!" Mrs. Peterson trotted past them to get to the head judge with her passel of women behind her. "Did you by chance see who won the sewing ribbons again this year? Really! Something must be done to change the rules. It's gotten so a *decent* person need not even enter anymore."

Jessa watched Nathan's face darken as he paused to take in the conversation.

"The judges make their determinations without the benefit of knowing the entrant's name, Merrietta." The doctor waved her off. "Every year you have the same complaint. The judging was done fair and square. The decisions stand as they are."

"She should not even be allowed to enter. You oversee the rulebook. You can change it."

The women passed around nods of agreement.

"Now, ladies, we agreed from the beginning to let anyone enter who could pay the fee. And what's more, they have equal opportunity to win. It's how this town is run. And I don't intend to sully the goodwill of our festival with jealous accusations." He leveled a stern look at each one of them over his wire spectacles. "Besides, Arlene sews circles around any one of you. Wouldn't be very Christian of us to disqualify her. Now, would it?"

Mrs. Peterson accepted his set down with a heavy sigh. "You're right, of course. Far be it from me to withhold charity this time of year. Even from the devil's own mistress."

Jessa felt Nathan tense next to her.

"Charity nothing. She won that ribbon because she works magic with a needle and thread. Now, I suggest you all go home and practice up for next year's competition." Tipping his stovetop hat, the doctor brushed past them.

"It just nags me that those Ramsey sisters win everything," one of the other women spoke up as soon as he was out of hearing range. "They take ribbons in nearly every division. And did you know they grew up without a ma? You know Judge Ramsey didn't teach them to sew and cook and do all the things they do so well."

"You are so right," Mrs. Apodaca threw in. "Didn't

Judge Ramsey's wife die just after that last girl was born?"

Jessa looked over to see if Nathan was listening. He pushed back his hat with a thumb and the frown on his brow told her he was indeed listening to every word.

"The way I heard it, Arlene took those other two to raise, her being the oldest and all." The woman clucked her tongue and a choir of others joined in. "A crying shame she turned out the way she did. After that no-good husband the judge hitched her to ran off with a gypsy and got himself killed stealing a horse. She lost every bit of respectability she ever had."

"I suppose she threw her lot to the wind and never looked back. Imagine, opening a cathouse right here under her own papa's nose. Why, they say the judge nearly flipped his wig."

"Yes, he did," Mrs. Peterson agreed. "And poor Alice. The woman can certainly cook like a dream, but she can't catch a man to save her soul." Raising her voice so Jessa could hear, she continued. "Thank goodness she has you and your family to look after. Did you hear? Her pear preserves took the grand prize again this year."

Jessa's gaze flew to lock with Nathan's.

Miss Ramsey and Arlene–sisters!

"Didn't the youngest sister, Alaina, win anything this year? Bless her heart. I almost feel sorriest for her over any of the others."

"She took honors for her Dutch tulip quilt."

"Oh, my! That was hers?"

"But don't go feeling sorry for her. She chose her path early on. I see the lot she's stuck with as her own personal cross to bear."

A third sister?

Jessa was nearly beside herself wanting to join the conversation and ask a million questions.

Nathan must have sensed it. He reached over and took her hand, holding it tight against himself.

This was just the information they'd needed. But out of consideration for him, she bit her bottom lip and listened quietly.

"Merrietta, where did you get that lovely brooch? I have a special pair of earrings that I am saving for the dance tonight."

The ladies had apparently exhausted their arsenal aimed at the Ramsey sisters and were ready to move on to other matters. As the chattering group continued down the street, Jessa stole a glance at Nathan.

He released her hand and something akin to hurt, or maybe just sadness, crossed his face before he resettled his hat.

She had to make him realize what this meant. They were on the threshold of finding his mother. When she opened her mouth to say so, his censoring gray gaze cautioned her to leave well enough alone.

Tonight, she decided. At the dance, she would get him alone and try again after he'd had a chance to think about it awhile.

In the meantime, he had an appointment with a newspaper man.

Chapter Thirty

THE FULL HARVEST moon appeared enormous on the horizon, silhouetting everything set before it.

Nathan stepped from the hotel and tipped his hat to a couple dressed in their Sunday best. A fiddle band played from an area cleared in the center of the square, and couples swarmed that direction like bees to a clover patch.

He stuffed a hand in the front pocket of his tailored black britches and crossed the courtyard to the Jamison ranch. A silver bolo tie hung from the collar of his crisp white dress shirt, which was topped by his black leather vest. He'd taken a brush to his Stetson until it was buffed up good as new.

Because the evening was a touch cool but mild, he'd put on his long duster coat. And because leaving them behind was never an option, his colts hung from their holsters on his gun belt.

He'd bet good money Jessa wouldn't be pleased about that.

Somewhere along the line, he'd started caring about what pleased her—or what didn't. She'd wheedled her way in until he found himself thinking about her even when they weren't together. And when they were together, Lord knows, she was impossible to ignore. Their easy friendship came as natural as breathing.

Glancing up at the moon, he decided it would be a shame to waste a pretty evening. It wouldn't hurt to do a turn around the dance floor a time or two, especially with the prettiest gal in Cimarron.

The case was moving along. They were inching closer to proving all the dirty dealings Hollinger and his associates had executed in the Territory, which, hopefully, would eventually lead to naming Augus's killer.

Earlier, he'd met with the newspaper reporter. Gave him all the hoopla that Lily thought necessary, and the man had eaten it up like a kid in a candy store. Just prior, the informant had provided some fairly convincing evidence against the validity of the shareholder's right to claim the land they'd stolen out from under countless families. The reporter had run off to the telegraph office and promised that the information would make the morning press.

What better way to catch a hornet than to stir up the nest?

News travels fast. Hollinger ought to be livid by tomorrow afternoon.

Out of courtesy to their informant, Lily refused to reveal the person's identity. Both Nathan and Jessa had a good idea of who she was, but if their hunch was correct, the less who knew for certain, the safer she'd be. If Hollinger had any inkling that his own wife had turned tail on him, she'd pay dearly.

For tonight, he'd just as soon put it all aside, if only for a couple of hours. Today, minus the careless talk of a few town busybodies, was among the most enjoyable days he'd had in years.

Rapping twice on the Jamisons's heavy wood door, he noticed a black-fringed surrey pull into the courtyard behind him. After bringing the horse to a halt, Mr. Phillips, the shopkeeper, stepped unsteadily from the ledge. Joining Nathan at the door, he nodded and adjusted his tie. In one hand he held a bouquet of flowers while he licked his other hand to smooth down each side of his hair, perfectly parted in the middle of his head. Clearing his throat, he again gave a self-conscious greeting.

Lily answered the door and graciously motioned for them to enter. She commented on how nice they both looked, and they returned the compliment. She did look nice. She had her hair wound up on top of her head and the pink dress she had on was obviously special ordered.

Miss Ramsey appeared from the parlor and blushed prettily when Mr. Phillips offered her the flowers. Nathan watched her closely. Knowing what he did about her, he couldn't help but look closer at her fine features.

This woman may be the closest thing he had to a blood relative.

He gave her a half-grin when she turned and smiled up at him. Then, when she reached up and patted his cheek, a warm sensation spread across his chest. The feeling was surprising, yet not altogether uncomfortable.

Taking Mr. Phillips's arm, the two said their goodbyes and disappeared out into the night.

Lily called for Jessa one more time.

Pulling a white flower off an arrangement on the table in the entry, she snapped the stem. A straight pin came from inside of her bodice, and she pinned it to the base of Nathan's lapel. "Gentlemen always wear a boutonniere."

"I was never accepted into Little Gentleman's School," Nathan replied smoothly.

Just then, Jessa appeared at the top of the stairway. As

Nathan turned to face her, he had to look twice. She was radiant. Her golden hair was pulled up on the sides with dozens of burnished ringlets cascading down the back. The turquoise-colored dress she wore, though modest, was cut lower than what she usually wore and was decidedly more fitted, complimenting her every curve.

This vision before him was right off the pages of some storybook.

Jessa lowered her dark lashes against the blush in her cheeks as she stepped down from the last stair. Some kind of rouge made her lips more pink and shinier than usual. The effect was staggering.

"Jessa, love, don't forget your wrap. The evening might prove chilly." Lily settled a lacy shawl around her shoulders then gave her a squeeze. "I'll be along shortly."

Nathan opened the door and allowed Jessa to precede him. Replacing the hat on his head, he offered his arm, and they made their way out to the town square.

It would seem the whole town was paired off as couples strolled leisurely about the square. Some were seated on bales of hay surrounding the dance area, some talked quietly beneath the cover of tall cottonwood trees.

The night air gently ruffled Jessa's curls and lifted her flowery scent onto the cool breeze. She greeted everyone they passed with a smile, and Nathan was quick to notice that he wasn't the only one awestruck by her transformation. She was causing quite a stir.

Pulling up beside an ancient oak, she slid her hand from his arm and turned to stand close in front of him. "Thank you for asking me tonight. I know you sort of got roped into it."

Nathan rubbed her arm. A shiver ran through her, so he

pulled her closer. "Nobody roped me into anything. I asked you because we need to keep an eye on Hollinger."

"Oh ..." Disappointment crossed her face as she looked away.

He lifted her chin to reclaim that intoxicating gaze. "And because I couldn't pass up a chance to dance with the most beautiful lady I know."

"Oh!" Her eyes widened. The sincerity of her surprise was almost more than he could take.

He wrapped his arms around her, and she leaned in snug against him.

There's no telling how long they stood holding each other that way. Neither seemed willing to let the other go. Music swirled around them, the familiar tempo of a timeless ballad, in perfect measure with the beating of their hearts. In that moment, nothing else mattered.

Two lonesome souls bound together by a common purpose. Almost as if the Almighty had seen to it from the beginning. Nathan might have neglected his prayers for years, but there was never any doubt in his mind that the God of heaven and earth still knew his name. The Padre made sure of it.

Jessa lifted her face, and the urge to lower his lips to hers nearly overwhelmed him. Too many casual observers. He wouldn't risk her reputation.

His jaw clenched as he looked out over the plaza. Standing here soaking up the moonlight only complicated things.

Nathan pulled her shawl up closer around her shoulders, then stepped back to tuck her hand in the crook of his arm. "Feel like dancing?"

"Not especially."

The sudden sound of his laughter attracted interest from

other couples close by. It wasn't hard to see which of them was bound to be the more sensible one tonight.

Nathan stepped over a bale of hay, then lifted Jessa and set her down on the other side. As soon as they entered the dance floor, the Hollinger girl made a beeline toward them. "Why, Jessa. I barely recognized you without your rope." Evidently, her stinger was poised and ready. "Meet my date, Mr. Claude Clark? He's the land surveyor for the entire territory. Papa says he has a very powerful position."

Claude was much more interested in surveying Jessa at the moment.

Before Nathan could call him on it, Jessa took the man's hand and gave it a good shake. "We have not met. Not officially, anyhow. But I do recall reading your name in a recent newspaper article. Something about a federal lawsuit. Some confusion about the illegal sale of thousands of acres of land."

While ol' Claude looked dumbfounded, Violet was openly vexed.

"I'm surprised at you, Miss Jamison." Jeb Hollinger sauntered up beside his daughter, touching a match to his expensive cigar. "You of all people should know how dangerous it can be to trust east coast newspapers. Your father should have taught you better." He blew a puff of smoke her direction, but Jessa didn't flinch.

"I've learned much from my father." Golden sparks flashed in her eyes.

"As have we all." Lily joined them with the east coast newspaper man at her side. "Jeb Hollinger, I don't believe you've met Peter McDonald. Head reporter for the Evening Star in Washington."

Hollinger slowly removed the cigar from his mouth and

leaned over, muttering to one of his hired guns who'd been staring down Nathan since their arrival.

Without delay the man set off to do his boss's bidding.

"Papa, you said Claude was destined to become rich. Doesn't seem much like it if—"

"Violet, go to the refreshment table and get a slice of your mama's apple pie. She made it especially for you and, far as I can tell, you haven't had a bite of it." He directed Claude with his cigar. "You, too. We'll talk later."

A commotion erupted across the road.

A pack of Hollinger's men stumbled through the batwings of the saloon, headed up by the one who'd obviously been sent to fetch them. Haphazardly shooting in the air, they were unmistakably drunk.

Out of sheer habit, Nathan's hand went to the hilt of his gun.

"Lobo! Just the man I want to see," one of Hollinger's men called out to him across the square.

Nathan recognized him from an altercation in Hays City over a year ago. He'd been part of a gang that Hickok ran out of town for shooting up the dance hall when one of the girls refused his advances. The buffoon was obnoxious when he was stone sober, much less after a few whiskies in his belly.

Standing right where he was, Nathan watched Hollinger's men make their way over to him. Five in all. Six including Hollinger, who hung back but was still well within shooting range.

Jessa stepped up to his side, and he realized that the music had stopped as a growing number of spectators drew in to witness the confrontation.

"The great *El Lobo* is a fraud," the man slurred, barely

able to walk a straight line.

Nathan said nothing. There was no use in egging him on. Too many innocent people could get hurt. He cautioned Jessa to step back. When she refused, Lily pulled her over, safely out of harm's way.

"Folks say you're the fastest gun this side of the Mississippi." His tone was loud and mocking, still Nathan held his tongue. He'd made it a point to never draw on a man too inebriated to make it a fair fight. "I say you ain't nothin' but lucky. Draw, mister!"

Folks laughed when he couldn't figure out how to unlatch his holster.

A familiar irritation ran up Nathan's spine. "Go home, Slade. Sleep it off. Come back when you're in your right mind."

The gunman struggled to get his gun free.

Before any others from Hollinger's posse could lend a hand, gunfire shattered the night and confusion broke loose in every direction.

Nathan felt the bullet whiz past him, missing him by mere inches. On instinct, he drew his gun.

Women shrieked and men shouted while fleeing to find shelter.

Another shot fired from the same direction, yet Nathan saw no one else wielding a gun. He dropped to a crouch in case whoever was doing the shooting had a clear sight aimed at his chest.

As the smoke began to clear, DeLaney lay crumpled in the middle of the street, lifeless in a pool of blood.

"Someone get doc. Miss Valentine's been hit."

Alarm surged through him as he spun to see Lily lying on the ground.

Jessa snatched the shawl covering her shoulders and carefully pressed it against the bloodstain at Lily's side.

As if caught in a strange nightmare, Nathan watched Jessa lift her eyes to him. Stark agony shone in their amber depths.

Blatant accusation fell down her cheek in the form of a single tear.

Chapter Thirty-One

GHOSTLY VISIONS OF another day and time rippled across Jessa's memory. As a child of twelve, pushing past a throng of onlookers to witness her father cradling her mother in his arms on the floor of the hotel lobby. The haunting sound of his wailing was still known to visit her dreams.

Exactly as back then, she found herself hoping—praying aloud—that the doctor would get there in time. Panic choked the very air from her lungs. Helpless to stop the bleeding, she was unable to hold back a sob that tore through her chest as she pressed shaking fingers against the ragged wound.

This could not be happening again.

Her mother. Then her father. Now Lily.

One by one, those she loved were plucked from her by the careless act of another, and she was utterly powerless to stop it.

Her mother had been shot with a bullet intended for someone else.

This time when she looked up, it was Nathan's gray eyes that met hers through a haze of smoke, a condemning revolver held in his hand. He searched her face so intently she had to look away.

"Jessa." Lily's haggard whisper captured her full attention.

"No, Lily, don't talk. Doc's on his way." Her voice caught in her throat.

"Jessa, love, listen to me." Lily grabbed the puffed sleeve of Jessa's gown and pulled her down closer. "You must take Lobo. Hide him. Take him to your papa's cabin."

"No." Jessa tried to pull away.

Lily again pulled her nearer and motioned for her to lower her voice. "They will hang him, Jessa. Before a circuit judge ever makes it to town. They have eliminated the sheriff." She winced in pain and took in a sharp breath. "They will hang Lobo for DeLaney's death and no one in Santa Fe will dispute—"

"Stop talking. You need to save your strength." Jessa was not going to let another loved one slip through her fingers. Lobo could hide himself. She couldn't even bear to look at him. She suddenly became desperate. "Where is Doc Jennings?"

"Do it *now*, Jessa." Though weak, her tone was firm. Lily's determination was as strong as ever. "You made a commitment to the Agency to see this through. To protect your fellow operatives. I don't need your help. Lobo does. Go. Before Hollinger puts together a mob of vigilantes." Lily coughed as she pushed at Jessa and mouthed the words, "Do it!"

Drawing a frazzled breath, Jessa nodded, slowly at first, then more convincingly as Lily squeezed her hand. Swiping at a tear on her cheek, she glanced around at the worried faces of friends and neighbors but didn't spot Nathan anywhere among them.

Letting go of Lily's hand was one of the hardest things she'd ever had to do. Father Miguel seemed to sense it.

"Go, *mija*. Time is short. I will see that she is taken care of."

Rising, she heard someone call for volunteers to form a posse. A collective yell went up as men began to gather in front of Phillips General Store. Not stopping to listen, she could only hear bits and pieces of Hollinger's boisterous demand for justice. "Sheriff shot ... cold blood ... women and children not safe ... Lobo ... killer ... savage ... half-breed ..."

They had little time to waste. Making her way past the crowd, she searched the shadows for Nathan.

The Nathan she knew would never leave them to fend for themselves.

The Nathan she knew would never shoot anyone in cold blood for no reason.

What if the Nathan she knew was nothing but a figment of her desperate imagination to believe in him, that he was every bit as good inside as she'd convinced herself that he was.

What if he'd fooled them all?

Coming around the Jamison Hotel, she caught sight of a shadow walking slowly toward the family stables where his horse was kept. She didn't dare call out to him. Hitching her skirt, she ran toward the figure, hoping to goodness it was Nathan.

He didn't look over his shoulder when she caught up with him. He just kept walking.

"Lily said you need to come with me." She moved in front of him and stopped short. He would either run over her or hear her out. "They're organizing a search for you. We can leave out the back way to the cabin I told you about in Rayado Canyon. It's hidden from the trail but we need to leave as soon as possible."

He hesitated, but only for a minute, then motioned for

her to lead the way. Keeping to the shadows, they wound their way to the stables. Quickly, they saddled their horses and walked them out the back door of the stable. A roar of approval came from the street, sounding like every man in town had joined Hollinger's improvised posse.

Jessa swung up onto her horse as Nathan did the same. With a hard nudge, both sprang forward into the night. If they could make it past the foothills into the mountainous pass of the Sangre de Cristos, they had a fair chance of losing anyone who may try and follow.

They rode low next to their horses' manes, not daring to look back. She knew as soon as her pony began to fly with no prodding that someone was on their heels. Gunfire erupted behind them, still too far away to be any real threat.

Nathan yelled for her to stay low in her saddle.

They rounded the mouth of the canyon as rifle fire blasted from behind. Jessa prayed Nathan had not been hit. At the clip they were going, if either of them were knocked from their horse, they'd surely break their neck.

She gestured for him to follow. Reining in hard, she took a sharp turn to split off from the pass and head up the mining path instead.

Relief flooded over her when Nathan moved right along with her.

The path would take them around the base of the mountain. Not many knew about the old miner's path so, hopefully, those behind them would assume they'd taken the high road like most folks did. Hopefully, they wouldn't realize their mistake until morning.

They could be long gone in the opposite direction by then.

Up against a craggy drop, Jessa slowed to rest her horse.

Waiting, she listened to the stillness of the night before finally allowing herself to breathe once again. No shouting or gunshots trailed behind them, so she reined her pony to a halt, trying not to give much thought to where she was. She'd avoided this path ever since her father's disappearance. Even before. Just north of Elizabethtown, they were coming up on the very spot where his packhorse had been found.

In the light of the moon, the steep cliffs and dense trees resembled mangled beasts waiting for an unsuspecting prey.

A chill ran up her back.

Nathan pulled up next to her, taking in the murky shadows of the overgrown path. "We'll have to walk the horses. Can't chance them breaking a leg on the underbrush in the dark." He slid from his saddle and went to help her down. "We go as far as we can by foot, then find a place to make camp. By the time the sun comes up, we'll ride again."

Dozens of biting responses flew to the tip of her tongue, until Lily's pale face, pained and pleading, filled her thoughts. Jessa had made a promise to help protect him. There was no time to nurse a broken heart. Tonight, they'd have to work together to get him safely hidden away at the cabin.

Tomorrow, in the light of day, she'd face the truth. Broken heart or not, she would find the courage to walk away. She had no future with a man who had such little regard for human life.

Her hair fluttered in the pine-scented breeze. After the harrowing ride across the high plains, the curls Lily had taken such care to pin into perfect ringlets were nothing but a mess of waves falling across her shoulders and down her back. Her turquoise dress fared no better. Looking down, she became aware of a jagged rip in her skirt next to dark stains of blood where Lily had rested on her lap.

Lord, please let Lily be all right.

There was no way of telling how long they walked except that the enormous moon was now high in the sky, and the air had become cold. It felt like hours. Always, when she and Papa came to his cabin, they'd taken this path in full daylight and ridden the whole way. It took less than a day to get there from Cimarron. But on foot, and in the dark, continuously stumbling over Lord knows what, the trip was brutal.

Nathan silently walked ahead of her. Only speaking softly to his horse now and again when the animal hesitated to take another step on the uneven ground. Otherwise, they said nothing. Thick pine crunched beneath the horses' hooves, amplified ten-fold in the hushed woodlands.

She was weary, and her toes were numb in the new shoes squeezing her feet. Never had she missed her boots as much as she did tonight. Though her aching feet was nothing compared to the ache she felt deep in her soul. Soon, prayer was all that kept Jessa from falling apart. At times she prayed aloud when the distress was too much to hold in. But mostly, she just spoke to the Lord in private, knowing He'd promised to listen to every word.

She poured her heart out there in the woods.

They discussed Lily and her desperate need for healing. They talked about Bucky and how he needed more than she felt able to give him. The Lord caused her to examine her true motives for wanting to run off to do good in a far away land. Truth was, she just wanted to feel in control of her own life and not have everything laid out for her. It was selfish, really. There were friends, family, and neighbors right here that needed her, depended on her, and now that she knew the depth of the corruption they faced, she decided it would be unconscionable to leave them to deal with all of this alone. The Lord had practically handed her their greatest weapon, the newspaper. As long as the people had freedom to read the truth, and the means to act on it, there was still hope for this territory.

Then she prayed for Nathan. She prayed to know truth. She prayed for the courage to face that truth, whatever it may be.

Eventually, as she walked and prayed, a strange compassion began to settle over her for the man walking in front of her. His shoulders hunched as if the weight of the world was his alone to bear. She imagined the grief he must feel. She had no idea what had made him draw his gun, but she did know that Nathan Wolfe was not a cold-blooded killer. At some point, in the stillness of the night, that became increasingly clear.

The thicket of trees gave way to a clearing with a sloping riverbank that led down to Comanche Creek. "It's not much farther," she called out. "Across the creek, there's a keyhole pass in the cascade. It leads to a hidden meadow."

Nathan nodded and kept walking, leading the horses down to the water for a much-needed drink.

Jessa couldn't wait to dip her poor, pinched toes in the icy water, even if for just a second.

The water burbled over rocks and twigs and the horses eagerly bowed their heads to have a taste.

"I never shot." His confession was low and quiet.

Jessa glanced over to where he was hunched down next to the water.

"I was set up, Jessa. My gun never fired." He slowly

looked up at her. The moon's reflection glowed in his eyes. "You can believe me or don't. But I didn't kill DeLaney."

Jessa couldn't say the words she knew he needed to hear. She wanted to believe him. Had no reason not to other than the fact that DeLaney fell directly in front of him, and he was the only one standing there holding a gun.

Nathan stood and led the horses to higher ground.

Jessa sat on the bank, reliving the awful incident in her mind. As she removed her shoes, a noise downstream caused the hair to stand up on the back of her neck.

An eerie moan that sounded almost human.

Her gaze shot over to Nathan who was crouched beside the stream. He slowly rose, his eyes trained in the direction of the awful groan. Moonlight glinted off the water, but whatever had made the strange sound was hidden in the shadows.

Biting her bottom lip, Jessa squelched the chattering of her teeth. Fear threatened to overtake her, and she squeezed her eyes shut to send up one last prayer.

Removing a matchstick from his saddlebag, Nathan flicked it with his thumb, then touched the lit end to a handful of kindling sticks. "Stay here." He strode past her as the sound came again.

Not on his life.

Jessa fell in behind him, with both hands holding onto his waist. "What do you think it is?" She tried to whisper but her shaking voice wouldn't stay quiet. So many legends of ghosts and ghouls in these parts. Not that she'd ever believed them. But *something* was out there, and it didn't sound happy. "Sweet Lord in heaven, forgive us of every sin ..." There was no sense in not being prepared. Just in case.

Nathan paused and frowned over his shoulder at her. Had she said that one aloud?

Jessa put a finger to her lips to caution him to be quiet.

The moan became louder as they got closer. And a whimpering as if someone was crying.

"Someone's huddled on the bank below. I'm going down. They may have a gun so if you're coming, you stay behind me, is that clear?"

He was so sure of himself. She had no choice but to trust he knew what he was doing.

They half walked, half slid down the rocky bank. Once down at the bottom, she could see that the form was a woman wrapped in a Mexican blanket. From every indication, she was very much among the living.

Nathan approached her carefully, not wanting to startle her. "Ma'am, is there something we can help you with?"

The woman jumped and so did Jessa.

"Away! Away!" She scrambled toward the water, but realized she was trapped.

Nathan held out his hands to steady her. "No one will hurt you. Just making sure you don't need some help."

Jessa looked closer, trying to make out her features in the waning moonlight.

Again, the woman wailed and broke into sobs.

Stepping around Nathan, Jessa went to the woman's side who hid her face behind a veil of dark hair. "Are you lost?"

"I run away." The blanket fell from her head and Jessa got enough of a look at her face to see that one eye was swollen shut and her lip was split open and bleeding. "After I kill him."

Chapter Thirty-Two

"She'll need a doctor." After much coaxing, Nathan was finally permitted to have a look at the shoulder she so fiercely guarded. The bone in her upper arm jutted through the skin, completely snapped in two. If she didn't get it tended to, she'd lose the use of her arm.

"No!" The girl skittered away from him, her eyes darting around her as if seeking a place to escape.

"Hold up, now. I have no intentions of hurting you." He came to his feet and took a step back, putting space between them. "But we need to get you help. That arm is broken. It'll have to be set."

She was sobbing again.

"It's plain to see you're scared." Inching closer, Jessa spoke softly. "But I promise, we only want to help."

The girl kept her chin tucked to her chest but peered over as Jessa knelt beside her. "My name is Jessa. And this man is ... Nathan."

She looked down at her hands which were clasped in her lap rather than up at him.

"He may look scary, but I don't believe he'd knowingly hurt anyone unless his life depended on it."

Nathan stared down at her until she lifted her gaze. Even in the dim light of the fizzling flame, he saw sincere faith shining on her face.

Her admission hit him hard, right in the chest, nearly knocking the breath from him.

"We can take you to my papa's cabin and bring the doc up to see you."

"She can't wait that long." Nathan tried again to move toward them. "That arm needs to be seen by someone who knows what they're doing."

"No." She protested once more, just quieter this time.

"You said you killed whoever did this to you?" Jessa laid a hand on her knee. "So he won't be coming after you, right? Is there more than one that you're afraid of?"

The girl shook her head.

On closer inspection, Nathan figured she couldn't be more than sixteen, seventeen at most. Ute Indian if he were guessing, at least in part. But the way she was battered wasn't done by the Ute people. Even if she'd been shunned and turned out, she would not have been beaten to a pulp first. She would have been given bread for the journey, and her hair would have been lopped off as an outward symbol of her shame.

"I'll take you to Elizabethtown myself. And I give you my word, I won't let anyone hurt you." He went to fetch his horse before she could protest.

Jessa had a better chance of gaining the girl's trust, so he left her to it.

Heading back toward Cimarron was dangerous. With Hollinger out for blood, he wouldn't be safe setting foot in Elizabethtown. But there was no other choice. The girl needed a doctor and there wasn't one for miles in the other direction.

They'd managed to lose Hollinger's men a good while back. At the breakneck pace they'd been traveling, they could be clear to Taos by now. One thing's for certain, they'd never expect Nathan to double back and ride toward town.

Funny how things worked out.

The echo of Jessa's prayers, desperate pleas into the quiet night, still played over and over in his mind. Something about the way she just talked to the Almighty like He was right there walking beside her.

After a while, Nathan truly began to believe He was.

Even said a prayer or two of his own. And as they'd walked, a peace he couldn't describe began to wash over him until he no longer felt the need to fight this thing himself. Something or *someone* bigger had taken up the fight.

He concluded that from here on out, whatever happened, he'd go to the grave declaring his innocence. He remembered something the padre used to say about the truth would set a man free. Thing was, no one else was inclined to listen to the truth.

He hadn't shot anyone. Checked the chamber of his gun and no bullets had been discharged. But his argument was lost in the wind.

Hollinger wasted no time pointing a finger. Since Nathan had drawn out of pure instinct, he was the only one standing there holding a gun. Given his past, it was a foregone conclusion that he was a menace to the good folks of Cimarron.

It would take an act of Divine Providence to get him out of this one.

Except Providence had just worked it out so he had no other choice but to go right back to face a lynch mob. If he were traveling alone, he'd lay low and disappear awhile until the dust settled. But he was not alone.

"Not much further." Jessa led the girl up the bank to where Nathan had the horses ready to ride. "Mariposa can ride with me."

Nathan was impressed she'd gotten the girl's name.

Jessa climbed up onto her pony and settled in behind the saddle, then held her arms out for Nathan to place the girl in front of her.

Mariposa had quit crying, an unquestionable relief. He hadn't been keen on listening to that loud groaning all the way back to Elizabethtown. Careful as he could, he lifted her onto the saddle, and still she winced in pain. Whoever had done this had left her completely battered.

The sky took on an indigo glow as a thin sliver of orange and pink stretched across the horizon. If they took the main mountain pass, they'd be to Elizabethtown by daylight.

Nathan swung up into his saddle and turned his horse toward the rising sun. With a nudge, they headed off to see what else Providence had up His sleeve.

JESSA OPENED THE flume inside a rock fireplace and lit the half-burnt wood on the grate. Extending the rustic pothook, she hung a dented kettle over the fire to boil.

E-town was a good bit livelier than Cimarron. As the mining town closest to Copper Mining Company, which operated near Mt. Baldy, the population was twice the size and twice as rowdy. Even early in the morning, the bustle outside the doctor's rustic shack was boisterous with flatbeds rolling through town and carts loaded down with fresh supplies.

Hopefully, it would be a great deal easier to blend into the crowd.

She hadn't bothered to try and persuade Nathan to go on to the cabin without her. He knew as well as she did that showing his face anywhere within Hollinger's reach was asking for trouble. He was one misstep away from the hangman's noose. With Hollinger calling the shots, he'd be lucky if he even made it that far.

She swept a sleeve over her brow, squeezing her eyes shut against the burn of exhaustion. Her entire body ached from lack of sleep. The pounding in her head was the only thing keeping her going.

Chiding herself, she returned her focus on Mariposa. The girl needed her, even more than Nathan did at the moment. Since bringing her in, she'd clung to Jessa, desperate not to be left there alone. Through bits and pieces, she relayed a most peculiar story.

The doctor, a slight, stern man, persuaded the girl to drink something to calm her nerves. He made it plain that he wasn't keen on listening to anymore of her far-fetched tale. "Out of her head," was what he'd called her.

But Jessa knew better. Something deep in her gut said the girl was telling the truth. Mariposa understood English better than she could speak it, still Jessa was sure this young woman held a key piece to the puzzle. Somehow, they needed to get her to Lily.

Panic instantly reared its ugly head at the thought of Lily, and the possibility of her dear friend suffering at the brink of death's door. Just as she'd done dozens of times through the night, Jessa whispered a prayer until peace overshadowed the worry. Lily was in God's hands. The absolute safest place she could be.

Now if she could only believe for Nathan the same way. Trusting the Lord to keep him safe had just become harder. Hollinger's dominance was far-reaching. Those he couldn't intimidate, he bought off or squashed like vermin. As a result, half the men in the county were indebted to him. Those who weren't, were terrified to cross him.

Nathan stood outside the back door out of regard for Mariposa's privacy.

He proved to be the greatest wonder of all.

For months she hadn't let herself think of him as a famous gunman. He was too decent and seemingly good to be the Lobo depicted in dime novels. But last night, she'd come face-to-face with who he really was.

Or so she'd thought.

From what she knew—or thought she knew—of gunmen, they were solely interested in themselves. Thirsty for power, greedy for attention. None of them cared a thing about the sanctity of life.

But when it came right down to it, time and again she'd seen Nathan put a stranger's well-being far ahead of his own. He risked everything to see that Mariposa was taken care of, not once considering the enormous sacrifice he was making in exchange.

Thinking on it, she hadn't actually seen him pull the trigger. There was a chance that the shots which killed DeLaney and hit Lily had not come from his gun. But he was the only one holding one.

Jessa rubbed her temples. Her heavy thoughts were too much to sort right now.

Taking up a tattered towel, she pulled in the kettle of boiling water. After filling a metal basin, she carried the steaming bowl over to a crude cot where the doctor tended to Mariposa. She laid strips of cloth out on a side table beside him.

Stubbornly, the girl pushed at his hands, speaking in a native language that neither of them could interpret, pausing only to sob uncontrollably when they clearly didn't understand.

A good hour later, the arm was set. Mariposa drifted in and out of an unnatural sleep, blessedly unaware of the pain. No easy task as a couple of prospectors, pounding on the door all the while, insisted the doctor come to camp where a wave of dysentery was causing a meyham.

The doctor shrugged into his overcoat and took up his worn case. "I don't expect you two'll be here when I return. Keep the arm in a sling and change out the bandages once or twice until everything begins to heal over." He stopped at the door and half turned. "Just leave a half dollar in the payment box over yonder for the bandages." With that, he pulled open the door and was immediately tugged outside by those waiting for his attention.

A clink of coins sounded behind her. Nathan must have come in from the back and added to the slotted box at the doctor's request.

"She's sleeping." Jessa smoothed a dark lock of hair which had fallen over her blackened eye. "But the doctor says she'll be fine."

"Have you gotten any more out of her as to where she came from or who did this to her?"

Jessa shook her head. "She cries for her baby now and then and is terrified every time someone knocks on the door. Unless we find someone who can speak her language, we'll only get a very rough version of it."

Nathan leaned against the crude windowsill, watching the shuffle going on outside on the street. "Who does she think she's killed?"

"Her husband." Jessa came up beside him at the window, too tired to care when she laid her head against his arm. The comfort of having him next to her eased any doubt she might have harbored against him. "She said he killed her baby."

Without hesitation, he slipped his arm over her shoulders.

She knew he wasn't one given to needless affection. He wasn't coddled as a child, nor brought up with the kind of bear hugs and gentle kisses she'd known with her own parents. The nuns were careful about seeing to the children's physical needs, but somewhat lacking when it came to providing a tender touch.

"We can't stay here." Though his voice was quiet, she heard the weariness in his deepened tone. "We'll have to take her back to Cimarron. Now that the dust has cleared, it's time we get this thing settled. I refuse to run scared. Lily or Cade or even Allan Pinkerton can't fix this mess with Hollinger unless I go back and prove I wasn't the one who shot DeLaney."

Jessa didn't trust herself to speak as she imagined what would await him the moment he dared show his face back in Cimarron.

She held a hand to her lips as tears began to overflow down her cheeks.

Nathan wrapped his arms around her, pulling her into himself. Unable to stop a floodgate of emotion, she wept hard from a place deep down inside. A well of grief that had, over time, taken in more than she was able to contain.

With her face buried in Nathan's solid chest, she cried until she was completely spent.

Chapter Thirty-Three

JESSA FIT PERFECTLY in his arms.

He'd never had a woman care enough to cry over him before. Knowing her tears were a result of her raw, honest feelings warmed his heart like nothing ever had.

Jessa, whether she'd admit it or not, cared deeply about him. *Genuinely* cared. The knowledge lit a determination that quickly engulfed him head to foot.

He was ready to take on Hollinger and his whole worthless gang. Shoot, the entire greedy bunch of them if need be. Whatever it took, he'd clear his name and make the town safe from the likes of Jeb Hollinger. Then he'd find a place to settle down with this weepy, sassy, irresistibly headstrong daughter of Augus Jamison.

"He hurt my baby."

Both of them turned to see Mariposa trying to sit up, pushing at the cot with her good arm.

"Lay back." Jessa was at her side in an instant. "We're taking you to find help."

Scanning the street for any sign of Hollinger or his men, Nathan spotted a couple of gunslingers he recognized from Hays City. Clay Allison and Crockett. Last he knew, neither had gone to work for Hollinger, but that could've changed by now. Both had been known to lend their gun to the highest bidder in the past.

They entered the saloon, and Allison motioned for their traveling companion to wait for them outside. The man sank to a step near next to where the horses were tied. He had beaded boots and unadorned double braids of the Ute.

Nathan threw open the door. "Hold tight, Jessa."

"No! It's not safe." The door closed on her warning.

Nathan tugged his hat low and crossed the road. Ten minutes later, he crossed it again with the Ute, Allison, and Crockett all in tow. He watched Mariposa's reaction carefully when they entered. If she showed particular fear to any one of them, he'd send them on their way.

Instead, she pushed away from Jessa and rattled off a string of Ute as soon as she spotted them.

Jack was what they called the big Ute but Nathan was certain it wasn't the name he was born with. All Nathan was interested in was that he spoke Mariposa's language and could get by well enough with broken English.

Jack went to the cot and looked her over.

The others in the room let the two of them talk. The girl gestured wildly through a barrage of tears. Allison, a southern gentleman before the war, stood with his hat in his hand, showing deference to the young woman's plight. "Something's got her good and spun up. Don't cotton to a man layin' into a woman like that. Little thing like that, coulda killed her."

"He tried," Jack spoke up. "He kill her baby then beat her and lock in room. He drink whiskey until sleep. She stick knife in back and run."

"This varmint got a name? Where do we find him?" Allison was better known for his temper than for his gunfighting skills.

"Husband kill many." Jack crossed his arms, appearing

angry. "He has rest stop at foot of Palo Flechado Pass. Many men stop for food and bed. He steal, then kill when sleep."

Frowning, Allison looked at Mariposa. "He killed his own baby?"

"Because baby cry." Jack's stone-faced answer was barely controlled. "She was stolen from Ute as she get water at stream. Not yet marry age. Have too much shame to go back to her people."

Nathan watched Jessa sink down on the cot next to the girl. "Mariposa, you said you already know me." Taking the girl's hand she made her look up at her. "How do you know me?"

At first he thought the girl didn't understand when she just stared from one to another until her gaze returned to Jessa. Reaching into the pocket of her skirt, she pulled out a gold locket.

"No," Jessa whispered.

Nathan took the piece and opened it to reveal the photo of a lovely woman on one side and a more recent photo of Jessa and Bucky on the other. "I take it this belonged to Augus?"

"It was attached to his watch fob. That's my mother. He carries this everywhere he goes."

Mariposa spoke to Jack then shook her head at Jessa with sorrow in her dark eyes.

"She say she sorry. Her husband take your papa and kill him, too."

Jessa turned her back to go stand at the window.

Nathan kept an eye on her but gave her time alone to absorb what she'd just heard. There could be no more denying it.

"This scoundrel got a name?" Crockett asked again.

"Charles Kennedy," Mariposa answered, then passionately pleaded with Jack in Ute.

"If he alive, she fears he will find her. He work for bad men. She afraid you leave her here."

"We won't leave you, I promise. We will take you to Cimarron." Jessa turned back to them, swiping at the moisture on her cheeks. "There are people there who need to hear your story. We will make sure that you are protected." The barely controlled tone of her voice didn't fool him for a minute. She was hurting. Lord help Hollinger if Mariposa pointed him out. If she had proof that he had anything to do with Augus's untimely death there wouldn't be anything left to hand over to the Feds.

"Jack, go with her." Clay Allison, grabbed his rifle. "Me and Crockett will take a ride out to Moreno Valley and see what we find out at that travel station. I'll bringing a few boys with me, but don't count on us hauling Kennedy back alive."

"If you come across any evidence that what she's said is true, I'll need you to come to Cimarron and give a full account. There will be a hefty reward for both of you for your time." Nathan offered a hand and Allison was quick to accept.

"You betcha."

Jessa wrapped Mariposa up in her blanket. "Jack, do you have a horse?"

He nodded.

"Go get him and bring him around back. We'll meet you out there." Nathan poured dirt from a bucket on what was left of the fire then turned down the oil lamp on a table. "We can be to Cimarron in an hour's time. I'll send Jack on to the hotel with a note for Miss Ramsey. She can get it to Lily. We'll wait down in the pecan grove until we hear from her."

Jessa led Mariposa to the back door but turned just before turning the knob.

"Just in case ... I mean, if ..."

Nathan leaned down and poured the love he felt for her into a fiery kiss.

Her hand came to rest on the side of his face as she kissed him back.

They may not have tomorrow, but for today neither of them were going to leave any doubt as to the feelings that had grown between them. Just in case ...

Chapter Thirty-Four

THE TEN O'CLOCK stage arrived just as Jessa, Jack, and Mariposa pulled up to the back door of the ranch. Several passengers departed the coach, while others stood by waiting to embark. The stir provided just enough diversion that the trio slipped unnoticed behind the hotel to a side door of the Jamison main house.

Nathan had split off in hopes of finding Father Miguel at the parish church at the edge of town. Until they could get ahold of Cade, the church was the best place to provide sanctuary against Hollinger's gang.

Other than passing a couple of drifters on the road from Elizabethtown, the ride in had been quiet. Mostly because Mariposa slept, and Jack wasn't much for talking. No telling what had transpired since they'd left the night before. Sheriff DeLaney had been shot down, that much she knew. A vision of Lily's beautiful face, so pallid and faint, stole across her thoughts until Jessa was again compelled to pray.

Jessa signaled for Jack to slow his pony and to keep the animals as quiet as possible. Hollinger had posted a man outside the back door. He lounged with his back to them against the old oak, eating an apple with his rifle tucked under his arm.

She slid from her horse. Jack lifted Mariposa as Jessa tried the double doors at the end of the main hall. Thankfully, they were left unlatched. Hurrying inside, she motioned for Jack to follow and wait for her in the hall.

She went straight to the kitchen where the aroma of warm bread and venison stew struck her as soon as she stepped inside, causing her empty stomach to churn. Miss Ramsey was nowhere to be found.

Jessa grabbed a loaf of bread that was laid out to cool on a rack. Tearing off a small piece, she then scavenged through the icebox. A plate of leftover ham would do nicely.

Quickly, she returned to where Jack had set Mariposa on her feet back in the hallway. She steered them toward her father's study. Heavy black curtains were pulled shut against the afternoon sun, leaving the room dark and chilled. She didn't dare light a fire. The least amount of attention drawn to the ranch house, the better. More than one or two chimneys giving off smoke would be a telltale sign more than just Lily and Miss Ramsey were staying under this roof.

Jessa helped Mariposa over to the sofa, covering her there with a fur blanket to help keep her warm. Jack accepted the meat and bread with a nod, then ripped it to share with his Ute sister.

While lighting a single chamberstick, she explained that she would leave them for a bit to see about getting some help. Jack positioned himself in the chair beside Mariposa. "I keep watch."

Jessa lifted the tattered hem of her turquoise skirt and darted up the stairs.

Once on the upper landing, she went straight to Lily's room and didn't bother to knock. Inside, she found Lily propped up on several lacy pillows, elegantly reading a novel. A current of relief surged through her causing her knees to go weak.

If Lily was startled to see Jessa come bounding in looking as though she'd wrestled a pack of wild hogs, she didn't show it. She slightly inclined her head toward the window which was open to the terrace below where Hollinger's man reclined against the tree.

Moving to the bed, Jessa silently leaned down and kissed her godmother's cheek. "How are you?" Jessa whispered next to her ear.

"Been better." Lily managed a tired grin. "And been worse."

As Jessa pulled back, they looked each other over. Lily's shining black hair hung down in waves well past her shoulders. Dark smudges shadowed under her eyes not normally there. It showed in her face that her body had been through a horrible ordeal. Although her color was not fully returned, she wasn't as deathly pale as she'd been last night.

Lily reached for her hand. "Where is Nathan?"

"The last place they'd look for him, at the mission with Father Miguel."

Lily didn't look happy to hear it, but whether she was too tired to fuss about it or simply resigned to the inevitable, she said no more.

Jessa crossed the room to the secretary for paper and pen. Dipping into the ink, she scribbled out Mariposa's statement, revealing their reason for returning to Cimarron.

Without a word, she fluttered the paper to dry as she returned to where Lily lay in the bed.

Lily accepted the message and read with increasing interest. She tried to sit forward, but grimaced as she fell back against her pillows.

Jessa watched her closely as she took in the information.

When she came to the part where the Kennedy man had killed her father and buried his body under the porch, her gaze shot back to Jessa.

Tears clouded their eyes.

Reaching out for Jessa's hand, they sat together as silent tears fell for the man who had once been so full of life. No words were necessary. Their depth of sorrow was beyond expression.

Miss Ramsey entered the room with a tray of tea and cookies. She stopped short when she saw Jessa but regained her composure when Lily cautioned her not to utter her name.

"Thank you, Miss Ramsey. I could use a cup of tea just now," Lily sniffed into a handkerchief. "But I find the afternoon breeze a bit chilly. Would you mind terribly shutting the window for me?"

"Not at all. I will do that right now." Miss Ramsey, Lord bless her, obviously thought she needed to yell in order to be heard down below. "I will shut the window, so you are not cold." Obediently, she went to the window and made a show of pulling the glass down to the sill.

Lily smiled at Jessa. The housekeeper had many talents, but theater wasn't one of them.

As soon as the window was closed, Miss Ramsey turned to Jessa. "Where is Nathaniel?"

"He's at the mission with Father Miguel and the children. He's worn out but he's just fine. We have guests in the parlor. I've already seen that they have refreshments and they are resting. But she's been hurt pretty bad. Have Harv check them into a room and make sure her door stays locked at all times."

Miss Ramsey poured Lily a cup of tea and stirred in a

splash of cream. "I can take them to the lobby myself."

"No, take them the back way. No one else must know she's here. Please don't say a thing to anyone. Warn Harv, too. Her life, and Nathan's, depend on it. Where's Bucky?"

"Playing with Wheezer over by the general store. Hank assures me they are welcome to stay where he can keep an eye on them all day."

Jessa wiped her eyes with a napkin. "Oh my heavens, Lily. I'm so happy to see you. I can't believe you were actually shot!"

"Yes, I was, wasn't I?" She took a long sip. "And the sheriff was gunned down in cold blood. Your doctor removed two small lead balls from deep in my left side. From the back, I might add. Apparently, whoever shot DeLaney used a short-barreled shotgun. Since I was standing next to him at the time, I was sprayed with buckshot as well."

"So Nathan couldn't have done it." Jessa jumped to her feet. "He had a revolver in his hand, not a shotgun."

"Yes, and he was standing in front of DeLaney and me. Not behind."

"So, he's cleared!" Jessa started for the door.

"Not as far as Hollinger is concerned. He still maintains it was Nathan's gun that shot us both." Lily handed her cup to Miss Ramsey to return to the tray. "The doctor did his best to explain, but by the time he had finished with my bandages, Hollinger already had a posse formed. The man's sway is astounding."

"We have to stop him." Jessa lifted the paper she had written on earlier. "Mari all but named him as the man behind her husband killing spree. Fourteen innocent men who all happened to have opposed Jeb Hollinger at one time or another."

"Yes, love, but she has yet to point him out specifically. Even if she does, it will be the word of a hysterical woman against a prominent citizen who is backed by a very powerful political ring."

Frustration caused Jessa's head to pound so hard it made her dizzy. "Surely Cade or Mr. Pinkerton can do something." A sob caught in her throat. She could blame it on exhaustion, but the truth was the thought of Nathan in the hands of a lynch mob was terrifying. The only thing he was guilty of was spurning Hollinger's offer to head up his elite force of triggermen.

"Cade is on his way with Rangers and Army. But they are powerless to take action against Hollinger unless we gather some viable evidence to serve formal charges against him."

Jessa sank back into her chair. She felt helpless.

"Allan is doing everything he can to get the attention of Washington on this case. But we must provide the proof." Lily set her cup and saucer on the night table. "The newspaper man is running your story. We can add another one to include the doctor's testimony. That may be enough to help clear Nathan should it go before a judge. We just have to keep him out of Hollinger's noose before a judge gets a chance to hear the case."

"For the time being, we must prove that Jeb Hollinger is behind the many, many evils he is accused of. Then Cade can place him under federal arrest, and we can put an end to this."

Almost too much to take in.

"So, I will find the evidence." A quiet determination took over Jessa's tattered senses. Mainly because the alternative was impossible to consider. "I'll send a note to Nathan telling him what we've discussed. As soon as I have a bath, I'll check on Mari and Jack. Then, I'll take a quick nap before dinner."

Glancing over at Lily, she saw her raised brow. "And after that?"

"After that, I will to pay a visit to the Hollingers'."

"I'll set a kettle to warm your bath and see to your friends." Miss Ramsey scurried from the room.

"I see that Nathan has gotten to you." Lily spoke softly, her hand laying over Jessa's.

Pulling in a deep breath, Jessa didn't answer.

"You are acting from a woman's heart. A woman in love. Nothing I say can change your mind."

Without a word, Jessa simply nodded in agreement.

"Be careful, passion makes a person behave recklessly sometimes. I need you safe until we get this resolved. You mustn't react hastily. Even with the best of intentions, you could get the both of you killed."

"I won't sit back and do nothing either." Jessa cut her eyes to where Lily studied her from the bed. "For whatever reason, Mrs. Hollinger has shown that she's not above helping us with evidence against her husband. I plan to make her see how crucial it is that I get every bit of proof I can on him before he ends up killing another innocent man."

The door came open once again as Miss Ramsey came in with a stack of towels in her arms. "Your bath is waiting for you in your room."

Arlene sauntered in behind her. "I hear you two have had a rough night."

"I wouldn't disagree with that."

"Lily, I brought you these pillowcases you were admiring, Thought they might cheer you up a bit while you're healing."

Seeing the familiar needlework made Jessa study the woman's painted face a closer than she had in the past. Her eyes were lined in kohl so it was hard to tell what their natural shape might be. Her bone structure was pleasing as was the chiseled shape of her red lips. But that still wasn't enough to go by.

She was just tired enough to not care how it might sound to just come out and ask the town madame what she was dying to know.

Arlene sighed and turned from Lily to clap a hand at her rounded hip. "Is there something you want to ask me?"

Jessa made no apologies for her question. Nathan had a right to know. "Are you his mother?"

Miss Ramsey gasped as her hand flew to cover her mouth.

Arlene pursed her perfectly drawn lips and looked Jessa over. A shimmer of something Jessa couldn't read lit the lady's blue-gray eyes. "No."

Jessa wasn't sure what she had expected but disappointment flooded over her. She had been so close to uncovering the truth. She looked over at Miss Ramsey, but Arlene answered for her, too.

"Alice isn't either."

Before Jessa could ask anything more, Arlene shook her head and took on a serious expression. "So, you fancy yourself in love with him, do you? It's written all over your face, honey."

How did everyone know except her?

"Nothing to be ashamed of. He's a fine specimen of a

man." Her powdered face broke into a warm tooth-bearing grin. "Look, I'm sorry I can't tell you what you want to know. I've always said he has a right to know the truth. But it's not my place to be tellin' it."

Jessa stood to her feet, ready to go soak in a hot bath.

"But if it helps any, even though he's not mine, I've always loved him as if he were."

"Me, too," Miss Ramsey added from near the door.

"Don't you worry, honey. We'll have Jeb's head on a platter with an apple in his mouth before this is over with. Wait and see."

As she walked to the door, Jessa spoke her thoughts aloud, not really meaning to. "It will take a miracle."

"Good thing love has a way of bringing about miracles when you least expect it."

Lily's words played in her head throughout her bath and even as she drifted into an exhausted sleep.

Chapter Thirty-Five

"L ILY! LILY!"

Downstairs was suddenly in an uproar as the front door crashed open, and the boys raced in, all screaming at once. "Lily, they snatched up Lobo."

"Parading him around town with a rope around his neck." That one sounded like Jacob, but in her present state of grogginess it was hard to tell one voice from another.

"They say they're gonna hang him before nightfall!"

Jessa's eyes flew open.

With shaking hands, she pulled on a robe and dashed down the stairs. "Who has him?"

All three boys began to talk at once.

"That 'forcers gang."

"They took his hat. Put it on a donkey." Wheezer's chin quivered. "Lobo kicked one in the stomach so hard, he threw up on his boots."

"They're gonna kill him, Jessa. We gotta stop 'em!"

Her pulse throbbed in her ears. "We won't let that happen. Bucky, take the boys and go tell Harv at the hotel to send a wire to Mr. Pinkerton. Tell him Nathan's in dire need of help. Mark it urgent."

"Jee hoshaphat!" Wheezer's eyes looked enormous in his spectacles as he caught sight of Jack frowning in the doorway. "Gray Wolf sent down the braves."

"Hurry up, now. There's no time to waste." Jessa shooed them back out the door. "Miss Ramsey!" She started for the kitchen, but the housekeeper was already halfway down the stairs.

"What can we do?" Her hands were red from wringing them so hard. "They've shot the sheriff. There's no one in town who can stop Jeb from …" Plainly, she was unable to even say it.

"Make sure you personally bring Mari her meals. Keep the shutters closed tight in her room. No one must know she's here. We need her safe until Cade can hear what she has to say."

Miss Ramsey didn't question her for a moment. Jessa had learned long ago that if the housekeeper felt like someone had control of the reins, she was content to merely carry out her part.

"And what will you do, love?" Lily stood at the top of the landing, her bedclothes discarded for a pair of stylish riding britches with a matching short jacket trimmed in gold. Her hair flowed in massive waves around her shoulders. The only sign that she'd been badly wounded was the slight way she leaned on the bannister, favoring her left side.

She looked like a swashbuckling pirate. Or a wild *conquistadora* ready to take on an army.

"You should be in bed." Jessa ran up the stairs to change into her buckskins.

"As should you, and yet, here we are."

They met at the top step.

"I won't let them string him up, Lily. I'll find a way to free him."

Jessa was fully prepared for an argument, but instead,

Lily's lips quirked into almost a smile.

"That's my girl. Go get changed, and we shall form our plan."

※

"Soon as Mr. Hollinger gets here, you gonna dangle from that hangman's noose right out there in the dead center of town." The sleazy saddle bum in charge of guarding him pointed through the barred window to where a crude wooden gallows was being erected by Hollinger's men. "Your fancy boots will be just a' kickin' in the wind."

Nathan stood beside the small opening in the jail's only cell, eyeing the single post with a crude crossbeam projecting from the top.

"That is if Cyrus can find him. Rode off with a whole posse last night looking for you and that purty girl. Might be a couple of days 'fore the boys can locate him." He dug something from between his front teeth with a grimy thumb. "I imagine he wasn't expectin' you to come crawling back home so soon."

Nathan turned a cool glare at him for an instant before looking out the window once more.

"Looks like there's a gully washer comin' over them mountains. That might hold 'em up a mite." The petty guard tromped out of the cell and shut the cell door behind him. Nathan could see the keys hanging from his wrist on a round ring. Taking him down wouldn't even be a challenge. But the rest of Hollinger's men were camped out all over the back of the tiny rock building with at least four on guard outside the front door.

The early evening seemed darker as storm clouds were

indeed brewing to the west. They were likely in for a good rain after sundown. He could only hope they may seek cover without Hollinger there to tell them not to. Good thing this crew was too afraid to make a move without their boss giving the direct order. Any delay at this point would buy him more time.

As they had brought him in, he'd heard the boys screaming down the street like banshees. Jessa and Lily had surely been informed by now. Trouble was, there wasn't a whole lot they could do about it. Even if every man in town opposed him, Hollinger could do as he pleased and his cohorts in Santa Fe would back him up.

Why he'd decided that Nathan was such a threat still made no sense at all.

Something red caught his eye, and he straightened to better see the street. Miss Arlene, followed by four of her scantily dressed ladies sashayed down the street, headed for the jailhouse. As she passed a darkened alleyway, she paused just long enough to acknowledge someone, or some*thing*, hidden in the shadows.

Arlene and her gaggle of doxies continued on, but Nathan's attention was focused on the corridor between the bank and the general store. It wasn't long before he caught a glimpse of Jessa, crossing to the other side of the alley on quick, light steps.

What was she up to?

The door to the jailhouse flung open, and Arlene flounced inside pretty as you please. Through the open door, he could see she'd left her ladies to distract the front guards while she walked right in unhindered, carrying a basket with a checkered towel over the top.

"Prisoner cain't have no visitors."

"Good thing he's not a prisoner, and I'm not here to visit." At that, she pulled a Smith and Wesson revolver from her basket and held it on the petrified guard. "Let him out."

As he fumbled with the keys, Miss Ramsey staggered in behind her, swatting off two men trying to stop her. "Don't touch me, you brute." Before either of them could react, she lifted her skirt and kicked one soundly in the shin with a heavy Brogan boot. An odd choice for a lady, considering they looked to be about five sizes too big and made for Army combat.

The gunman's yelp was heard for blocks, and lights began popping on in every window in town, like a dried ear of corn over a campfire.

Just as his jailer swung the door open to his cell, Father Miguel pushed through, reading from a thick volume he held in both hands. "It's the law of the Territory! Every man or woman condemned to death has the right to speak to a priest." He hit the page with the back of his hand. "I am here to speak to this man on the authority of the Treaty of Guadalupe Hildalgo."

"Yes, it surely does," Miss Ramsey chimed in.

"That's clearly what the law says. Look it up yourself." Arlene nudged the man with the keys, then handed her gun over to Nathan. She pulled him down so only he could hear. "Sorry, I couldn't find any bullets."

"Bilk, you ignoramus!" One of Hollinger's big guns pushed past a brothel woman to get inside. "The rest of you, clear this place out."

A crowd gathered in the street to see what the commotion was all about. "You can't arrest Lobo or anyone else. Ain't none of you the law," a balding man with lambchop sideburns called out but was immediately silenced by a fist in his midsection.

The rest murmured among themselves, but none dared to confront the gang again.

If he was going to make a move in all of this mess, now was the time to do it. "Stand back." He shoved Bilk toward the door and held his gun trained on the man who considered himself in charge. As soon as he crossed the threshold of the jail, he yelled for the rest of them to drop their guns.

Nathan saw Jessa dash across the street, rushing toward the jail. "Jessa, stay where you are. Miss Arlene, I thank you for your help. But now you and your girls need to back away before you get hurt. Padre, you and Miss Ramsey, too."

"I'll take that." Hollinger came from somewhere behind them, followed by at least ten men. Every one of them had both guns drawn.

"Your gripe isn't with her, Hollinger, it's with me." He wasn't sure how long he could hold off twenty guns with only one of his own. One that held no bullets. But he was prepared to bluff as long as he needed to.

"Lock him back up. Post four guards inside and five at each end of the building. No one—and I mean *no one*—will be allowed to see this man until he hangs at dawn. That's when the real show begins. Bright and early."

Nathan was shoved back inside the jail as Hollinger continued to bully his men. "Make plenty of coffee. If I catch even one of you sleeping, you'll hang right beside him."

A dog barked endlessly in the distance.

Nathan turned for just an instant to try and find Jessa in the dispersing crowd.

She stood exactly where she'd been before. As their

gazes locked, he saw the battle she fought to be brave.

"I love you." Her words were whispered, but they hit his heart as fiercely as if she'd shouted it.

With another hard prod, he was forced inside, and the door slammed shut behind him.

And a crack of thunder split the air.

Chapter Thirty-Six

"CLEAR A PATH."
Head held high, Nathan's wide shoulders filled the doorway as he squinted into the first beaming rays of early daylight. With hands bound in front of him, he set foot outside the rock structure that served as Cimarron's jailhouse.

It would appear the whole town turned out to see Cimarron's most infamous son sacrificed to the greed and grandeur of Jeb Hollinger. As he passed them by, some stared in amazement while others openly wept. The evils of greed, and all it had taken from them, had finally won out. They could do nothing but stand by and watch.

Nathan's breath was visible in the crisp, rain-cleansed air. A sidelong glance revealed Hollinger gloating at the foot of the small platform. As usual, he surrounded himself with half a dozen men with rifles.

The two old codgers left their checkerboard to push through the crowd for a firsthand look. A hard shove sent Nathan parading out onto the center of town where Hollinger sent a satisfied sneer as he passed. The two steps of the platform creaked under Nathan's boots as he took them one by one to stand before a swinging noose. He scanned clusters of pained expressions dotting the street and boardwalks intently looking for Jessa's face in the crowd.

Almost frantic to gaze into those golden eyes one more time.

Hard as he searched, she was nowhere to be found. From the looks of it, neither Lily nor the Padre had shown up either. Just as well. Hollinger was determined to make his killing the biggest spectacle the county had seen thus far, warning of what was to be expected should anyone dare to cross him.

Nathan's attention lifted to a second-story verandah of the hotel. Jack reclined on the rail with his gun, lowering his hat in greeting. He pointed the end of his rifle toward a bluff just outside of town.

Narrowing an eye, Nathan viewed Gray Wolf atop his powerful black horse. To his right, a row of Apache warriors. To his left, Utes. The chief sat tall, arrayed for war in full-feather headdress with a decorated spear in his hand.

The knot in his stomach intensified. This didn't bode well for the citizens of Cimarron.

Hollinger wasn't about to back off, even if it meant the shedding of innocent blood. Neither would Gray Wolf. He had a score to settle for the murder of his son. Add the Utes out to avenge Mariposa's abduction and this had the makings of an all-out Indian war—with a town full of unsuspecting people caught in the crosshairs.

Nathan clenched his hands, twisting at the leather bindings. Raucous laughter surrounded him as he tugged to get free.

A desperate prayer rose from his very depths, stealing all other thought:

> *God, spare these folks. They don't deserve this.*
> *They've never been anything but kind.*
> *I have nothing meaningful to show for my life.*

But Jessa ... and the others ... save them. Don't let this be the end for them, too.

"Open your eyes. Face death like a man." The big gunman shoved Nathan beneath the heavy rope.

Suddenly, his would-be executioner let out a bellow as a lasso sailed over his head and tightened with a lurch around his middle. Hauling him from the platform to the ground, Nathan watched Jessa back her horse down the alley until the man jerking the end of her rope was strung tight as a fiddle. Bucky, Jacob, and Wheezer darted from the general store where they threw a flour sack over his head and hogtied his feet before Hollinger could even issue the order to shoot.

Miss Ramsey and Mr. Phillips waved them back into the general store as squeals of surprise from the onlookers created just the diversion he needed. Nathan vaulted over the side of the platform and made a dash for the hotel.

Hollinger barked orders while his gang of enforcers began running in circles.

The crowd scattered in every direction.

Lily met Nathan at the door and quickly pulled him inside. With one upward slice of her pearl-handled dagger, his bindings fell to the floor.

Harvey Chavez busted out a window in the lobby for the waitress named Conchita. She thanked him then rested a rifle taller than she was against the sill.

It would seem the whole town was prepared for a fight.

Peering out the door, he even saw the peace-loving padre wielding a tree limb, whacking down a gunman who aimed for Jessa. Then, crossing himself, he quickly stepped over the rubble.

Jessa made her way back to the hotel from the alley. Nathan tensed as he watched Hollinger turn and catch sight of her.

Nathan's hands went for his guns, but they weren't there. He started to go back out but was stopped by Lily's hand on his arm. "You stay here. We've got this."

Arlene made a dash to retrieve a fallen six-shooter in the middle of the road. Keeping her aim directly on Hollinger, she quickly moved to shield Jessa as they hurried toward the hotel.

Once they ducked inside, a cheer went up from the windows of every establishment in town where gun barrels protruded from each pane.

Nathan pulled her into his arms, and she clung to him.

Hollinger and his men were left alone in the street.

The embarrassed gunmen began to regather back to where Hollinger stood by the empty hangman's noose with nostrils flared in a murderous rage. "Lobo, you can't hide behind the women's skirts forever. You're outnumbered."

"What a ridiculous thing to say," Lily spoke next to Nathan. "The man obviously can't count. He's trying to goad you. We have enough to hold them off until Cade gets here with reinforcements."

"That could be days." Arlene crouched beside a window. "Even with a formal pardon, you know Jeb won't let this go. He'll find a way to get what he wants regardless of who he must trample down to get it. Cade best watch his own back."

"Major Matlock's wire said they were just about to cross the Texas border. Nearly a week ago," Harv Chavez provided from his position at the telegraph desk. "I'd say the storm last night might have slowed them down a bit, but they'll be here. You'll see."

"Lobo! You coward. Come out and fight like a man!" Hollinger sounded more and more desperate. No telling how long before he gave the command to storm the hotel.

"Lily, you know where I could get my hands on a spare Colt?"

"I do." He nearly missed Jessa's soft answer and still wasn't sure he'd heard her right. She left his embrace to go behind the registry desk. From somewhere down below, she lifted a double-barrel Coach gun. "It was Papa's."

As she held it out to him, he searched her face for a clue as to what she may be thinking in handing over the gun. He knew it went against everything in her. Yet still, she trusted it in his hands. "As long as you have men who want to kill you, you'll need to protect yourself."

"Incoming wire, Miss Valentine," Harv called across the lobby. "From the Territory's own Senator Crutchfield. This is a big day, yes siree!" The tapping continued as Harv read aloud as he took note. "Jeb Hollinger is commanded to surrender office. Court-appointed replacements to follow." He ripped the paper from its pad and brought it directly to Lily.

"Bold move by Santa Fe, wouldn't you say?" Lily reread the missive as if she needed reassurance that he had gotten it right.

"Hollinger's a loose cannon. With the evidence we have against him, he's more of a liability than he's worth." Nathan checked his weapon for ammunition then clicked the barrels back in place.

"The corporation will just replace him with another landgrabber hand-picked by the ring," Arlene remarked from the window.

Nathan peered out at Hollinger now in a huddle with his men out in the center of the road. Moving to another window, he looked to see if Gray Wolf still held vigil out on the northern ridge.

The line of warriors had not moved.

"I have it on good authority that Allan Pinkerton is working closely with congress to appoint more of their own hand-picked individuals to governing positions in the Territory." Lily refastened her white gloves. "Divide and conquer. The first step to dissolving this so-called ring."

"In the meantime, who will look out for the people here? Surely, they will replace DeLaney first," Jessa replied. "While they go through more underhanded bankers and land commissioners, trying to figure out who can be bought off and who can't, who's going to help these people stay on their land and keep their homes?"

A valid question in Nathan's estimation. One that would have to be addressed at some point.

Hollinger's men began to move toward the front of the hotel. His final grandstand was about to take place.

"Jessa, get away from the door." Nathan spoke quietly, motioning for her to take cover behind a sofa.

The heavy door rattled against a thickset fist as the big man pounded furiously. "Mr. Hollinger orders you to surrender. If you disregard his order, we will take over the hotel and leave no prisoners. Any bloodshed is on your hands, Lobo. You've been warned."

Arlene fired off three consecutive shots. He could see she'd aimed for a pickle barrel to put a good scare into them. She quirked a grin at Nathan. "Just a warning not to get too close."

"You've been advised, Lobo!" Hollinger yelled from the

street.

Nathan jumped back when a bullet splintered through the front door.

"We're coming in!"

"It really wouldn't be to your best interest," Lily called out through the broken window.

Hollinger gave another order to open fire. No immediate gunfire erupted. "Boss, there's women in there." The muffled complaint was met with a fatal gunshot at close range from Hollinger's own gun.

Jessa sprang from the protection of the sofa when Conchita dropped her weapon and scrambled to a corner. With an arm around her friend, she peered out the window. "He's killing his own men now."

"Rather impulsive," Lily observed with a frown. "The actions of a rabid animal before it throws itself from a cliff."

A move like that was downright reckless. These were paid killers, with more arrogance than brains. If they chose to turn on him, he'd never leave the street alive.

"I don't pay you to ask questions." Hollinger was still ranting, red in the face with fists clenched. "Get Lobo!"

Nathan spun and fired as a man broke through the side window.

The warning was taken.

Shots again fired at the door as it flung open, and three gunmen stormed inside.

Nathan pulled off a round of shots that managed to scare back their intruders. One fled back out the door while two ducked for cover. Unfortunately for one, he rolled headlong into Lily's blade which she pressed firmly against his chest. The weapon dropped from his hand as he pled for his life.

The other begged as well. Nathan swiveled to see Arlene holding Conchita's discarded rifle on the man.

"Jessa!"

The scream came from outside. Through the open door, Nathan saw the big gunman holding Bucky against his leg with the barrel of his gun at the boy's temple.

"Bucky." Jessa flew out the door before anyone could stop her.

Even as Nathan called out to her, his heart sank to his stomach.

It was a trap.

Chapter Thirty-Seven

Jessa bolted from the hotel at full speed. Seized by panic, she screamed for the killer to release her brother.

Several others appeared in the doorways of surrounding businesses with rifles in hand.

"This has gone too far." Mr. Phillips held his weapon against one shoulder, poised and ready to shoot. "Let the boy go!"

"He's just a child," Mrs. Apodaca called out from the bakery.

"Let him go!" Shouts rang out from every doorway.

"Stay back, or the kid dies." The big man sneered as he hauled Bucky up by the scruff of his neck.

Catching the look of wild terror in Bucky's eyes, Jessa skidded to a stop. She lowered her voice to speak directly to her brother. "Stay calm. Don't do anything rash. He won't dare hurt you or every law-abiding citizen in this town will fill him full of lead."

Without warning, Jessa was yanked from behind, the hard steel of a gun jabbed under her chin. "Drop your weapons! Every one of you. Lay them down." Jeb Hollinger's hot, foul breath on the back of her neck made her skin crawl.

On first instinct, she thought to go limp like Lily had taught her, but the man holding Bucky needed no encouragement to do him harm.

Spinning her to face the hotel, Hollinger tightened his grip. "Come out or I'll kill her, Lobo. You hear me? I'll kill her."

"You have been relieved of your duties as bank commissioner—effective immediately," Lily called from the entrance. Her voice sounded tight and furious. "Should anyone be harmed in any way by this stunt of yours, Senator Crutchfield will see that you suffer full consequences."

"Get out here, you worthless mongrel," Hollinger growled. His hand shook with fury.

"Jeb Hollinger had the sheriff killed," Mrs. Peterson called down from a second-story window of the bakery. "Two witnesses saw that big goon there pull the trigger of his rifle. He's the one who needs to be arrested!"

Shouts of agreement flooded into the street from every building.

Jessa spied movement on the hotel verandah as Jack crouched behind a railing, the end of his revolver trained on Hollinger.

"A coward move, Lobo. Leaving a woman to take your bullet." Hollinger jerked her jaw with his hand. "Take a good look at her face. Remember her disgust for you, knowing she's about to die because you aren't man enough to stand up for yourself."

Nathan stepped from the doorway of the hotel, hands showing he held no weapon.

No! Jessa wanted to cry out to him, but her jaw was held tight. Hollinger was desperate, baiting him to come out unarmed. Squeezing her eyes shut, she prayed he wouldn't make any sudden moves.

"Face me without a woman between us." Nathan's demand seethed with anger. "One on one, Hollinger. You and me."

"Ah, but there will always be a woman between us." He ran cold fingers down Jessa's face and farther down the side of her neck until she shivered with revulsion. "How would you feel if she were taken from you? Pawed and ravaged by a filthy beast."

Panic slithered over her at his touch.

Behind her, the big man gave a pained howl. From the corner of her eye she saw Bucky skitter to the boardwalk, throwing his arms around Miss Ramsey's waist.

Nathan started toward Jessa, but Lily was at his side, holding him back with a hand. "No need to respond. That's exactly what he's hoping for."

"So young and lovely. Like another I once knew." Hollinger seemed oblivious to anything else around him as he mindlessly continued his taunt with his face pressed against her temple. "Never mine. Never did I win her heart."

Feral rage flashed in Nathan's eye.

Jessa was frantic. She had to do something before Hollinger pushed him too far. With an arm, she shoved his trigger hand away from her chin. Turning her head, she brought the heel of her boot down hard against his shin.

Gunfire split the air.

Her breath froze in her throat as she spun in search of Nathan. Momentarily numbed by shock, she finally broke free, rushing to his side. The click of revolvers sounded all around as Hollinger's men took aim at them both.

Nathan's fist clenched as a muscle worked his jaw.

Jeb Hollinger remained in the same spot holding his upper arm as blood oozed from between his fingers. "Shoot them! And this time don't miss."

"This ends here, Jeb." A lady in a fashionable day dress walked toward them. Her features were shadowed from beneath by a matching hat with curled plumes. The pistol held with both of her hands was aimed directly at Jeb Hollinger's chest. "I won't let you hurt anymore of those I love."

His laugh was ugly. "Ah, yes. The many loves of Mrs. Jeb Hollinger."

Mrs. Hollinger?

"Alaina Ramsey Hollinger," she corrected.

The enormity of her revelation took a minute to sink in. Mrs. Hollinger was Nathan's mother.

Looking up at Nathan, Jessa saw that he was clearly as taken aback as she was.

"Didn't I warn you, Alaina? The day the judge paid me to take you off his hands, I swore I'd find your illegitimate whelp and make him pay for his father's sins." Hollinger ground out his contempt as he took slow, menacing steps toward his wife. "I vowed he would die for everything taken from me. You think they don't know what you are in Santa Fe? You think they don't whisper about you in the finest drawing rooms? You don't care that my *legitimate* daughter will never be accepted in their circles because her mother is a—"

Just as he reached her, hands poised to choke, Hollinger contorted violently. His eyes bulged as his face turned crimson, and his hand fell limp at his side. Slumping forward, he fell face down in the dirt.

A red-feathered arrow jutted from between his shoulder blades.

At the end of the main road, Gray Wolf lowered his

bow as the rest of his war party fanned out behind him. At least a hundred of them armed with bows and spears.

Jessa was quick to notice that everything about the Apache chief was commanding. The way he sat atop his horse, powerful and unyielding, his black hair falling well below his strong arms. The dark glint in his narrowed gaze, so much like his son standing next to her.

No one moved for a full minute.

If the chief chose to take revenge on the rest of the town, there wasn't much they could do about it. They would be in for a bloodbath. Jessa pled for Divine assistance in keeping both sides in check.

Finally, he presented his hand, flat and palm down, toward Mrs. Hollinger. He brought two fingers to point from his broad chest and then to her. A symbolic gesture of some kind.

Clearly dazed, she hesitated for just a moment before returning the gesture with tears shimmering in her gray eyes.

His features were set in a hard line, except when he regarded a woman who unmistakably held a piece of his heart. Without a word, he wheeled his horse and the entire line turned their mounts with him. They kicked up dirt in a fast gallop, and then they were gone.

Nathan caught her watching him and kissed the top of her head.

Folks peering from every window gradually emerged from their homes and businesses. A few gathered around Jeb Hollinger's body, shaking their heads and relaying events as they had seen them from their various vantage points.

Without their boss, Hollinger's men holstered their guns. Throwing nervous glances at the citizens of Cimarron, they made quick steps toward their horses. Not one person tried to stop them as they rode fast out of town. Odds were Colfax County would see them again.

"Cade will be sorry he missed the excitement." Lily was business as usual. "He had a federal warrant for Hollinger's arrest on Mariposa's testimony. For now, at least, these good people's homes are safe from forcible eviction." She disappeared again into the hotel lobby.

A tangible current of relief ran through the gathering of local landowners.

Chapter Thirty-Eight

A FULL THREE days passed before Nathan returned to Cimarron.

With all that transpired, he'd needed time away to clear his head. Away from the hubbub of Hollinger's standoff. Away from Alaina Hollinger and the soul-churning emotion her gray gaze stirred every time she looked at him.

What's more, until he could come up with a plan to make Jessa a permanent fixture in his life, he needed to steer clear of her, too.

He'd offered Father Miguel a hand in getting the children settled back in at the mission. A perfect excuse to put some distance between what he'd learned about his past and the gnawing uncertainties of his future.

Thankfully, the Padre gave him plenty of time to mull it over.

Finally last night, before a blazing campfire, the two of them hashed it all out well into the wee hours of the morning. All that weighed heavy on Nathan's mind was laid open right there under the stars. He'd admitted the shame of every promise he'd broken over the years. They discussed the possibility that dreams were never truly lost.

Sometime before they'd called it a night, they'd even concluded that Nathan would be utterly foolish to underestimate Jessa's vast ability to love. By assuming she was incapable of loving a wretch like himself, he was denying her the privilege of making up her own mind on the matter. The Padre had a good point. You'd never meet anyone more devoted to the people she believed in.

Just like the old days, the profound wisdom of the small parish priest lifted and restored him. He had a way of speaking directly to the heart of things. Nathan could only guess it came from spending so much time in deliberate prayer. The Good Lord must figure anyone who stops to ask Him the best course to take can be trusted to guide others down the right path as well.

His thoughts immediately turned to the way Jessa had frequent, out loud talks with the Almighty.

That night they'd walked together through the woods, listening to her pour her heart out in desperate petition, changed him somehow. She hadn't recited a memorized prayer. Not that anything was wrong with the way he'd been taught to connect with heaven. Growing up, the Padre's common prayers never failed to bring him peace.

But Jessa came right out and spoke to God like He was walking right there alongside them. The deeper they traversed into the woods, a peculiar feeling had fallen over him. Nathan had the distinct feeling that the Lord not only walked right there with them, but He listened to every word.

Still brought a sense of awe just thinking about it.

When he relayed the strange event to the Padre, the priest explained that communicating with the true and living God is our greatest privilege. He can always be found in our everyday tasks. "We must seek Him there, *mijo*."

Although, it was a typical Padre answer, this time it had made perfect sense.

By the time they'd turned in, Nathan was at peace. Not sure if it was because of the Padre's words or maybe it came from having spoken at length about his own deep misgivings. But this morning, his future didn't feel near as bleak as it had six months ago.

"Nathaniel, pull over, *por favor*. I will not be long."

They'd started out for the hotel early this morning after Lily sent a note saying Cade and his company of Rangers had arrived. They'd taken statements from just about everyone in town except Nathan. They needed him to come in so they could officially bring a close to this case.

Father Miguel brought the old buckboard to take back a few supplies from the general store. Nathan rode his horse beside the wagon, enjoying an abundance of clear blue skies and easy conversation.

As they pulled off, he could see the Padre's brows were drawn as he looked out across the road at the graveyard. Following his line of vision, Nathan spotted a female in black standing over a fresh grave marked by a single wooden cross.

As they neared, he recognized Mrs. Hollinger.

Nathan paused, allowing the Padre time to speak with her alone at what he could only assume was her husband's final resting place. Her small shoulders were bent, and her head reverently bowed. Oddly, his heart went out to her. In a matter of moments, she'd been left a widow. All her past sins were laid bare in front of everyone in town, sure to be the topic at every dinner table from now 'til something else scandalous came along to take its place.

Lord knows, that daughter of hers would be no comfort.

Mercifully, she had her sisters. The three of them proved they'd take on the whole county if one of them was in trouble. He certainly wouldn't want to cross them.

Nathan watched them talk quietly for several minutes, turning every now and again to look over at him sitting atop his horse. She was smaller than the other two sisters. Fine-boned but sturdy. Her hair was graying at the temples but light-colored and neatly pulled back into a bun at the back of her neck. He supposed most would consider her attractive, but since the first time he'd met her, the thing that stood out most about the lady was the kind way she treated folks.

As a person spoke, she gave the distinct impression that she really cared about what they had to say. Not just Nathan, but he'd watched her do the same with Lily, and Jessa, and even now with Father Miguel.

The fact that she'd bothered to bring flowers to the grave of a man like Hollinger, who never seemed to give her the time of day unless he was berating her like she was one of his hired men. The woman deserved sainthood if you asked him, just for living with the man as long as she had.

Once they left the graveyard, she returned to her surrey with the fringed canopy while Father Miguel ambled up to the road where Nathan waited beside the buckboard.

"Tu madre would like a private word with you, *mijo*." Slightly out of breath, he climbed up to the bench and took up the reins. "Leave your horse. I will wait here."

When the Padre took on that no-nonsense tone, Nathan didn't bother to argue. Besides, this meeting was a long time coming. No more avoiding the inevitable. The woman who'd given him life wasn't some faceless image in the back of his mind anymore. She was a living, breathing human whose heart had already taken quite a beating the past several days. He didn't intend to add any more to it.

"Ma'am." He approached her small carriage, and she shifted to make room beside her on the tufted leather seat.

"Thank you for seeing me, Nathaniel. Please join me."

As he climbed in, she steadied her horses with a firm hand on the reins.

"I won't take too much of your time. I know you have somewhere to be." She was much more composed than she had been that day in the street. Certainly understandable given the circumstances. Still, it was good to see her smiling again. "I have an offer I'd like to make to you."

He was intrigued but not ready for any type of commitments just yet.

"With Jeb's demise, I'm left with an enormous number of responsibilities. The bank, of course, will find his replacement. But his shares in the land corporation fall to me. We have the grain mill in Cimarron along with a spread with forty head of cattle just north of Elizabethtown. We also have a townhome in Santa Fe, and Jeb recently acquired a lovely home in Denver."

Nathan wasn't sure why she was giving him the rundown of Jeb Hollinger's assets, but out of consideration he let her talk.

"As you know, Violet has gone to college and will, I'm certain, choose to remain with Jeb's sister to attend society parties at every holiday until she finds a husband." The lady scanned the horizon as if searching for the right words. "I would very much like for you to stay in Cimarron, Nathaniel. I feel there is so much we need to catch up on. So much time lost. So many things yet to say." A side glance seemed to remind her that he was still there, listening to every word. She gave a shrug with an embarrassed smile. "I'd like for the ranch to go to you."

Whatever he'd thought she might say, that was not it.

"I realize this is a decision you'll want to think over. The house is only five years old. The cattle can be kept or sold off. There are a hundred acres to do with as you please."

Nathan readjusted his hat, mostly so she wouldn't see the stunned look on his face.

A hundred acres of prime land. Who wouldn't be interested in such an outlandish offer? But what, exactly, was she looking for in return? "Why?" It's all he could think to ask.

"I-I'm afraid I'm bungling this apology into an awful mess." The way she wrung her hands reminded him of the Ramsey woman. "Perhaps I should start over."

"You don't owe me an apology." Nathan stilled her hands by putting his hand over them. "I was never looking for an apology. I read your letter. I recognized a long time ago that you were acting on what you thought was best. No one's to blame." He fought that old rise of frustration that made him want to walk away. He would see this out once and for all. They both needed to be free. Until they met this thing head on, regret would continue to tear them to shreds.

"But I must. I need you to hear me." She turned her hand to clasp onto his. "I was so very young. So very afraid. And desperate to do whatever I could to keep you from harm. I truly believe God pointed me to the mission." Her voice suddenly caught on a sob causing Nathan to look closer at her gray eyes filling with tears. "Walking away from you that day…" She shook her head, seemingly unable to go on.

He slid an arm over her shoulders.

He'd always tried to imagine his mother in his mind's eye. She was tall like him. Stern and sour like Sister Helena.

Too busy to be bothered.

Nothing like the lady sitting next to him.

"I had a good upbringing. The Padre made good on his promise to you."

"Father Miguel has been a godsend. I owe him an immense debt of gratitude." Moisture shone on her cheeks as she searched her bag for something but came up empty.

Nathan pulled his handkerchief from his vest pocket and handed it to her.

With a tearful smile, she laid her head against his shoulder for a brief moment and dried her eyes. "Arlene made this for my sixteenth birthday. I thought it was the most beautiful handiwork I'd ever seen." She gave him a weak smile. "It was all I had to leave with you."

"It's always meant something special to me."

"You know, I used to sit down the road from your mission and paint you as you played in the side yard. You had no way of knowing it. Father Miguel always kept my secret. But I was never far. I saw the scrapes and bruises from playing stickball. I saw the many, many rocks you skimmed across the river whenever you needed time alone to think something through. I prayed for you every night. And while I couldn't openly be a part of your life, I was determined not to miss a thing."

"I would have kept your secret." He wasn't sure why he'd said it, but he wasn't entirely sorry that he had. What he would have given to have had a friend like Mrs. Hollinger as a kid. "Even if you never told me who you were to me, I would have liked to have known you."

She sat up in her seat, away from the comfort of his arm. "My father was adamant that you would hold no claim to our family. Which is ludicrous in my book. You had every right to anything I had. But he was a hard man." On a ragged sigh, she worried the cloth between her hands in her lap. "He sold me off to Jeb Hollinger when I was eighteen, and Jeb was even more eaten up with contempt for you than Papa was."

She threw a glance over at him. "I needn't say why. Even as a child you were so like Gray Wolf. Strong, strapping, intense and so beautifully handsome."

He looked out over the mesa, oddly enjoying her tender estimation of him. Made him feel warm inside.

"So, there you have it. The land belonged to my father and to his father before him and was deeded to Jeb when we married. As far as Arlene, Alice and I are concerned, it rightfully belongs to you now."

He didn't know what to say. Having a spread of his own was a lifelong dream. It wasn't like he was taking anything of Jeb Hollinger's. This was land that had belonged to his mother's family for generations.

His mother.

His family.

Chapter Thirty-Nine

NATHAN ENTERED THE kitchen just as Cade Matlock held out his cup for Miss Ramsey to refill.

"From the looks of it, Clay Allison already took care of the situation. Found Kennedy dangling from an elm tree about twenty feet away from the house. Everything was just as Mariposa, here, described. The body of a child was found near the hearth. Nearly ten thousand dollars found in a cigar box under the bed. Same brand Hollinger favored I might add."

"Allan received clearance for the money to be returned to Mariposa." Lily crossed the kitchen to sit beside the Ute girl on a bench near the backdoor. "We have no hard evidence the money was stolen, or where to return it even if it was. Mariposa, on the other hand can use it to rebuild her life wherever she so chooses."

Nathan was glad to see the girl hadn't forgotten how to smile. She looked a whole lot different than she had the last time he'd seen her. Hair clean and brushed to an ebony shine. She was dressed in blue calico with a matching homemade sling to hold her arm. Most likely Jessa's doing with help from Lily and maybe even Miss Ramsey. Thus far, her sixteen years had been a nightmare. It was about time something good happened for her.

"Lobo, about time you got here." Cade set aside his cup

to come shake Nathan's hand with his customary slap on the back. "I hear you dodged the noose with minutes to spare."

"I had help." Nathan grinned looking around as he stepped farther into the room. Jessa was nowhere to be found. "You came alone?"

"Brought a unit of Rangers with me, figuring on making some arrests. Turns out, we weren't needed after all. You two took care of things just fine without me."

"Not just us. Jessa handled more than her fair share." Again, Nathan looked around for Jessa. "Where is she?"

"She's gone to fetch Bucky and bring Miss Peterson a rhubarb pie," Lily provided with the quirk of a grin. "Seems the dear woman's cat is suddenly purple."

Miss Ramsey handed Nathan a steaming cup of coffee. "She'll be back shortly. Have you had breakfast?"

"Yes, ma'am. Ate before we left." He never was one to turn down a good cup of coffee though.

"I'd like it very much if you'd call me Aunt Alice." Her face immediately turned crimson when Nathan's cup froze halfway to his lips. "I mean, only if you want to, of course. I don't mind ma'am at all if that's what you prefer."

Nathan passed a look to Father Miguel, hoping for a little graceful assistance. "I'd be pleased, but all this is going to take some getting used to."

"Such a lovely gesture, dear lady. Would you care to come along with me to the general store? I must replenish our supplies, and I would enjoy the company." The Padre didn't disappoint.

"Certainly, Father. We can talk later, Nathaniel." She gave him a sweet smile before the two of them left down the hall.

Nathan moved to take a seat at the table facing Cade.

"Like I was saying, Charles Kennedy's place up at Palo Flechado Pass provided all the evidence we needed. Letters and bank drafts from Hollinger himself made out to Kennedy in exchange for eliminating anyone who got in the way of Hollinger and his buddies from the land corporation. Kennedy lured them into his travel stop, and they were never heard from again."

"Anything on Augus?" For Jessa's sake, Nathan had hoped they'd find something.

With a heavy sigh, Cade settled back into his chair. "His body was laid out underneath the floorboards of the porch. Along with at least ten more in the cellar. Most were already reduced to bones. I don't know how anyone within a quarter mile of the place didn't notice the stench. Augus must've been onto him. He never was one to seek out a travel stop."

Nathan's gaze rose to where Jack stood in the corner with arms crossed. Obviously leery of the white man, though he refused to leave Mariposa alone. "Jack, you planning on taking Mariposa home to your people?"

Jack shook his head. "I am her people now. We will make a home with the Pueblos, who accept all. There, I will build her a safe place. We will live together."

Mariposa rose to stand beside him. They spoke quietly in the Ute language before Jack addressed Cade. "She asks if she is free to go. She has told all she knows. She is ready now to forget."

"Because of your bravery, countless lives have been spared." Lily handed them an envelope as she walked with them to the door. "I do hope you will accept our gratitude and know we wish you all the best, love."

"Where do you go from here, Lobo?" Cade sat forward and rested his forearms on the table, as it was just the two of them left in the room. "I can't imagine you'd be wanting to head back up to Kansas. Not while Jessa's down here anyhow."

"I'm not leaving without her." Nathan had to grin at the teasing note in his voice.

"So happens, I have direction from the US Attorney General to try and entice you to stay in the Territory."

An odd request. Especially considering he'd never had any dealings with whoever the Attorney General was. "Another warrant for my arrest?"

Cade's hoot of laughter caught the attention of Lily as soon as she came back into the kitchen. "I can't tell you how glad I am to see you two in such good humor."

"I was just getting around to telling him about the offer from the new Department of Justice."

"Quite an honor, really," she agreed.

"You bet it is. I have men who'd give their eye teeth for such an opportunity."

"Care to fill me in?" Nathan looked from one to the other letting them have their fun. "Or you want me to guess?"

From behind Cade, Nathan spotted Jessa who must've slipped in the back door.

"They want you to head up law duties for the entire northern part of the Territory." Though she was dressed in a black mourning dress, her smile was brilliant as she moved toward him. "Based out of Cimarron as a US Marshal. Looks like my prayers were answered after all."

Although it had only been three days since he'd last seen her, he pulled her into his arms and held on tight as if a part of himself had been missing without her. Breathing deep from the flowery scent of her hair, he gave no thought to anyone else in the room.

"I missed you," she whispered against his chest.

"Same." He placed a kiss at her temple.

Without her, his life had been dark and hopelessly grim. Now that this bundle of sunshine had warmed his heart, he'd do whatever he could to make sure she stayed beside him forever. He couldn't imagine a future without her.

In a way, he had to admit his own prayers had been answered, too. When words aren't enough, God reads a man's innermost longings and provides the very thing he didn't even know to ask for.

With eyes closed, Nathan was overcome with a moment of pure gratitude as he gave a nod of thanks to the Almighty.

"Jessa, I believe you have a bit of news." Lily stood back, leaning against the counter with her arms folded across her chest. "I'd love to hear what you've decided to do about it."

Jessa didn't immediately respond, content to stay still wrapped in the security of Nathan's arms. Considering his hold tightened, she'd say he wasn't ready to let her go either.

Now that he was back, she planned to keep him here with her where he belonged.

"You reckon they want us to leave?" Cade chuckled from his place at the table.

Reluctantly, Jessa took a step back, taking Nathan's hand and leading him over to the table. "You remember that newspaper man? The one from the Washington paper who came to town looking to put a face to their anonymous contributor?"

"I met the man." Nathan chose to keep her hand nestled inside of his atop the table as they each took a seat. "You think he ever put two and two together?"

"He was sent by his newspaper bosses to validate the outrageous charges that were coming out against the corporation. We were putting out some heavy allegations against high-powered political figures in Santa Fe. Unless they could get someone to admit to having firsthand knowledge of the situation, they were going to have to put Papa's column on hold. All that work he did, and all the danger Mrs. Hollinger put herself in to get us evidence would have been for nothing."

"So, you told him," Nathan finished her thought.

"I did."

Lily joined them at the table. "And because she did, the Washington Star has offered to syndicate her column with a front-page exclusive if she will allow them to use her name. With her latest entry telling the sensational events of finding Augus's body and all that Charles Kennedy's widow had to tell. Jessa will become the premier source of news from the Territory."

Jessa searched Nathan's face to gauge how he was taking all this. He kept his gaze centered on the cup of coffee in front of him but made no visible indication he had an opinion one way or the other.

"You and I both know, things around here are only going to get worse before they get better. Now that you all turned over the hornet's nest, they'll be out for blood." Cade took a silver star from his vest pocket and tossed it to the table. "You'll need the backing of the whole United States judicial system to keep folks around here safe."

Lily was quick to agree. "And knowing that every misdeed they commit stands a chance of being reported in every newspaper west of Abilene will certainly give them pause next time they decide to swindle the folks in Colfax County."

"Having an advocate in the two of you, I'm guessing the tribes will be treated a mite fairer than they are used to as well. These Indian agents can start towing the line or be replaced. Jessa's articles can see to that." Cade tossed a wink at her.

"Never live with regrets, love. You've had your chance to explore the world. There's plenty of time for that." Lily reached over and placed her hand on top of both of theirs. "For now, every road leading to a purposeful, fulfilling life is leading to these beautiful hills of your home. As much as I've loved working with you, I believe with all my heart your adventure is just beginning right here in Cimarron. You are deeply loved by some of the finest of people I've ever met. I daresay, they've come to depend on you both."

What Lily said made perfect sense. Since the final realization that her papa really was never coming home, Jessa had looked around her with a whole new perspective. This is where her mother and father were now laid to rest. All they'd worked so hard for, all the people they'd considered family, was worth fighting for. Life in the Territory was never considered an easy one, but it took a special breed to love it, embrace it, and ultimately make it better to pass on to the next generation.

"I'm in." Jessa gave Nathan's hand a squeeze.

His gray gaze rose to meet hers. So bold, yet so gentle.

"Me, too. On one condition." He came to his feet, and this time when he reached into his vest pocket, instead of pulling out his mama's handkerchief, he held something gold and shiny. Bracing one hand on the table, he leaned down to kiss her forehead. "You'd do me the honor—"

"Down on your knee, Lobo. If you're gonna do it, do it right." Cade moved to watch from the other side of the kitchen. Lily joined him there.

Jessa still wasn't a hundred percent certain what she thought was about to happen, really was about to happen.

With a look of consternation, Nathan dropped to one knee in front of her. "Listen, Jessa, I love you. That's about all I know for certain right now. I don't want to ever be without you, and the surest way I know how to make sure that doesn't happen is to make you my wife. Where I go, you go. Where I stay, you stay. We're in it together forever from this day on."

"Ask her," Lily prompted.

"Yes!" Jessa didn't need any more asking than he'd already done. Hopping to her feet, she threw her arms around his neck. Nathan stood and spun her as a cheer went up from every doorway and window. From the looks of it nearly everyone in town had turned out to witness Lobo pop the question to Jessa Jamison.

"Absolutely, yes." She spoke loudly next to his ear to be heard over the excitement. "I loved you first, remember?"

"Here's to a lifetime of answered prayers." With a grin, he set her down on her feet and kissed her like they were the only ones in the room.

"See, Wheezer," Bucky's voice carried over the noise. "I told you she liked him."

"Jee hoshaphat!"

Epilogue

*Chicago
11 December 1870*

"A Scottish blessing for the happy couple." Allan Pinkerton raised a glass toward the table where Nathan and Jessa were seated as his guests of honor. "May your joys be as sweet as flowers that blossom in spring, radiant as the summer sun. May the shower of autumn leaves bring you faith and fortune, and may your love be resilient amidst the long winter nights."

"Here, here!" Distinguished guests filling the private dining room at Chicago's famous Lake House restaurant lifted a toast to the newly married couple.

Jessa had never been happier in all her life.

At her special request, Nathan wore a dashing black evening jacket and silver brocade vest, just like the ones advertised in Harper's Bazaar. In thanks to Mr. Pinkerton's kind words, he tipped his Stetson, sending a thrill through the crowd of dime novel admirers.

She could hardly believe this wonderfully enchanting man had been her husband for two whole months now. Their wedding had taken place at Mission San Gabriel with the entire town in attendance. Oh, how beautiful the old mission had been with hundreds of flickering luminarias outlining its high walls and bell tower, spilling down to the lower walls surrounding the cobblestone courtyard.

At the urging of the Washington Star's editor, the latest installment of her column had included a photograph of the bride and groom. To his delight, an extra edition had been printed after the first run completely sold out.

Then in early November, the ten-twenty stage from Amarillo delivered a staggering surprise. A stately woman with amber-colored eyes stepped off that coach, presenting herself as Mrs. Franklin O. Murphy.

Their maternal grandmother from Philadelphia.

With no warning whatsoever, Jessa had no time to prepare for such a momentous occasion. To her astonishment, however, no special preparation was necessary. The moment they sat down to become better acquainted, they found common ground. Her grandmother had a familiar way about her, a comfortable disposition that reminded Jessa so much of her own mother.

She'd been searching for her daughter ever since her husband had passed away last spring, taking with him the last of the heart-wrenching grudge he'd held against Augus Jamison. It wasn't until Jessa's articles in the newspaper became the talk of Philadelphia, with the name of the anonymous reporter finally revealed, that she found a place to begin her search.

Her traveling companion was a niece, or a friend's niece, or maybe her niece's friend. Jessa never could remember. Her name was Gretta, and she kept her nose in a book for the most part until most everyone forgot she was in the room.

"Bucky, do you really think it wise to catapult an olive from your spoon aimed directly at our honorable mayor?" Lily sipped from her flute to hide a smile.

"Surely, not," her grandmother looked shocked that Lily would even suggest such a thing just as Bucky let it fly, thumping the poor, unsuspecting man in the back of his neck. "Oh, dear heavens."

Nathan reached over and gave her hand a squeeze. "Should be a memorable Christmas if nothing else."

He grinned when Jessa gave him and Bucky both a look of warning.

Her grandmother left her place at the table to make small talk with the mayor's wife. Hoping to smooth over any ruffled feathers, Jessa would guess. Good thing this stop in Chicago was only for one night. The poor mayor might have them run out of town if they were to stay any longer.

They were due to leave again in the morning for Philadelphia to spend Christmas at her grandmother's home at her request. Jessa would have yet another firm talk with Bucky before they got there, then pray for it to take hold.

"Lily, your special delivery has arrived." Allan Pinkerton reclaimed his seat beside Jessa. Taking up a knife and fork, he cut into the delicious prime rib. "Have you told our newlyweds about your next assignment?"

"I leave for New Orleans tonight. The special delivery is actually for a doctor there." Lily summoned a young woman standing in the doorway over to their table. "I've chosen to personally deliver this one."

Just then a small voice babbled from beneath a blanket in the young woman's arms.

Even Gretta looked up from her book to see what could have made such an adorable sound.

As Lily pulled back the covering, a small child, not more than six or seven months if Jessa had to guess, peered up at all the strange faces. Grinning with only two bottom teeth, she was the sweetest little thing Jessa had ever seen.

Lily lifted the baby and carried her over to reclaim her chair beside Allan Pinkerton. "Would you like a slice of apple, love?"

Lily reached over and took a slice from Allan Pinkerton's plate.

"That, Miss Valentine, is part of my dinner." Pinkerton informed her.

"Expense it, Mr. Pinkerton," was her response.

"Who is she?" Jessa removed her shiny bracelet and jiggled it to catch the baby's attention.

"Her name is Olivia de Beaulieu. She's the special delivery." Lily smoothed the baby's curls. "I have a court order to allow that I stay on as her nurse. At least until I figure out whether the good doctor is the one responsible for her mother's sudden demise. As far as we know, he hasn't a clue that his niece was ever with child."

"Somehow, I don't see you as the type for changing diapers." Nathan spoke to Lily, but his attention stayed on the child.

Jessa watched the baby's sweet blue eyes glance up at her as she gnawed on her apple. Who would do such a thing? If Lily suspected foul play in the mother's death, that meant someone intentionally took this sweet child's mama.

Lily lifted what was left of the slimy apple slice and handed it back to Pinkerton who looked appalled but set it on his plate.

"I will bring in a real nurse as soon as we are settled." Lily was clearly out of her element. "I plan to convince him to hire me on as the child's governess so that I can oversee her care from a loftier perspective."

Lily never settled for anything less than full control.

"The sooner, the better." Pinkerton lifted the napkin from his lap to swipe at his hands. "I will arrange to have one sent to you in New Orleans."

Guests began to make their way to the door as the dishes were cleared from the tables.

"I know you two have a train to catch so we won't keep you. Again, let me express our appreciation for the fine work you put forth on the Hollinger case. You both deserve a restful holiday." The chief detective rose but refrained from shaking Nathan's hand. "Enjoy time with your new family.

Lily held the baby in one arm as she accepted a leather portfolio from Pinkerton.

Jessa stood to give her a hug. "Keep in touch, Lily, and thank you for everything. I will miss you."

"You will hardly notice I'm not there. I promise to write often." With the child in her arms, she retrieved her bag and they disappeared out the door.

"If you'll excuse me, I must go wash my hands." With a pained expression, Allan Pinkerton tossed his suit jacket over one arm and also made his way toward the door.

"If Lily's still there in March, maybe we can take the train home by way of New Orleans. I've always wanted to go there." Jessa reclaimed her chair.

"I see no reason why not." Nathan looked down into the eyes of his bride as he took his seat and slipped an arm around the back of her chair. "I promised to provide you a lifetime of adventure. Might as well start now." When he grinned like that, her heart melted all over again.

"Nathaniel Wolfe, I have a feeling life with you will always be an adventure, even when we're old and gray sitting out on the porch in our rocking chairs." She shamelessly sidled in next to her husband.

"Long as we're together, I don't care where we are." He gave her a wink.

For once, in as long as she could remember, she felt no need to chase down her own happiness. This time happiness found her—roped her in, tied the knot, and promised to never let her go.

A Note From The Author

For many reasons, this book will remain close to my heart.

First of all, I was born and raised in New Mexico, surrounded by the beautiful Sandia mountains. My grandfather's family owned a ranch near Cimarron and our family history in northern New Mexico goes back to the 1700s. My papaw was an old cowboy at heart, part Mexican/Spanish, part English, and, yes, part Jicarilla Apache. His grandmother's family really did own the local restaurant/saloon/hotel in Cimarron.

Secondly, in my research for *The Adventuress*, I discovered so much history during this time period. The Civil War had come to an end. Hundreds of soldiers came home to find they had no home anymore. They were broken and many were bitter about the terrible losses they had suffered. They migrated westward to New Mexico Territory, which encompassed modern day New Mexico, Arizona, and parts of Nevada and Colorado. Lawlessness became the norm, and corrupt government soon took over. Hired guns took sides and before long some of the best-known showdowns took place within the counties of New Mexico Territory. The mass murders that occurred on the property of Charles Kennedy in the Sangre de Cristo mountains really did happen. His young Ute wife escaped to Elizabethtown to relay a story that still sends chills down the back of every local resident. Jeb Hollinger in this book was purely fictional, though he was based on many land bosses, bankers, and investors who were determined to drive the farmers from their land at any cost.

Lastly, I'll always remember *The Adventuress* as "the book" I was writing when covid paid a visit to our household in October 2021. I managed to avoid the worst of it, but my husband spent three unforgettable days in the hospital while I wrote on my laptop in the parking lot because I wasn't allowed to go in. Cimarron provided a familiar place where I could go to ease my worried thoughts. Jessa's prayers were my prayers and the peace that filled her was a merely a reflection of what God did in my own heart. I sincerely hope you enjoyed Nathan's and Jessa's story as much as I loved writing it.

~ Much love, Lori

ADDITIONAL READING:

Caffey, Donald L. *Chasing the Santa Fe Ring: Power and Privilege in Territorial New Mexico*, University of New Mexico Press; 2014

Serna, Louis *Clay Allison and the Colfax County War*, independently published, 2020

Weiser, Kathy *Charles Kennedy – Old West Serial Killer*, www.legendsofamerica.com/we-charleskennedy/2020

Montoya, Maria E. *Translating Property: The Maxwell Land Grant and the Conflict over Land in the American West, 1840-1900*, University Press of Kansas, 2005

Reynolds, R. Clay *The Hero of a Hundred Fights: Collected Stories from the Dime Novel King, from Buffalo Bill to Wild Bill Hickok*, Union Square Press, 2011

My Heartfelt Appreciation

With deep gratitude, I thank my prayer team, design and marketing masterminds, talented editors, and patient beta readers who went above and beyond to help accommodate the release of this book.

Special thanks to my editors:

Ashley Espinoza (developmental), your instinctive knack for knowing what is missing and exactly how to fix it, your eagle eye for inconsistencies, your sense of organization that keeps everything in pace, and your uncanny grasp of each character and what makes them tick.

Denise Harmer (copy editor and proof reader), thank you for fitting me into your busy schedule (twice) and for making my elusive question marks, capitalizations, and commas behave. Your attention to detail helps me focus on the fun stuff.

To Roseanna White of Roseanna White Designs for another gorgeous cover design.

To Jaime Jo Wright of MadLit Assist for help with marketing, social media, newsletters, cool graphics, and so much more. You are truly a blessing.

Thank you for the prayers: Kerry, Betty, Toni, and my dad, Don. Keep 'em coming! I depend on your prayers and feel every one.

Thank you to my wonderful first readers, Carol Bates,

Sheri Raymer, Cindi Cannon, Erica Wright, and Laurie Westlake. Your eagerness to help and invaluable feedback is truly a gift.

Thank you to my husband, Daryl and to Jarod, Eli, and my four fellas. You have my heart forever.

Father, to You be the glory. Always.

I am so excited to bring you
The Governess
Book Three of A Matter of Intrigue
Coming in spring 2023
Lady Lily Valentine's
mysterious past
finally comes to light
in the dramatic series finale

You won't want to miss this one!

Let's stay in touch! Visit my website:
www.loribateswright.com

Made in the USA
Middletown, DE
27 November 2022